# where there is *Life*

# ALSO BY CHARLENE CARR

**A New Start Series**
*When Comes The Joy*
*By What We Love*
*Forever In My Heart*
*Whispers of Hope*

**Behind Our Lives Trilogy**
*Behind Our Lives*
*What We See*
*The Stories We Tell*

**Standalone**
*Beneath the Silence*
*Before I Knew You*

# Where There Is Life

## A New Start, Book 2

Charlene Carr

Published by Coastal Lines, 2019.

Published in Canada by Coastal Lines
www.coastallines.ca



Library and Archives Canada

Where There Is Life
Book Two of the A New Start Series
ISBN: 978-1-988232-16-4

This novel is a work of fiction. Names, characters, places, and incidents either are the product of the author's imagination or are used fictitiously. Any resemblance to actual events, locales, organizations, or persons living or dead is entirely coincidental and beyond the intent of the author.

Typography by Coastal Lines
Cover Design by Coastal Lines

Second Edition, September 2019

This work is also available in electronic format:
Where There Is Life
ISBN: 978-0-9939238-2-1

*For Sarah,*

*One of the few people I've never felt the need to prepare a face for.*

CHAPTER ONE

My head fills with the sound of metal crunching into
metal, the sensation of my body flinging forward
then back, a scream I'm not sure emerges from my
throat.

"Autumn, can you hear me?" My mother's voice filters
through the noise. "Leo, I think she's waking up!" Bright
light shoots into my eyes. Stabs of pain, like a million nails,
drive into my head. "Autumn? Are you awake?"

I try to speak but my throat is dry. I swallow, working up
enough saliva to let my tongue move naturally. "Mom?"

"Leo, Leo! She's awake." My mother's voice makes the
nails drive deeper. She leaps from her chair and races to a
door. In a moment she's back at my side. "Can you hear
me?"

"I hear you." The words are less than a whisper as my
eyes adjust to the light. The room I'm in is tiny, bare. Pale
yellow curtains sway gently in the breeze. They remind me
of the curtains I had as a girl. I turn my head at the sound of
my father entering the room, then groan at the shoots of
pain that accompany the motion.

My parents hunch over me with expectant, nervous
faces. My father doesn't look like himself. His hair is
dishevelled, his face unshaven. "Dad?"

"It's me, baby."

"Where am I?" My parents look at each other—their
expressions scare me. I try to prop myself up but can't move

my right arm. Something holds it rigid. A plastic sleeve of some sort keeps it in place. "Mom?" My voice shakes.

"Honey." Mom looks away from my father and back at me. "What's the last thing you remember?" I close my eyes and try to think. It's difficult. Pain clouds my mind. The throbbing pushes itself against my skull. I remember the sound—the metal—but it's all so fuzzy. My mind travels to the last clear moment.

"The wedding." A feeling of warmth caresses me. "I remember the wedding."

"Oh, dear." Mom's voice wavers. My head feels heavy and I drift back into sleep.

"Why?" I force the word out, fighting the sleep that calls, but don't hear an answer.

❧

WHEN I WAKE AGAIN, the room is dark, the only light trickling in from the hallway. The window has been closed, the blinds drawn, and the curtains lay perfectly still. I scan the room and see my mother sitting in the corner, her head resting on a sweater, leaning against a wall. I think of calling out to her, but she looks so peaceful.

My head still throbs, my mouth is still dry, and my face feels tight. A glass sets on the table beside me and I reach for it, surprised again by the weight of the contraption on my right arm. A stainless-steel sink and a counter make up one wall of the small room. My bed has metal railings and is propped up slightly. It's a hospital room. No beeping machines or I.V. stands surround my bed the way they did in Billy's room, but this is definitely a hospital.

My throat feels blocked and my mind fights to piece together this information. "Mom," I say in a panicked whisper, but she doesn't move. "Mom," I repeat, louder this time, but she doesn't hear. Her question, the last thing I remember, comes back to me—the wedding. As I ease into that memory, my panic lessens.

We couldn't have asked for a better day. Bright sunlight filtered over everything. It was warm but not too warm—a wonderful 25 degrees Celsius. I'd feared rain. A beach wedding could be tricky, but every cloud in sight was white and fluffy and perfect. My dress flowed in the light breeze. My happiness was so intense it seemed surreal. I can almost feel it now. As the music started, I turned to my bridesmaids—Allison, Julianne, Eloise, Tracey, and then there was Jennifer, holding my hand.

When it was my turn to walk from behind the sackcloth barricade, I looped my arm in my father's, stepped out with a deep breath, and there he was. Matt, my love, waiting at the end of the satin aisle…Matt.

"Matt." I break from my reverie. "Matt!" If I was in a hospital room, a hospital room where I'd seen Mom and Dad, where was Matt? Mom rouses from the corner and rushes over to me. She slips into a chair and grasps my hand. "Shh, calm down, baby, calm down." Her other hand traces over my head, soothing. "It's okay, baby."

"Where's Matt?" My voice strains with the words, terrified I know the answer.

Mom lets out a breath and I can see her eyes crinkle, her lips purse the way they do when she's prepping to say words she doesn't want to speak. "What do you remember?"

"The wedding," I breathe the words, "and then earlier today, here, you and Dad, you asking me…Where is Matt?"

"There was an accident," she says, then pauses too long. He's gone, I think. He's gone. But I don't want to accept it. I can't accept it. I won't. The last thing I remember is the wedding—walking toward him, the way he looked at me, the tears in his eyes. I remember the vows, the kiss, our first dance…everything after that is a blur. "You've been," she hesitates, "well, we've explained it all already."

"What do you mean?" My breath comes quicker now.

Mom wrings her hands, like she's washing them, like I've seen her do so many times before. I try to focus on this action, to let it hold me steady. I start to shake. "What do you mean?" I ask again, as the panic returns.

"You've been in and out. Sometimes you seem to remember and sometimes—"

"Mom—" Anger flares in me like a raging fire. "Where is Matt?"

"There was an accident," she says again, and I want to scream, but I don't. Instead, I cry.

"Mom?" I remember now, how she explained this all before.

Memories trickle back as she speaks. "After the flight from Halifax, you landed in London and were headed to the hotel…" We were headed to the hotel. Matt had been nervous on the plane. I'd teased him and tickled his side, told him he needed to get used to it—there'd be a lot of flying in our lives. He kissed me then, on my temple, the scent of his shampoo wafting over us as he brushed the hair off his forehead. My flesh tingled.

'Pinch me,' I said, looking into his amazing blue eyes.

'Pinch you?'

'I'm so happy.' I grinned. 'I need to know it's real.'

"It was rush hour," says Mom.

He pinched me then, and I swatted him for it. 'Not that hard.' I leaned into his side and watched him hail a cab. He picked up our luggage with such ease and I admired his muscles as he carefully placed the bags in the trunk. Matt wasn't the first man I'd dated who looked like a Greek god, but he was entirely unique in other ways. It was his heart I'd fallen in love with, his mind.

"The truck ahead of you, its load slid off."

We slid into the backseat. He squeezed my thigh. 'London,' he said.

'Europe.' I replied. We drove along the highway and then suddenly we weren't driving anymore.

"The car—"

"Stop," I say. "Stop." The pain flies back at me. Such pain. Pain that made today's agony seem like nothing. Again I see Matt's body fling forward and back, and as it does our eyes meet. A shard of something, a metal tube maybe, flies from the front of the cab, pinning his neck into the headrest. Blackness crowds in then, which transforms into a fuzzy veil. I have flashes of clarity—words, images—but the next thing I fully remember is Mom leaning over me, running to the door, calling for Dad. "He's gone?" My voice sounds so tiny, so soft, I'm not even sure I've actually spoken. "Matt?" I say louder, as my skin grows cold.

"Yes, baby," says Mom, crying so hard now, hugging me, crushing me. My whole body aches and I want her off of me. I want to get out of here, to get anywhere, to go back. I have to go back. I have to make this not real. Matt is my life, my future. We could get in a different taxi, a different plane.

"No."

"What?" She looks up, pulling her head from my chest, easing her grip on me.

"No." I say more firmly. "No. He's not gone."

"Autumn," she wipes her hands under her eyes, smearing the tears. "I'm sorry, baby. It's—"

"This didn't happen." I swallow and raise my voice. "Matt's okay. Matt's—"

"No," she says with a tone that makes my confidence waver. "It did happen. We all wish—"

"I want to see him." It's a bad joke. That's all it is. Or a mix-up, a confusion. This happened to someone else. Some other couple. Not us. "Now. I want to see him now."

"Baby." She shakes her head. "You can't see him. He's not here."

"What do you mean?" I chest constricts. "Where is he? I want to see him. Now."

"They shipped his body—"

"Now!" I scream and start to push myself off of the bed.

Her hands grasp my shoulders, pinning me down while she cries for the nurse. I try to push her away but the effort sends shards of pain through my body. A woman runs in then dashes away again as my mother and I struggle. She returns with two other women, all in scrubs, and they join my mother in this battle to restrain me. One woman stabs my arm and almost instantly the fight leaks out of me. I raise my arm one final time, trying to swat my mother away but she grasps my wrist and sets my arm down. She rubs my hair, the side of my face, saying, "Shh, shh," as the tears coat my cheeks. They're warm and I want to wipe them away, but I don't have the strength to move. I want to get out of the bed, but my body isn't listening. Soon I can't even keep my eyes open. One of the women says I'll be out for a couple of hours and my mother gently thanks her. I try to say Matt's name but can't form the word.

WHEN I WAKE NEXT, MY mother and father are sitting next to my bed, their hands clasped, my mother's head on my father's shoulder, his head on hers.

The tears return before they even realize I've joined them. "Autumn?" My mother questions. I keep silent as she glances at my father then looks back at me. "You remember?" I nod. "Oh, baby," she reaches her free hand to clasp mine. "I'm so sorry."

"What happened to him?"

"He didn't make it," my father says. "He—"

"I know." I snap. "But how, how did he? Was it the—"

"You don't want to focus on that," says Mom. "You just need to focus on getting better."

"But—"

"Listen to your mother," says Dad. I'm too weak to fight back so I nod, close my eyes, and cry until there are no tears left. When I've laid silent long enough that I'm sure my parents assume I've drifted back into sleep, with my eyes still closed I ask, "What happened to my arm? Where am I? How long have I been here, and when can I leave?"

"Eight days," says my mother. "You've been here eight days. You're in London still, in the hospital." These answers don't surprise me, they seem like remnants of something I already knew. My father notices the doctor in the hallway and waves him over.

"She's awake, is she?" The doctor smiles gently. "Do you remember me, Autumn?"

"No." I've been in here eight days, which means Matt's been…his body, it would be…

"I'm Dr. Fassbend. Do you remember the accident?"

I shrug and look away. I don't want to talk about the accident, don't want to think about it. I don't want to know about the driver…if Matt didn't make it and he did, and I did…it's better not to know.

"What does she remember?" The doctor addresses my parents and they relay the information.

He's young and has a lovely accent. Jennifer would find him sexy.

"That arm is mighty uncomfortable, I imagine," says Dr. Fassbend, "it's been crushed in several places. The vehicle rolled."

If I'd just happened across this man at a café or in a park, I would have told Jenn about him when we got back home…

"The reconstruction went well. You've got steel rods in you now—the bionic woman."

…joked she should take a flight to England, try to find him. He may just be the man she was waiting for.

"What we were really concerned about was your head injury and the internal bleeding that caused swelling and pressure those first few days. We just didn't know. But you're a fighter. You've pulled through."

Jenn probably wouldn't be interested in this doctor though; another accented man seems to be drawing her attention.

"The fact that you're starting to remember, that's brilliant. A very good sign."

At the wedding reception Rajeev and she were alone on the deck. They took a walk on the beach.

"You've got cuts and contusions—stitches in several places." He glances to my parents and they shake their heads for some reason. "But nothing life threatening. That's what you need to be thankful for."

Matt came up behind me as I watched them.

"You've been stable for several days now. All we were waiting for was your memory. Since it seems you've got it back—"

He squeezed his arms around my middle, whispered in my ear, the sweet citrus scent of Grand Marnier on his breath. 'Hmm, well look at that.' He kissed my temple so gently I wasn't even positive he really had.

"—we won't have to keep you much longer. We'll do a few more tests, make sure all the pressure against your brain has dissipated."

Matt, whose voice I'll never hear again, who lies trapped in some coffin, who—

"You'll get to go home."

Home? I stare at the doctor. Matt and I can't move into our new apartment for three months. We…

"You'll need some rehab, but with your background as a trainer that shouldn't be—"

The tears start quickly, cutting off his words, and turn into choking sobs. The doctor stares at me, his mouth slightly agape. "We can discuss this later," he says. "Tomorrow."

My mother nods at him. "Thank you, Doctor." She puts her hand against his upper arm in that way she has and all I can think about is Matt. I squeeze my eyes and try to will myself back to the reality that was supposed to be, instead of the reality that is—the one I can't believe.

If I've been here eight days, in the reality that was supposed to be, Matt and I would have finished our tour of England by now. We would have arrived in Scotland yesterday. We'd be cuddling near a castle, holding hands as we explored a Moor, or enjoying a few pints at a pub. I keep my eyes closed tight and hold on to these hopes, these dreams. At last the tension releases, but I keep my lids down. Dreams, that's all they are and all they'll ever be. Only dreams.

I stay this way for some time, aware of my parents' presence. Even with my eyes closed, I feel them looking at me. I search for something to say, something so they don't look at me the way they must be, feel the way they must feel, but I have nothing. I open my eyes and there they are. They seem almost comical standing there like that, so eager with worry, staring at me like I'm this fragile thing, ready to crack at any moment. But I am this fragile thing. The realization makes me queasy, and cracking doesn't seem like such an impossibility as I thrust myself to the side of the bed, purging whatever food I can't even remember eating.

My mother is immediately at my side, holding my hair back, making her soothing noises, but I don't want any of it. I don't want to be soothed. I don't want to *need* to be soothed. None of this can be real. This is not my life. My life is wonderful. My life is beautiful. My life is just about to turn into a brand new adventure. I'm supposed to tour Europe with the man of my dreams then go back home to open a fitness studio with that same man, the man I love. We're going to be successful, have babies, do all the things we talked about. I rest my head on the pillow, shutting out my parents and their stares as I shut my eyes.

That's not my life anymore. All of the plans that were mere dreams before Matt are nothing now. I'd been talking about opening my own studio for years, about travelling

Europe for even longer, but I never took a step to do either until Matt was there to do them with me. I was too frightened something would go wrong, that I'd fail. Knowing Matt would be beside me gave me the courage to make concrete plans. Without him, these dreams are nothing.

I try to roll onto my side, away from my parents, but this blasted whatever it is around my arm prevents me, sending a streak of pain at every motion. I stay on my back and stare at the ceiling, wanting to sink through the bed, through the floor, through the earth, and join Matt wherever he is. I breathe, but the air seems hollow, seems somehow not enough. I don't speak when my parents talk to me, I just stare at the ceiling. The off-white, water-stained ceiling. I eat when they ask me to eat, letting my mother spoon feed me. I take the pills the smiling nurse hands over and hate her like I've never hated anyone before. Really, I have never hated anyone before, and I know I don't hate her either, not really. But concentrating on that emotion feels better than the alternative.

Once the woman leaves the room, I turn to my mother. "I need to use the washroom."

"Do you want a bed pan or..."

"I can walk, can't I?"

"Yes," says Dad. "Yes, you can walk. They just didn't want you to for the first few days—the head swelling and all."

"Oh."

"But the doctor says everything seems fine now." My mother's smile wobbles like jello. "Here, let me help you."

"I can do it," I say as she reaches for me. Grasping the bed remote, I raise my torso as high as it'll go then move my legs over to the edge and let them dangle. They feel heavy. Lazy. I stand, using my good arm to help prop myself up, and the room spins. My father is beside me, his arms under mine as I lose my footing.

"Oh, just a moment," Mom says. Rushing to the bathroom, she opens the door then closes it behind her. The sound of rustling emerges just before she does, all jello-y smiles. I look at my father with a question. He shrugs.

He supports me as I make my way to the bathroom. "I've got it from here," I say. "Thanks." Dad smiles at me. He looks so tender. It's unnerving and puts me in danger of another round of tears. I turn from him and step into the bathroom. "Mom?"

"Yes, Honey?" She's at the door in an instant.

"What's this?" A towel hangs over what I imagine is the bathroom mirror.

She stands between me and the towel, looking sheepish. "I just thought we could save that for later."

"Save what for later?"

"Well, the bruises, the cuts, your face, the," she hesitates, "the hair."

"Hair?" I lift my good hand and feel my head. The left side, the side she'd always touched as she soothed me, is fine, but as I move my hand over I feel the right is shorn in spiky clumps with a bandage of some sort covering a spot almost as big as my palm. I reach for the towel and she blocks me.

"Honey, don't. You've got enough to deal with right now."

Pushing her arm away, I pull the towel down. As it falls, I whip my head away from the reflection. Mom's arms are waiting for me and I bury my head on her shoulder, trying to breathe. This is some mistake, some…this isn't me. This isn't my life. Mom pats my back then steps away from me. She grabs the towel and starts to put it back up. "No." I step back to the mirror. The woman there isn't me, or she is, but only half of her. My left side is pretty normal. A little haggard looking, with a stitch above my eyebrow, but nothing alarming. My right side is a monster. The skin is a disgusting mix of purples, greens, and yellows. The flesh swells with these colours that make their way down to my lip, which puffs out with a grotesque, scabbed over cut. Within the mess of colour is a large gash that starts just above my jaw, around my eye, and under the bandage on my head. Small stitches hold it together, making me look like some kid dressed up as Frankenstein's monster. My hair is shorn—basically Bic'd—around the bandage. A little further out is about a week's growth and then shorter clumps stick up here and there on the whole right side. I start to peel the bandage away, but Mom grabs my wrist. I shoot her a look and she lets go. The skin is bumpy and swollen. Large black stitches keep the flesh together. It's clear it's starting to heal, but it's so rigid looking. So raised. This will be more than a scar.

"The hair will grow over it," she says. "It'll be hardly noticeable." She's quiet for a moment and so am I. She smiles. "Before you know it, you'll be just as beautiful as you always were." I place the bandage back down, smoothing the edges and making sure it sticks. "It would have looked better by now," she says, "but they had to open it again once or twice…the bleeding."

I nod. "And my face?"

"It's just a scar. Everyone has scars."

"I'm going to use the washroom now."

"Oh," she looks sheepish, embarrassed, "yes," and backs out of the small room. I close the door and stare at myself a little longer. I'm glad Matt isn't here to see me like this, I think, and then realize…I'd take this. I'd take worse, far worse, to have him here. To see me. To let me see him. I sit on the closed toilet lid and stare at the tiles.

"Autumn?" Mom knocks at the door. "Are you okay, baby? Do you need help?"

"I'm okay." I stand and try to ease my pyjama pants down. It's only at this moment that I realize I'm even in pyjamas. They're not mine. I didn't bring any pyjama pants with me—just sexy lingerie. I lean forward on the sink, using my good arm to brace myself. My right arm is essentially useless. It just hangs there, straight and rigid in its plastic prison. Matt hadn't even seen my new lingerie, so carefully purchased for what I thought he'd like best. We hadn't even gotten a chance to—I slam my hand on the counter. I was so tired after the reception. We didn't get back to the hotel room until after three in the morning. 'You wanna?' He'd said, a gleam to his eye.

'I'm exhausted,' I'd replied. 'Let's wait till we get there. Till it can be really special.'

'All right.' He wrapped his arms around me. 'A kiss?'

I stand again, avoiding my reflection, and work my bottoms up with one hand. When I exit the bathroom, my parents are standing in the middle of the room, eyes upon me. My father takes several steps closer. "You need help?"

"I'm fine," I say, with a snap to my voice that I instantly regret. They're just trying to help me. "Thanks though," I add, my voice softer this time. He nods, always a man of few words. I think back to several years ago when it was him in the hospital room, him looking scared and weak. It was the hardest thing I'd ever gone through, seeing Dad like that. It was terrifying. He'd lost thirty pounds and only looked like the shell of my father.

It was the first time in my life things hadn't really gone according to plan, but then they did, and here he is—cancer free for over eight years—healthy and robust. I smile at him, but it feels like a betrayal to Matt; the smile leaves my face almost as quickly as it arrived. With effort, I ease myself back onto the bed.

"Do you need anything?" Mom asks.

"What?"

"Anything—food, a book, a movie, anything?"

"No." I look at the ceiling. Mom and Dad take their seats beside me. "Am I a widow?" I ask.

Out of the corner of my eye, I see them look at each other. Neither one says a word. They don't need to.

# CHAPTER TWO

I'm a widow at twenty-eight. I'm a widow at twenty-eight who had less than twenty-four hours with her husband. Does that even count? It has to count. If it doesn't, it's like what Matt and I had doesn't count. When the doctor comes back the next day, I try to pay attention to his instructions for rehab, but my focus keeps drifting.

"Do you think you have all that?" asks Dr. Fassbend, a broad smile on his face. I shake my head and look to Mom, who has been making notes.

She pats my arm. "I'm getting it, don't you worry."

The doctor looks between us. "Well, the physiotherapist will have access to her files."

"Perfect," says Mom, and ushers him out. I couldn't be more thankful. Once he's gone, my father pushes over a wheelchair.

"I can walk."

"We know, Honey." Mom pats the back of the chair. "Hospital policy."

I sigh and let Dad roll me out of the building. When the cab pulls up Dad opens the door for me, but I stay seated.

"You can have the window," says Mom. I shake my head, not wanting to get in that cab, not wanting to look out those windows and see anything I should have seen with him. I tell myself it'll hurt less if I don't say or think his name, but I know I'm fooling myself. It hurts no matter what.

Mom looks at me curiously but doesn't question. She crawls in and slides across the seat, then sits there, waiting for me with wide eyes. I sigh, stand, and maneuver myself onto the seat beside her. Dad sits down beside me and pats my leg. We all buckle up.

"Everyone is so excited to see you." Mom wears a pasted-on smile as we wait in the airport lobby. "They've all been so worried." She pauses between her sentences, perhaps waiting to see if I'll respond. "And it will feel good to go home to your old bed. That hospital room was so bland." She nods, crossing one hand across the other on her lap. "You'll be better before you know it, and it's so great that the doctor said your arm may—" Dad puts his hand on Mom's leg and squeezes it gently. She stops talking as I turn my head from them, watching the people rushing around, sitting, reading, talking on the phone, texting. "They had the wake, of course. But they're saving the actual funeral service, the internment for when you—"

I stand and gesture to the washroom as I walk away. Inside, I lean against the row of sinks, my head turned to avoid my reflection. I don't want to hear anything about back home. I especially don't want to hear anything about Matt. How do they expect me to handle a funeral? What do they expect me to say? I don't want to go back. What is there to go back to? We both quit our jobs a few weeks before the wedding. We both gave up our apartments. The plan was to travel Europe for three months then return to Halifax, move into the apartment we had lined up, and start working full time on setting up our own studio. So, I have no job, no apartment, and no Matt. I also have no plan.

One step at a time is what I always tell my clients when they're struggling with their weight-loss or fitness goals, struggling with whatever it is in life that holds them back. I didn't know what the hell I was talking about. One step at a time, I'd say, as if it were so simple. So doable. You need a plan, I'd say, a goal, something you're working toward. I don't have any of that. I don't want any of that. I don't want to go home…not that I want to stay here. All I want is to crawl in a hole and stop being. I don't want to die, just not exist. If I don't exist, then it won't matter that Matt doesn't either.

I turn my body toward the mirror and look critically at the image that stares back at me—what I see is not the monster that looked back at me just days ago. The bruises are fading, the cut on my lip is nearly healed, the gash across my cheek isn't quite as bad as I first thought—it's settling down, though still incredibly obvious. I pretend to smile and it scrunches up, crinkling and pulling the surrounding skin. The doctor said I was lucky about that too, said it's probably going to heal into a darkened line, that it shouldn't be raised very much, not like it is now. Eventually, he said, it may be smooth enough that people assume it's a birthmark—long and slightly textured. Lucky indeed.

Wearing a large knit cap that fully covers my ragamuffin locks and shadows my face, a passerby probably wouldn't even give me a second look—minus the arm brace. So I broke my arm? So what? People break arms all the time. I'm hardly a spectacle.

This more realistic view of myself is almost disappointing. I should be more of a spectacle. I should be a walking sign. People should see me and think, *oh that poor girl. She must have been in a horrible accident. Did she lose someone she loved? Is she damaged on the inside as much as the outside? More?* Instead, I'm unnoticeable. No one would guess. No one would wonder. Instead, I'm practically fine. It's not right. It's not fair. This is all I get, and Matt…

Minutes pass as I hide out in the bathroom, but not so many that Mom would feel the need to come check on me. When I sit back down across from my parents neither speaks, and I'm grateful for the silence. I go back to watching people, not wanting to see my parents' faces. We board the plane and I pull on an eye mask, blocking out everything around me, ignoring the flight attendant's offers of drinks and snacks, as well as Mom and Dad's hushed tones.

Daniel meets us at the baggage carrel. He doesn't say anything. He just hugs me, kisses my forehead, and holds me while I try unsuccessfully to stifle back fresh tears. When he releases me, he hugs Mom and Dad.

"How's the traffic?" asks my father.

"It's fine," says Daniel. If things weren't as they are, he would have given me a look, rolled his eyes at Dad's obsession about the traffic, and I would have rolled mine right back. He doesn't do this though. He doesn't make eye contact with me while we wait for the luggage, while we make our way to the car, or when he takes my bag up to my old bedroom. Finally, as he turns to leave, he says, "If you need anything, anything at all. If you want to get away from here or something, I'm just a phone call away."

"A phone call?" I say, alarmed and immediately shamed that this teasing tone can still come out of me, that for that brief second I forgot.

"A text." He grins, not catching my alarm.

"Thanks." The moment he leaves, I plop down on the bed. Mom enters my room a few minutes later, asking if I need anything. I shake my head and roll so my back is facing her. I feel her hesitating by the door, deciding whether to enter. Relief washes over me when her padded footsteps make their way down the hall. I want to be alone.

A couple of hours later I hear footsteps again. By the weight of them, I know it's Dad. "Supper's ready if you want to come down."

"No thanks."

He's silent for a moment. "You must be hungry. You didn't eat anything on the plane."

"I'm fine."

He shuffles his feet on the old shag carpet. "I'll bring you up a plate. You can have a few bites later on…if you want." He waits another few moments then closes the door.

Several hours later Mom is back again. "You have to eat something," she says. "You didn't eat anything."

I roll over. She's still wearing that same smile, the one that does nothing to hide all the worry breaking through. "I'll eat tomorrow."

She dry washes her hands for about the millionth time since I woke up in the hospital. "Okay, Honey. Okay. Autumn," she says my name as if I might be uncertain she's talking to me, "the funeral is tomorrow. At three. Do you have any idea what box your dresses are in? You have a few black ones, don't you? Your father could bring the right box up for you." She pauses. "So you could look. Or I could. I wouldn't mind if you just—"

I take a deep breath and look toward the closet. Not much is left in there—just clothes I'd probably never wear again, a few items I was saving for my future daughter. "Do I have to wear black?" Matt liked me in colours. Bright, sexy colours.

"I think you should."

"I don't know." My throat tightens and my chest constricts. It feels as if she's asked me a complex question I have no hope of knowing the answer to. "It could be anywhere."

"Oh, well—" She continues the dry washing and I want to scream at her and hug her and curl up in her lap and have her tell me this is all just a dream and everything is going to be okay in the morning. "I'm sure the boxes are labelled. He'll just bring up the ones marked bedroom."

"No." I sit up so fast my head spins. "What if it's from his bedroom? All the boxes were just put in the truck together."

She nods. "I'll look through them. I'll find a dress for you."

"I don't…" She can't look through his stuff. No one

should touch it but me. No one should take in those last whiffs of his scent, that mix of Ocean Surf deodorant, Aussie shampoo, and something else I could never quite pinpoint, which must have just been him. But I'm not about to look through it either, so what can I say? My travel backpack consists of clothes more suited for hiking and exploring old dusty streets than a funeral. I only even packed two dresses—one for a romantic evening out, the other for a nightclub. "Okay. Thanks, Mom."

"It's my pleasure."

"Just…if you open one of Matt's boxes, close it back up again. Right away. With tape."

"Of course." She wrings her hands once more. "We're going to bed soon. Is there anything you need before—"

"I'm fine."

She closes the door and I stare at the ceiling again. I've never felt this kind of lethargy, this pointlessness. This isn't me. I always have plans, goals, something to keep me moving and active. I reach into my purse and turn on my phone for the first time since Matt and I boarded the plane to London. While the screen loads, I stare ahead of me and focus on the collage above my old desk. I'm smiling in every picture. Why wouldn't I be? There's me winning the 100-metre dash in grade twelve at the school track meet. Me accepting flowers after I had the lead in the production of *My Fair Lady*. Me at prom with my super hot boyfriend, and then the whole gang in front of the limo. I look at this girl and see all her dreams. She didn't know it was Matt who would make those dreams worthwhile—at that point she didn't even know she wanted a studio, that she'd be a personal trainer. She just wanted to be happy, and she had been. Everything came easy to her and what didn't, she dismissed. Why focus on art projects when you could be the theatre program queen? Why take advanced English and History courses when you could breeze through any of the advanced sciences with barely even trying? That girl wasn't afraid of failure; she pursued the things she knew she'd succeed at, so failure wasn't an option. That girl in the pictures didn't know what she wanted to do with her life, but she wasn't worried about it. Ranked among the top of her class, voted best smile three years running in the yearbook, the girl in the photos believed she'd get whatever she wanted. Her life had a way of working out. Even the few minor heartbreaks she'd suffered were barely memorable when, in a few days, another handsome face was ready and waiting to make her feel desired.

I turn my head from the collage. That had been high school. University had brought challenges. Showed me, to a degree, what fear was, and failure. Steven, my first college boyfriend, swept me off my feet the first day of Orientation. He was a third year—sexy, exciting, intoxicating. My obsession with him had taken precedence over everything else in my life, leading me to almost fail out of two of my classes and actually fail a third. I gave him my whole heart, my virginity, and in return he taught me how easy it was to slip into an emotionally abusive relationship, how a trusting person could so easily be deceived. It took seeing him in bed with another girl to finally believe the hunches I'd had that I wasn't his only love.

After him I held myself back, only having simple, surface relationships. My obsession with Steven taught me how to fear. Years later, when the dream of the studio came, of travelling Europe, that's when fear really crept back into my life. Those dreams represented new and unchartered territory, things I could fail at. I couldn't protect myself from them the way I protected myself from every other guy, not opening my heart to a single one—not until Matt.

Matt turned my fears into exciting possibilities. His strength, his smile, broke through the walls I'd built. He gave me back the faith that my life would work out. With Matt I saw my future as bright and gleaming, just like I had before Steven taught me life could bring other outcomes.

With Matt I'd believed in real love again. I vowed to be his forever. I look back at the collage, at the smiling face looking back at me. And now I'll be no one's.

I turn to the phone and the menu is popping. Forty-five Facebook notifications, seventeen text messages, twenty-nine emails. Setting the phone back down, I crawl under the covers and lie there for hours, watching the numbers on my alarm clock click by. Tomorrow I have to face all those people, all those people who last saw me smiling and happy and about to embark on a grand adventure. Morning is hours away, but still it comes too quickly.

# CHAPTER THREE

gentle knocking, followed by my mother's voice, rouses me from a fitful sleep. "Autumn, sweetheart, I have breakfast ready for you."

"I'm not—" The door opens and Mom picks up my untouched plate from last night.

"It's time to get up."

"The funeral's not for hours," I groan, my body still aching.

"You haven't eaten since we left the hospital. It's been a whole day."

"I'll eat later."

"Autumn."

"Mom."

She stares at me, then shakes her head and steps back into the hall. "You're having lunch." She gently closes the door. I sit up, simply because I can't bear to lie down anymore. I've never been this sedentary and, although it's what my mind wants, I feel my body rebelling. When I stand, the spinning in my head worsens and I sway. Maybe Mom's right. Maybe I need food. Through the open window, I see my father in the backyard weeding the lawn. Why isn't he at work? Is it the weekend? I reach for my phone to check, but let my hand fall away from all those waiting messages. The knowledge isn't worth it. I pull on a pair of shorts, glance into the hall to make sure Mom isn't lurking, head down the stairs, then stand at the back door, transfixed by the concentration on my father's face, the focus. He can't be focusing on the weeds that intently.

When I slide open the door and step onto the deck, he looks up at me, relief washing over his features. "You're up."

"I'm up."

"You need anything? Anything at all?" It's unnerving, this urgency, this need to satisfy. I love my father and I know he loves me, but he's a man of few words. He doesn't usually add much to a conversation and isn't overly involved in our affairs—except when he's drinking, of course, then it's hard to shut him up. He must be scared for me, to be so attentive.

"No." I take the few steps to the railing. "A lot of weeds this summer?"

"I'm killin' 'em off good." A shell-shocked look of terror covers his face. "I'm diggin' 'em up. I'm—"

"That's good." I turn toward the door. "I should take a shower."

"Autumn." He drops his weeder and rushes toward me. "It's…" His voice is gruff, hard. "It's going to be okay. I mean, I know it doesn't seem like it. I know it's hard, but you're going to be okay."

His words make me angry. They also make me want to be a little girl, believing every word my daddy says. I nod too many times then hurry inside. It will not be okay. It can't be. Matt's dead. That will never be okay.

I peek into the fridge and see some donuts there—my father's, obviously. I haven't eaten a donut in years. But who cares? I bite in and let the sticky sweetness soothe me…only it doesn't soothe. It's just sweet, nothing more. I follow it with a glass of milk and decide I should shower before my mother takes that into her own hands too. It's difficult. This is my first shower since the accident. The doctor gave me a bag to put over the arm brace and after a few minutes I have it secured. That seems to be the least of my problems. I stand for a moment, letting the water pour over me as I try to figure out how to wash my hair. At last, I hold the shampoo bottle over my head and squeeze. Washing my body is even worse. I don't think it will work very well to just plop body wash on me, so I take my loofah, prop it between my chest and the shower wall, and squeeze the gel onto it. I then try to foam the soap through with one hand. Eventually, I have success and step out of the shower after about twice the time it normally would have taken me. I even managed to shave my legs with no cuts. I felt ridiculous doing it, though. Shaving my legs—is that what's important right now? Stubble free legs? But it's been over a week. The last thing I want is people to have another reason to pity me.

When I return to my old bedroom four dress options lay across the bed. I choose a three-quarter length, simple black dress and put it on. My reflection seems almost comical, so different from what I remember myself looking like in this outfit. The doctor said to leave the bandage on for several more days. I can't hide my face, but perhaps I can at least make the bandage less obvious. A search through my closet and drawers only yields a tie-dyed scarf. Not happening. So I grab one of the other dresses and try to fashion it around my head. My mother's reflection appears in the mirror. When I turn toward her, she holds up a hat that looks like something my grandma would have worn. It's black though. I take it from her, place it on my head, and turn back to the mirror. After this day, I never want to wear black again.

"AUTUMN." JENNIFER WALKS over, hugs me, holds my hand. I'm not sure why, but I don't want to cry. I really don't want to cry today, and so I just kind of turn myself off. I nod or shake my head when those motions will suffice. I use as few words as possible and avoid eye contact whenever I can. People seem to accept this, but what do they really think? What would my old self would have thought? She probably would have tried to cheer me up. She would have held my hand, like Jenn is doing. She would have said, 'You'll get through this.'

"Oh, Darling." Carol, Matt's mom, wraps her arms around me, drawing me away from Jennifer's grasp, and is crying before I've even fully realized who it is. Maybe she was crying already. I close my eyes and sink deeper into this shell I've created. "Are you okay? Your arm."

I shrug and nod, in danger of losing the battle against my tears.

"We're so glad you're okay." She looks at me as if she's trying to see Matt inside of me, or trying to see why it's me and not him that stands in front of her. I want to tell her so many things—to say I'm sorry and I'd take his place if I could, and it's my fault because I'm the one who wanted to start the trip in London, and—

"You'll always be our daughter." Her lips quiver. "Always." She hugs me again, "You're all we have left of him," and sobs on my shoulder. I watch all this, gently patting her back, as if I'm not there, not part of it. I can't be all they have left of him. I can't be enough for them. I'm not even enough for myself.

Mike, Matt's father, walks over, puts his hand on Carol's shoulder, eases his way into the embrace, and kisses the side of my forehead, just inches away from the scar. Here we are, the three people who loved Matt most in the world. The three people he loved most, and I don't want to be here, touching them, feeling their pain. It isn't right for this much grief to be in such close proximity.

I pull away and they release me, then head to the front of the room to take their seats, shaking hands and accepting hugs along the way. I watch them, and then realize Jenn is holding my hand again, that my mom and dad and Daniel have formed this little huddle around me as they usher me forward to sit down the row from Matt's family. I glance over and see Matt's older brother, Charlie, with his arm around his mother. He's not looking my way and I turn back before he can—he looks so much like Matt.

I keep my head down, not wanting to see the friends and family that must be here, then just as I'm about to take my seat I notice the casket. Pulling away from my family, I walk toward it and place my hand on the cool wood. A man walks over to stand a few feet away from me. He's probably the funeral director, making sure I don't do anything I shouldn't, but his closeness feels invasive. After a few moments I glance his way. "Can I see him?" He shakes his head and purses his lips.

"It's a closed casket," my father says.

"I know but…" I look to my dad, to the man, then back to the casket. "I just want to see him. I didn't get to see him."

"The family decided on a closed casket," the funeral director says as he takes several steps forward.

"I'm his family," I say, a plea to my voice.

"Well, his family—"

"I'm his wife," I say, sharper this time.

My father's hands are on my shoulders, pulling me away. "I want to see him." I fling myself on top of the casket, hugging it—my plastic arm awkwardly trying to grasp. That other self sees me do this and tells me to stop, screams at me, but I don't. I hold on, push my face into the wood, and wait for someone to pull me off. Someone does. I don't resist but keep my eyes on the casket. I say his name for the first time since I woke up in the hospital bed, then wish I hadn't, because more than anything else, saying his name is what makes this all real.

As soon as the word crosses my lips, "Matt," he's really dead, and this really is his coffin. I sink to my knees and a hush settles over the room as the sound of my bawling takes over. That other self, the one that's separate and aware, realizes I'm making a spectacle, but I can't help it. I can't stop it. I'm guessing no one knows what to do because I'm allowed to keep on. At last, I realize my cousin Billy is kneeling beside me, his hand on my shoulder. "Cry all you want," he says in that firm voice he's only recently starting to reclaim. This permission stops me from bawling.

I look into his face that is still somewhat gaunt from his own ordeal last year, and wrap my arms around him, crying more softly now. After a minute or two my tears slow, and he helps me to my feet and then to my seat. A few moments later, the funeral director makes an unnecessary announcement asking everyone to take their seats. My crying stops. Matt's cousin walks to the podium. A few other people have words to say. I'm guessing they tell some stories because trickles of laughter reverberate off the walls. I'm guessing they talk about Matt and me because I pick up on my name once or twice. Through it all I'm trying to stay safe within that shell—tuning out as many of the words as I can.

I'm so weak. Everyone loved Matt. No one else is this pathetic. I should be up there talking about him, sharing the little tidbits that were special to us, honouring him and what we had, but I'm not. I can't.

When Matt's parents walk up to the podium, I finally open my ears. "Matt was our baby," says his father, and I can't help thinking back to a little over a week ago when the two were standing together in front of another podium, toasting our marriage. "He was bright. He was loving. He was adventurous." Mike starts to choke up and I can hear sniffles through the crowd behind me. "He was a good man and we are proud of him." He looks right at me, and I resist the urge to look away. "Just days ago, he made us more proud than we've ever been by choosing to devote his love and his life to this beautiful woman right here." He takes a breath and sends me a slight smile. "For those of you who were at the wedding, you already heard what Matt said to me the night before he married Autumn. The night of the wedding though, just before the two of them headed to the hotel, I shook my son's hand and told him he'd done good. He smiled, in that way he had, and said, 'Dad, all I've done is not mess it up, and I'm going to spend the rest of my days making sure I never do.'

"He told me it'd been the best day of his life and he couldn't wait to spend the rest of his days with you." Mike's talking directly to me now, and despite my effort to hold back, new streams pass down my cheeks. This time, just about everyone around me is crying too, so it seems okay. "Autumn, you may have only had a day as his wife, but I know you filled my son with enough love to last a lifetime, and so I want to say thank you. Matt's life may have ended too soon, but because of you I know it ended happy." He stops here, hesitates, as if he has more to say, but then nods at me. I nod back and he and Carol return to their seats, her crying worse than mine now, as she lets out these little choking sobs.

The director gives some information about the burial site and I stop listening. All I have to do now is follow along with my family, shake the hands of the people I should shake hands with as we leave the building, and hug the people I should hug. Again, I get by with as few words as possible, 'Thank you,' being my go-to phrase.

When I step outside the building, I notice the sun is shining. The old me would be happy for this, feel it's wonderful, enjoy the fact that Matt adored the sun and so this is the perfect send off. The new me wants to shade myself from it and, for the first time, is glad for the ridiculous hat I'm wearing.

After Carol and Mike, it's my turn to toss a rose on Matt's casket. It slips from my hand and lands gently. It's the second time I've given him a rose. The first was on our one-year anniversary. He'd smiled, delighted, and said he thought that was his job. I told him there were no jobs, and if I wanted to give him a rose, I would every year 'till the day we died.

I concentrate on breathing evenly as a progression of people follow suit. Carol and Mike invite me and my family to a small gathering they're having at their place to commemorate Matt—relatives and close friends only, but I decline, saying my head is hurting and I need to lie down. After saying this, I realize my head really is hurting. I hug them both and nod when they try to make me promise I'll keep in touch. As I sit in the backseat on the drive to my parents' house, watching the trees and houses zoom by, I wish that I was going home. The problem is, home for me has just been buried.

# CHAPTER FOUR

Over the next two weeks, despite her obvious frustration, my mother still smiles at me, brings me meals when I don't feel like going down to eat, and screens the calls that keep coming for me. She tries to encourage me to go for a run, to shower every day, to go out with my friends. Most of the time her efforts are pointless. My father doesn't know what to do, so he tiptoes around me, making random offers— 'I can redecorate your room.' Another day, he says, 'Haven't you always wanted to go to Jamaica? Maybe you should do that. Grab a few girlfriends. Your mother and I would be happy to fund the trip,' and then smiles sheepishly as if he's worried I'm worried he's trying to get me out of his house. When he makes these offers I smile back, thank him, and say, 'Not right now.'

I know I can't go on like this forever, but there doesn't seem to be a clear alternative. My feelings aren't unique. People exist who know what I know, have felt what I feel and, presumably, many of them have made it through. But at the moment, making it through seems impossible. Some days even the thought of walking out my parents' front door makes me break out in a cold sweat.

The best part of my day is the instant I wake up in the morning, before I realize where I am, before I realize anything. In that brief moment none of this has happened. I'm still happy. I'm still me. I'm not this sullen, quiet, lost shell of a person. It only lasts the span of a breath though, and then the worst part of my day comes, when I remember he's gone.

"Autumn?"

"Yes?" I open my eyes and look at the clock. It's the worst moment.

"Eloise is on the phone."

I squeeze my eyes shut and try to fight off this morning's tears. "I'm still in bed."

"I see that." My mother steps into the room. "But this is the third time she's called this week."

"Tell her I'll call her back later."

"Autumn," her voice deepens, "get up."

"Mom."

"Get up." I haven't seen that look in years. Not since I was a child.

I stare at her, wide eyed, and without my consent the tears start streaming again. She doesn't come to me. She just shakes her head, like she's never been more disappointed in her life. "What would Matt think of this?" she whispers before stepping out of my room. She shuts the door so gently I can barely hear it. After grabbing a tissue and wiping my face, I lug myself out of bed and go to the mirror. The girl who looks back at me has only a shadow of the bruises that defined my reflection just weeks ago. Fuzzy short waves of hair are completely counter to the long flowing tendrils on the other side. The scar on my face is more defined now, without the green and purple blotches next to it. It's much more evident than the doctor implied it would be, but not hideous. Not grotesque. "You're fine," I say. "Just like always."

I screw up my face and try again. "You'll be okay." That doesn't sound any better. "You're pathetic," I say. "You're weak." I take a deep breath, stare deeply into this unfamiliar person's eyes, "You're lost."

This is not what or who I want to be. Closing my eyes, I turn from the reflection then pull on a pair of jeans and a t-shirt. The waist is loose. This surprises me at first, especially seeing as I haven't worked out since…it happened. But I guess that's what barely eating for almost three weeks will do. It's not good. I don't have excess weight to lose. My mother's words come back to me—What would Matt think of this? But it doesn't matter what Matt would think. He's not here.

Trying not to let my legs shake, I walk past the kitchen toward the front door. My mother intercepts my journey. "What are you doing?"

"I'm going for a walk."

"Where?"

"I don't know, Mom." Trying to curb the bite to my voice, I smile. "Just a walk."

"Do you want to eat first? You haven't—"

"I'm fine." I tug at my shirt. "Thanks."

"I can come. Just a sec—"

"It's fine," I repeat, "really," and place a hand on her shoulder, give a gentle squeeze.

"Your hat," she says as I turn to the door, her voice lilting ever so slightly.

"Oh." I stop and feel my shoulders slump. "Thanks." I step to the closet and grab a toque. It's ridiculous. It has to be at least 21 degrees outside, but I pull it over my head and then give her the surest, bravest smile I can muster. "I won't be too long," I say, having no idea if this is true.

I don't know where I'm headed. I just know that as much as it scares me to leave, I can't be in that house a moment longer. My parents live pretty far from the downtown core—a good five or six kilometres. The opposite direction doesn't have much but subdivisions—for as long as I could walk, anyway. So I head toward the city centre. As I'm walking, I turn off my thoughts as much as I can and try to take in the good things around me—

flowering lawns, children riding bicycles, the sky.

It's been weeks yet I still feel baffled by the absence of Matt. None of it seems real. I keep expecting my phone to buzz and the screen to light up with his smiling face. I keep thinking if I head to his old apartment I'll find him waiting, eager to tell me it was all a bad dream.

Avoiding the streets I would usually take makes the walk more like seven or eight kilometres, but it's worth it. It means I don't have to walk directly past the gym—mine or Matt's—or my old apartment. Eventually I find myself in the Commons, a large green space in the middle of the city. A group of people play softball in what must be a local league. It's the type of thing Matt and I used to do, only soccer was our sport of choice. It's how we met.

I take a seat on the near empty bleachers. As I watch the softball game, see the players cheer each other on, I let myself sink back into memory. When that first game ended, Matt, the team captain, suggested the team go out for victory wings and beer. We sat across from each other and I couldn't help smiling every time he looked my way. He was confident, sure, but not cocky. Never cocky. Though he was friendly with everyone, he paid extra attention to me. His single-dimpled smile made my stomach flutter. Matt was the first man to give me butterflies…the only man.

I close my eyes as the softball game finishes and the field clears. We barely had two years. "It wasn't enough time," I whisper. A lifetime wouldn't have been enough time. As dark approaches, I rise from the bench and make my way back to my parents' house. A couple passes, hand in hand, and I'm shocked at the bitter envy that rises within me. I clench my fist, wanting something to pummel. This isn't me.

❧

As I enter the house, the sound of Jennifer's voice makes my body tense. She's sitting at the island with my mother, a cup of tea in her hands, cradling it, like she can't let go. She doesn't even drink tea. "Hey," I say.

"Hi." She stands awkwardly, both hands still around the cup. I can tell she's debating whether or not to hug me. She doesn't. "How's it going?" Alarm passing through her eyes—presumably the embarrassment of asking such a stupid question.

I shrug. "It was good to walk."

"Yeah, that's good." She puts down the teacup. "Where'd you go?"

"Just downtown."

She nods. My mother smiles. I stand there, the three of us staring at each other, then take off my hat, rub a hand over the dampness of my scalp. "It's coming in well," says Jenn.

I shrug again and brush my fingers through the mess. She gets that look now, the I don't know what to say, I don't want to cry, it hurts too bad, what am I supposed to do look. "I think I'm going to head on up," I say. She keeps looking at me with that look. "The walk. It wore me out."

"I'll join you."

When we get to the hall, I hold my breath as we pass by the sewing room, like I always do, not wanting to think of the contents inside. I sit down on the bed and she slips into the desk chair. "Your mom says this is the first time you've left the house since the funeral."

"Yeah."

"She says you're not taking any calls."

"Uh huh."

"She's really worried."

I shrug.

"I'm worried too."

I nod. She watches me and I put my head down, gazing at my little plastic arm prison. It itches so badly. "Can you help?" I motion to it. "I can't get it off on my own and I just—" She's beside me before I can get the sentence out. "Can you grab a cloth? From the bathroom. A damp cloth?" She nods and is back in a moment. She gingerly undoes the clamp as I use my other hand to brace my arm and hold the weight so it doesn't bend. The doctor said this was important. I'm not to move it for two more weeks. Jenn smooths the cloth over my arm, washing it gently. The touch is so tender, so intimate, that the shell I've been working to maintain is in danger of crumbling. Knowing I need to keep supporting my arm is the only thing that lets me keep it together.

"Is that better?" she asks once she's finished.

"Yeah, it is. Thanks."

"Some of the girls are going out this weekend." She folds the cloth then cradles it in her hands. "Nothing big. Nothing fancy. Just some appetizers and then a movie. I was wondering if—" My shaking head cuts her off. "That's all right." She gives a gentle nod. "Maybe next time." She's quiet for a few moments as we sit, looking at the rug. At least that's what I'm looking at.

"When I lost my mom, I really sank into myself," she says. "I had no job, no purpose. I felt…I don't know…lost, angry, alone." She looks over at me, gives this little half smile. "I'm not saying you need to be okay yet or that you'll ever be completely okay. I'm not saying I know how you feel. But I just want you to know I'm here for you. Even if you want me to just sit in a room with you, I'll do that."

"Thanks."

"I miss him too," she says, and I can hear she's fighting tears now. I look over and our eyes meet. "I loved him too." Her voice cracks. I remember running into her apartment, fuming, accusing her of trying to get in between Matt and me, of lying to me about their relationship. She easily dissuaded my fears, but now I expect there was more behind it than I realized. Not that I think she'd cheated or anything, not that she'd tried to, but seeing her eyes, the pain there, I'm certain I had reason to be angry.

But what does it matter now?

"I know," I say. "He loved you too. He was really proud of you and—"

"Don't." She rests her hand on my knee. "I'm here to comfort you."

I nod. "How's your Dad? And Billy?"

"Good. Billy's getting his own place. Moving out next week actually. He's a little nervous to be on his own again, but I think he's ready."

"He seems it," I say, thinking of how his own brush with death made him a stronger, better man.

"He's started training again on his own. He doesn't even use the cane most days."

"Excellent," I say.

"Autumn."

"Yeah?"

"If you want to come stay with me for a while, you're welcome to."

"No, I—"

"I know your mom is going back to work next week. I could help you out with the cast, your meals, keep you company."

"I don't need help," I say. "I'm fine." I hesitate. "Is that why you're here? Did Mom ask? Does she want me to—"

"No, no. I was just wondering. I just wanted to offer. I mean, I know it must be difficult for you. The cast is still on for a few more weeks, right?"

"Two more weeks." I know when Jenn is lying. She's always been bad at it…except, perhaps, where Matt was concerned. She lied about the training with ease. I feel that sense of betrayal again, like she's been in cahoots with my mom. Or maybe she's just a pawn Mom played in an effort to get me out of her house. "I'm pretty tired." I stifle a forced yawn. "You mind heading out? I'd like to take a nap."

"No problem." Jenn rises. "You need anything or you want to get away—even just to come over for dinner, watch one of our old favourites, you'll let me know?"

"Yeah."

"I don't know if it's the same thing…I mean, it's not the same thing—you and Matt—but at least for me it's gotten better. You know? I don't pick up the phone to call her so much…It's just gotten better."

I nod at her again and squeeze out a smile. Jenn didn't live with her mom. Jenn wasn't about to start a life with her mom. Jenn hadn't built her future and all her dreams around her mom.

I'm relieved when she leaves. My stomach growls, but I ignore it and turn off the light.

# CHAPTER FIVE

**D**ays blur one into another, with nothing overly distinctive to separate them.

"Autumn," my mom says one afternoon, "now that your cast is off, don't you think you should start thinking about work? I found some job ads for you." She places a printed sheet of paper down in front of me.

"I'll look at it later," I say, and switch the channel on the TV.

The next week at dinner she mentions a visit with an old friend. "She was telling me about this woman's entrepreneurial group. Apparently they help women branch out on their own. They provide career and business counselling and help women through any loan processes. It sounds splendid." She looks at me, a broad smile on her face. I nod.

Dad takes a long draw of his beer. It's been years since he had a beer with dinner, now he has two or three. "Sounds great, Lucille. You should look into it, Autumn." I offer my dad a noncommittal smile. He spends the evenings outside, doing pointless, unnecessary repairs and spruce-ups around the property. When he comes in, he looks at me like I'm this broken thing he's helpless to fix, which I guess I am.

My friends come over and try to draw me out of the house. I go with them, just to avoid more hours of my parents' pity and frustration. I wear big hats that are too warm for the season, but sweatiness is better than the stares. The stitches on my cheek have dissolved, leaving a scar no one would ever mistake for a birthmark. I avoid mirrors when I can, but windows along storefronts, reflecting my deformity, are harder to escape. My visit with Allison and Tracey consists of a movie at Allison's apartment, rather than the theatre, as they wanted. With Eloise, we have a picnic in a poorly visited park. They try to get me to go to the gym—but mirrors line those walls. It's not just the mirrors though, I can't work out at home or outside either…any routine I think of, any exercise, has memories of Matt plastered all over it.

At rehab, where mirrors reign supreme and I have no choice but to do the exercises I'm assigned, I put on a smiling face and a positive attitude. "I'm doing so well," I tell my physiotherapist. "I don't even think I need to keep coming. I mean, I know about rehabilitation."

"People don't always do the things they know they should do," my therapist smiles back, "sometimes it's good to have someone guide us through the motions."

"Oh, well—"

"Have you thought of seeing someone?" she asks, while manipulating my arm through the exercises of the day's session. "To talk to," she adds as I grimace through the pain.

"I'm fine."

She nods in a way that says, 'We both know you're not.' And it's true. I'm failing. But I don't like admitting this. I don't want people to know. If my physiotherapist is concerned with how slowly I'm 'healing,' what must my friends and family think? I need to at least start faking that I'm getting better, for their sakes.

Over the next few days, I wake up earlier, eat full meals, shower every day, and put on makeup when I leave the house. Still, my body feels restless, as if a blanket of lethargy constantly enshrouds me. From the look on my parents' faces, I'm still not fooling anyone. The more I try, the heavier the blanket becomes. It's vicious. Even the effort to smile wears me out.

One afternoon I'm sitting at the kitchen table dabbling with a bowl of porridge, trying to force it into me, happy to be alone, no need to pretend I'm getting better, when Daniel saunters in. "Hey, Sis," he says, ultra-casual. "How's it going?" I shrug, then remember my efforts and paste on a smile. "I was thinking, I'm out of the condo now almost two weeks a month for work. It's silly, really, letting the place just sit there empty. And I've got that extra room. It'd be cool if you wanted to shuffle over to my place, keep an eye on it while I'm away. Just until you figure out what you want to do next, of course."

I stare at him.

"Really, it'd be doing me a favour. I've been nervous about break-ins, someone could be casing the joint, keeping track of my travels…"

His voice peters off and I wonder if he realizes how ridiculous he sounds. He probably couldn't sound more forced, more fake, if he were trying. Casing the joint? Really? "I'm all right here," I say. "You should consider a roommate."

"I don't want a roommate." He gives me one of his world class grins. "I want my sister."

"No, you don't." I get up from the table, the bowl half full, and leave the room. He doesn't follow me and I'm thankful for this. If my parents want me out of the house so badly, I wish they'd just tell me. First they enlisted Jenn, now Daniel. They probably think they're enabling me or something by letting me stay here…and maybe they are.

I need to do something big to show them I'm okay. I'm not okay—but something that will fool them. Clearly, the forced smiles and daily showers aren't working. On the way back to my room, I walk by the sewing room. Not that, not yet. I decide to finally get that haircut everybody has been suggesting. The new growth is covering the scar decently well, but it's still a mess. On one side of my head hair flows past my shoulders, on the other I look like a limp porcupine.

When I get to my room, I notice my phone flashing. It shows a missed call from Jennifer. For the first time since before the wedding, I call her back.

"Autumn, hi." She sounds startled to hear my voice. "It's good to hear from you."

"I'm returning your call," I say, wondering how in such a short time I've lost my ability to interact like a normal human being.

"Yeah, I know. That's great." We both ignore the implication in her overly bright tone that I'm apparently so far gone it's an accomplishment that I actually returned a phone call. "So, what's up?" she says.

"I'm returning your call," I repeat, only realizing after the words come out how stupid they are.

"Yes, I was just calling to check in. And I thought maybe you'd want to hang out?"

"I could tonight," I say quickly, before I can stop myself.

She's quiet for a moment. "Rajeev and I are going out tonight with Tammy and Colin," she pauses, "and a few other people too. Some of the girls, some of the guys. You're more than welcome to come."

I ignore the possibility. Matt's memory would loom like a spectre. "You're going out with Rajeev? Like, *out* out with Rajeev?"

"Yeah," she says, a softness entering her voice. "At the—" She stops. "He asked me out a few weeks ago."

"That's great." I hesitate. "So, is it a date or…"

"Well," I can hear the grin in her voice, "we've been seeing each other a couple of times a week. In my mind it was exclusive, but he actually asked last week. He asked if I'd see only him." She sounds so happy. "Is it…" Her voice is hesitant now. "I don't know. Is it okay to be telling you this?"

"Yes." I spew the word out.

"I mean I've wanted to tell you for weeks now, but I didn't know if I should…if it was okay."

"It's okay," I say, fighting to keep my voice even. "That's awesome, Jennifer. I want you to tell me these things. I want you to tell me all of it." I don't, not really, not yet. But I want to want it, so I figure that's good enough for now.

"He's really sweet," she says.

"I know. He's a good guy."

"He makes me feel beautiful."

"You are beautiful." I smile now, the most genuine one I've had in weeks. And something reminiscent of happiness flutters over me.

"Thanks." She gives a little sigh. "He makes me believe it. Even now, I don't always feel it. It's like some days I see the old me. I put a few pounds back on—I seem to yo-yo— and I know it doesn't really matter, but at the same time, it just does…Not in his eyes, though."

"That's wonderful, Jenn," I say. "We always…" I stop at these words and the happiness vanishes. It'd been Matt who'd first thought of Rajeev as a good match for Jenn. He'd met Rajeev at Daniel's birthday dinner almost two years ago, and when the fellas went out that night, Matt and Rajeev hit it off. When he noticed Rajeev seemed to have a bit of an interest in Jenn, he made it his mission to get them at the same events. In the process, Rajeev and his relationship had grown. He'd even been one of Matt's groomsmen.

"I know," Jenn says. "I feel really good about it all. I think he may be what I've been waiting for. It's taken long enough," she says with a laugh that cuts off. "Really though, you should come tonight. Everyone would love to see you. It'll just be casual. We're going to Rockbottom—wings, some drinks, trivia. Daniel might come. He's thinking of bringing this new girl he's been seeing."

"Daniel's been seeing someone?"

"Apparently so."

"I didn't know."

"If you come, maybe you'll meet her."

"No." I hesitate. "I can't."

She must hear in my voice that I'm at the tip of a breaking point. She doesn't push. "How about tomorrow night? Just you and me. I'll make this avocado and feta dip recipe I found, and we can watch the new Channing Tatum movie. Have you seen it yet?"

I have no idea what movie she's talking about. "That sounds good."

"Six o'clock." A pause. "And Autumn?"

"Yeah?"

"Thanks for calling."

"Sure," I say and lay back on my bed, exhausted.

A COUPLE OF HOURS later, Mom knocks on my door.

"Come in."

"Hi, Honey." She steps to the bed and straightens my pillows. "How's your day been?"

"Same old."

"Mm-hmm." She smooths my comforter. "Daniel said he offered for you to move into his place, keep an eye on it when he's travelling."

"Yep."

"Well, do you think you will?"

"No."

"I think it'd be good for you."

"Or you just want to get me out of your hair."

"No," she gives her head a soft shake, "of course not."

"Then why, Mom?"

"Because I think a change of scenery would be good for you. You're welcome here as long as you want. You're always welcome here, but you've never been a homebody, Autumn. I think moving would be a good first step. You'd be downtown. You'd be in the heart of things. It's so boring for a young person out in the suburbs."

"Fairview's not that far out."

"Well." She smooths the comforter again. "I just think you need to start taking steps forward. You need to start making plans. You're just kind of existing here and—"

"If you want me gone just say so," I snap.

"Honey."

"What? What, Mom? Yes," I say, my voice becoming shrill, "I'm just existing, okay? I don't know what else to do. I don't know how else to be. I don't know anything anymore."

She steps toward me, wringing those hands again. "Autumn, I know it hurts. I know it's hard, but—"

"No, you don't know." I clench my fists, my fingernails digging into my palms. "You have no idea—"

"I've had loss," she snaps back. "I know—"

"Can you leave, please." I slump into my desk chair. "Just leave."

She shakes her head and turns to the door. She leaves. And yet again I'm lying in the dark, alone.

I've taken to reading history books. Sometimes I even pull out my old kinesiology textbooks. I need something to make the hours go by. I've given up on novels. I've given up on the radio. I've given up on most movies. They remind me too much of what I can't help being reminded of, anyway. Listening, watching, or reading it, the romance plots or subplots that seem to make their way into every song, movie, or book, is not good for my mental health. Love seems to be everywhere. Love and loss. I guess that's the human condition. It's more frustrating than encouraging. On one hand, I'm not the only one who has gone through this, but on the other hand, I'm not the only one who has gone through this. How depressing is that?

I'd rather be unique. I'd rather not know there are so many others hurting. Also, it would make my inability to think, to plan, to hope, more justified. I don't like spending all this time in my head; the voices battling inside me. One tells me I need to move on, to make choices, to act—the other tells me there's no point in anything. If I could, I'd silence both voices and pretend this never happened. If one or two seconds in the course of history had played out differently, it wouldn't have happened. I would have been finishing out the last couple weeks of my honeymoon—fulfilling a lifelong dream with the man I'd always dreamed of.

My gnawing stomach finally propels me out of bed and down the hall. When I get back to my room, a book sits on my desk—not mine. Self-help books started popping up around the house a week or two ago. First there was one on the coffee table in the living room. Then another in the bathroom reading rack. Finally, there is this. It's incredibly specific—not just about loss and grieving. The sub-title informs me it's about grieving the death of a spouse. Of every senseless, overbearing thing my mother has done, this hurts the most. He hadn't even had a chance to be my spouse. Not really. "Mom!" I yell.

Light footsteps tread down the hallway. "Yes, Honey?"

"What is this?"

"What's what?" She smiles.

I pick up the book and shake it in her face. "What's this?"

"It's a book."

"I can see that. Why is it here?"

"Because I thought it could help you."

"Did I ask for help?" I toss the book and she catches it against her chest.

"You need help." Her own voice rises. "It's not like you listen to—"

"This is not going to help!"

"You don't know that."

"I do know that, okay? Just…mind your own business?" Her face couldn't look more stricken if I slapped her. My voice softens. "If I want your advice, or the advice of some book, I'll ask for it."

"You are my business." She lifts her chin, her jaw set. "I have to do something." She places the book back on my desk. "Just skim through it. If it's trash, you can toss it." Without a parting word, she turns from me, exits the room, and treads back down the hall. I sit, staring at the book just inches from me. Its presence seems to suck the oxygen out of the air.

❧

I DON'T LEAVE MY ROOM for hours, and when at last I creep down the stairs, expecting Mom and Dad to be safe in bed, a noise from the living room startles me. I tiptoe further and peek my head in. The lights are off, but I make out the figure of my mother. As my eyes adjust to the darkness, I see that her head is propped in her hands, her shoulders slumped. She looks old. Those slumped shoulders shake. She's crying like I haven't seen her cry since the death of her sister. I watch for a few minutes, wanting to ask her what's the matter, wanting to wrap my arms around her, but I can't.

When I start to tiptoe away her head rises. "Autumn? Autumn, is that you?"

I step back. "Yeah."

"What is it? What's wrong?" she says, trying to mask the catch in her voice.

"Nothing. I'm just grabbing a snack."

"Oh, okay. Okay." She stands. "You want me to fix you something?"

"No." This is my chance to be a normal human, to offer

my shoulder. "I can get it."

"Okay." She sits back down, collects a book and her reading glasses. "I was just going to bed. You sure everything is all right?"

"Yeah, Mom." This is the moment. This is when I ask her if she's all right. If there's anything I can do for her…only I know the one thing I can do, and I just can't do it, no matter how much I wish I could. "It's fine." I push out a smile. "Night."

"Goodnight, Darling."

The fridge light pours onto my face as I look blindly at the contents. My mother is mourning me. I don't want to be this burden to the people I love. I hate it. I don't want to make them hurt just because I hurt. Something has to change. I can't stay here. Matt was…I can't do it. I can't think about him in the past tense. It'd be better not to think about him at all, to pretend he never existed. And then it hits me. That's the solution. That's the way to let go of all of this misery, all of this ridiculousness. Matt no longer exists. The only way to be free of this pain is to live like he never has.

# CHAPTER SIX

The next morning I wake to sun streaming through my blinds, the sound of birds chirping outside my window, but not that wondrous moment of ignorant bliss. Last night's resolution hasn't left my mind. The burden of it sits like a weight on my chest. Not that the resolution is a burden…it's what I need to do first that weighs me down. But after I do it, I'll be free. Fake it till you make it, Jennifer said to me once when she was on her weight loss journey. Good thing I have all that high school drama club experience.

I get out of bed, take a shower, put on actual clothes—not the gym pants and t-shirt I've been living in most days—and set a reminder on my phone to call the hair salon when they open.

My parents are still asleep, so I head to the kitchen and pull down pots and pans and measuring utensils, eager to surprise them. By the time my father enters the room, groggy and rubbing his eyes, bacon sizzles and bounces in the pan, and a small pile of pancakes waits on the warmer.

"I thought it was your mother," he says through a sleepy grin.

"Nope." I reply, trying to remember how I used to speak, to call forth the cheeriness that once came naturally.

"It smells good." He smiles broader now.

"Sit down. I'll serve you a plate."

He sits, looking hesitant but hopeful, and I fight the urge

to throw up my hands, say, it's all a ruse, Dad, and curl up in his lap. "How has work been?" I ask.

"Oh, you know, same old same old. It's hard work, and on top of that the boss has been on everyone's backs about having a social media presence, letting our contacts know about our services on Facebook and Twitter. It's beyond me."

I nod. "It could help though. A lot of people post on Facebook or put out a tweet when they're trying to find a company."

Dad makes a noise somewhere between a snort and a groan, then tells me the pancakes are good. I watch him eat, noticing how old he's looking. He's in his mid-60s and he's starting to look it. His tiredness brings back post chemotherapy memories. That was a rough time overall— not only did he fear losing his life, he lost the moving company he'd worked his whole career to establish. Selling the company to pay the medical bills then going to work at a competitor's business wasn't easy. Looking at him, bent over his plate like this, I wonder how much longer he'll be able to do such a labour-intensive job and how much of the fatigue I see is a direct result of me, not the work. "Is it stressing you out?"

"No, no," he says. "It's no big deal. I don't want you worrying about it." He smiles at me, that tender smile that's become so familiar in recent weeks. "I'm just being a stubborn old goat. I'll do the tweeping. I may even like it. You never know."

I almost laugh at his slip. Instead, it's more an intake of breath, but it's the closest I've come to laughter in a long time. Just as I sit down to eat, Mom walks into the kitchen.

"Autumn?" She doesn't even try to hide the surprise in her voice. "Did you make this?"

"Yep." hate her surprise, her incredulity, but sound as cheery as I can, anyway.

"Thank you." She takes the plate I've set out for her. "It

smells wonderful."

"It tastes wonderful too," says Dad.

We eat in silence for a few minutes. "So," Mom says, and I can tell she's been debating her words since she sat down. "Do you have any special plans for today?"

"Well," I say, "I'm going to book an appointment at the salon."

"That's wonderful!" she exclaims. "That'll be good. Really great."

Her tone drips with pride, an acknowledgement of how pathetic I've been if booking a hair appointment is deserving of pride. "And I'm going to open the gifts, the cards." Both of my parents look up. They look at me, then at each other, then back at me.

"Are you sure?" says Mom.

"I'm sure." I shrug. "You need your sewing room back."

"That's not a problem," she says. "You don't need to do that yet. You have time."

"I thought you wanted me to start doing stuff, to get on with things."

"We do. For you, but that..." Her voice drifts as she looks again at my father. "I'll call work," she says. "I'll take a sick day."

"You don't have any more sick days left."

"I'll make it work." She hesitates.

"No." I take a deep breath. "I want to do this on my own. I need to do this on my own." My mother nods in response, her head dipping up and down in slow motion. I sit taller in my chair. "I did want your advice though. What do I do? Do I send things back? Do I keep them? The gifts, the money...and...thank you cards?"

"You keep it," she says. "Or you sell it. Your choice. But no, you don't have to worry about giving anything back. And the cards...I can write them if you want. I'd be happy to. People will understand."

I smile at Mom. I'm the one nodding slowly this time.

"I'll see," I say. "I'll think about it."

❧

I PUT IN THE FIRST FIVE numbers of my salon then change my mind. If they don't know about the funeral, they'll be asking questions about the wedding. Either way, I don't want to deal with it. I look up another salon with good reviews and book the appointment for four o'clock. That should give me time to do what I've got to do and won't make me late for Jenn's. Grabbing my fourth-year kinesiology textbook, I sit in the living room waiting for Mom and Dad to leave for work. When they do, I head upstairs and open the sewing room door then take a step back, shocked at the massive amount of wrapped boxes and bows that crowd the floor and love seat. We'd expected mostly money as people knew we'd be travelling for several months and because we both already had our own places. Still, there are a lot of gifts. I step into the room and make my way around the boxes to our card cage. It's half full.
As I survey the room, I wonder if I'll even have enough time to get through it all before four. The original plan was for Mom to open all the cards while we were travelling and cash any cheques so people wouldn't worry—it looks like she didn't have the chance. I decide to open everything, read all the cards, and make one pile for items I want to keep and one for items I'd like Mom to return or sell or do with as she pleases. I'll place all the cash and cheques back in the proper cards to let her handle thank-you notes. She offered, after all. I sit down, pull over the nearest box and open the card. It's from Julianne, one of my closest friends since kindergarten. Before I've even made it to the bottom of the card, her words have me in tears yet again.

Five and a half hours and a full box of Kleenex later, I've gone through it all and feel more physically exhausted than the time I ran a marathon. All the love and affection people have for me and Matt is overwhelming, and I'm heartbroken over their hopes and dreams for our future. After opening the last card, I sit for several minutes and close my eyes, trying to let go of the pain as best I can while going through every minute of that last day—every smile, every laugh, every touch of his hand on mine, every stolen glance—things I never plan to think of again. I can almost feel him, hear him, smell him, and it makes my whole body ache. When I open my eyes all that beauty disappears. I rise from my cross-legged spot on the floor, step out of the room, and make a resolution. From this moment forward, I'm going to live like I never knew Matt, like, as far I'm concerned, he never was. From this moment forward, my life is my own.

WHEN I GET TO THE salon, the stylist is friendly but hesitant. "I had surgery," I say. "Clearly, the doctors had no idea of this season's styles." She laughs and is put at ease. She doesn't question me further but commences with the usual salon talk. I stay out of it as much as possible, letting her chit chat with the other stylists and clients. When she swivels my chair around, I can't say it's a style I ever would have chosen, but I like it. It's chic. It's a style I can walk around with without feeling the need for a hat.

The stylist was quick, which gives me an hour before I'm supposed to be at Jenn's, so I decide a new outfit is just what I need. I choose black skinny jeans, a peek-a-boo sleeved purple top, and then, to complete the outfit, heels. I look more like I'm going to a stylish restaurant than to a movie night in, but it feels good. As I sashay out of the shopping district, I can't help but notice the testosterone-filled eyes on me. It's not an unfamiliar feeling—but it has been for the last few months. Not that I care. Not that I want roaming eyes on me, but it's better than averted ones. I wonder how many of the eyes that watch me pass are shocked or repelled when I get close enough for them to see my marred face. There's no more redness, no more swelling, but I'll always be scarred.

When Jenn opens the door, I do a little spin. "Wow," she says. "You're looking great. I love the hair."

"Why, thank you." I lay the levity on thick. "I thought it was time for something a little more stylish."

"It's working. We're just staying in, right?" she says. "Or do you want to go out?"

"We can stay in…unless you want to go out."

She looks at me, hesitant. "I'll go out," she says, "if you want to go out."

"Yeah, let's do it!" I say, holding onto my resolve to act like everything is normal, like I'm not dying a little inside just by letting these happy words out of my mouth. "Why not?"

"Just give me a few minutes to change." I wait in her living room, tapping my toe to the funk that plays on the stereo and telling myself I'll be fine. I'll be better than fine. I'll be great. I'll be me. "All right," Jenn comes back into the room. "I'm ready if you are."

"I'm ready."

We go to a new restaurant that I look up on my phone. This is calculated, of course. If I go to any of our regular places, I'm more likely to run into someone I know. Just because I've decided to live like Matt wasn't this huge part of my life, that doesn't mean anyone else will go along with it. This fact is evidenced by Jenn's forced smile, her hesitancy. Of course she thinks this is an act. Of course she's worried I'm going to crack and break down into a bawling mess at any moment. I won't though.

We order cosmos and I ask her how last night went. "It was great," she says. "Lots of fun."

"And was Daniel there? With his new lady?"

"Yup." She takes a sip of her drink.

"What's she like?"

"Oh, she's nice."

"Come on, Jenn." I lean toward her. "Give me the deets." I don't think I've ever said 'deets' in my life.

"She seems good for Danny. She's sweet. A teacher. Grade two. She's a little shy, but she opened up once she got more comfortable. She seems smitten with him, and him with her."

"That's great." I smile broadly. "It's about time Daniel found someone good. He deserves it."

Jenn nods.

"And what about you?" I ask. "Tell me more about how things are progressing with Rajeev."

"Well," her smile brightens, "I really like him. He treats me so well, too. He's respectful. Almost too respectful." She giggles at this. "I wouldn't mind if things progressed a little faster than they have. Last night when he walked me home, he came up for a few minutes. That was the first time he'd ever even been in my apartment." She grins. "It was also the first time we had a proper make-out session. It had only been quick pecks before." She blushes. "He knows what he's doing."

"That's awesome. That's really good. I'm happy for you, Jenn."

"Thanks. And thank you for…" She seems to debate her words. "Thanks for coming out tonight."

"No, thank you!" I almost shout. "We're young, right? This is what we should be doing. Going out. Having a good time. Living life." She nods, though not as enthusiastically as I would like. I finish my drink and signal to the waiter for another. I look at Jenn and she shakes her head. "So, how's work going?"

"It's good," she says. "I've started thinking about going out on my own—getting writing contracts independently from the company. I think it'd be more profitable. I've also been dabbling with the idea of a novel—just on the side, of course."

"Oh yeah? That's great. Look at you," I grin, "living the dream."

"I don't know if I'd call writing stories for ESL kids the dream," she laughs, "but it's good work."

"Work you can do from home, that isn't stressful, and that only takes up, what, twenty to thirty hours a week?"

"Yeah, it's pretty good." She takes another sip of her drink. "What about you? Have you thought about going back to work anytime soon? Will your arm be able to handle it?"

"My arm's doing okay," I say, moving it back and forth. "I guess I'll get stopped in airport security for the rest of my life," I laugh, "but it's functional." Jenn nods. "I don't know about going back to training," I say and can feel my resolve failing me. My love of fitness and dream of owning my studio came before Matt, but the actual planning of it was something we'd been doing together. "I mean I left my old job and—"

"I'm sure they'd take you back."

"I don't want to go back." I say too sharply.

"Well, you could get on somewhere else or get started on your own studio. Wasn't Allison thinking of joining you once it was established? Maybe now she'd want to be a partner."

"No."

"Well, maybe—"

"No." I force a smile, knowing it's unfair to snap at her like that. "I think I may pursue something entirely different. Something new. There are other things I could do."

"Well, yeah, of course."

"I could..." I hesitate. I've got nothing. My head drops and I push the drink away.

"You want something Matt wasn't connected to?" she asks.

"Don't say his name," I whisper.

"What?"

"Please. Just don't say his name."

Jenn gives me this look like she pities me. It's miserable. "Okay."

"He's gone, right? He no longer exists. I need to act like that. I need to live like he never was."

"Autumn. I don't think that—"

"I need to, Jenn. I need to get away from everything and everyone that connects me to him."

"What do you—"

"I need to."

"Okay," she says, resting her hand on my arm. "I don't know what that means though."

"I don't either. I just…no training, okay? And no more talk of him. Not tonight. Not ever."

She looks almost frightened, but she nods. "Okay," she says, "okay."

I trace my finger along the rim of my glass then look up at her and smile. "How 'bout some food? I'm hungry. Let's eat."

"Okay," she says again, then watches in apparent shock as I order items I usually avoid—nachos and deep-fried pickles. If I'm not going to be a trainer, what does it matter? Nothing matters at this moment. My life is a clean slate and I can fill it with whatever I want, maybe even cheesecake.

As we go through the rest of the night, only half of me is present. The other half doesn't know what the hell I'm trying to pull. How am I supposed to live like Matt never was? He's everywhere. We head to the movies after our meal and he's in line at the concessions stand. He's in the rows ahead of me and behind me at the theatre, where we cuddled or held hands. He's in the parking lot laughing with our friends after a show. I know when I get home it'll be the same thing. He'll be in the kitchen chatting with my father, at the table laughing with Daniel, on the back porch commenting on my mother's new garden design. Even if I say goodbye to training, if I can erase that whole portion of my life, he'll still be around every corner. He'll still be behind every smile of every person I love. They all knew Matt. They all know how lost I've been. Even if I can fake it till I make it, I'm not sure they can. If Jennifer is any indication, it'll take some time before anyone even trusts my newfound smiles.

I envision finding a new apartment, setting it up, and the men I enlist to help—Matt's old buddies from his gym—they'll be falsely chipper, thinking how they were supposed to be helping out the both of us. My brother or Daniel, or Dad—all of them, too, would think how Matt should have been there, directing, sharing the load.

Maybe one day I'll meet someone new, it seems impossible that I'll ever want to, but suppose one day I do. Everyone I tell will wonder if I'm ready, wonder if I'm comparing this new man to Matt, wonder if I'll make it through. It's not going to work. None of it. Trying to forget about Matt, "it's not going to work."

"What?" Jennifer looks over at me. She almost trips. We're minutes from her apartment, minutes from the room where I first showed her my ring, where I asked her to be my maid of honour.

"It's not going to work," I repeat. "Living like Matt never was."

"Living like Matt never what?"

"Like he never was. Like he never existed, like I never even knew him—what I was saying in the restaurant."

"I'm still not really following you."

"I decided yesterday," I say, "that I can't go on…the way I am. And Matt's the problem. But Matt is gone. He no longer exists, yet I'm living like he's around every corner, like he still matters."

"Of course he matters."

"No," I say. "No. He mattered. But he doesn't exist anymore and there's nothing I can do to change that. The only thing I can do is start living like he never existed, like I don't have this huge hole in my life where he is supposed to be."

"Autumn, I don't think—"

"It's the only way, Jenn." I glance at her then look straight ahead as I continue walking. "But it's not going to work. Not here. Here…well, it's just not going to work."

"Autumn. You can't just pretend Matt never existed. He did exist, he—"

"It's my only choice."

"It's not right, it…" her voice rises. I hear the pain. "You can't do that. You can't pretend—"

"It's really not your business." I cut her off again. "You can think about Matt all you want. You mourn him all you want. My mourning's over."

"But, Autumn—"

"I can't keep living like this, Jenn. I can't keep making my family live with—" My voice catches. "This is my decision."

"You can't just—"

"I've made up my mind," I say with resignation. "And I know what I have to do about it."

"What, what do you—"?

"I'm leaving."

"Huh?" We're outside her apartment now, standing in front of the steps to the lobby. "Don't leave. Let's talk about this."

"That's not what I meant, but yeah, I'm not coming in. I don't need to talk." I smile, finally feeling like I have a plan, like there's a chance I can be me again. All I need to do is put it into action.

"Autumn."

"Thanks for a fun night." I lean in for a quick hug, turn, and head down the street.

"Autumn, come back. I'll call you a cab. Stop."

"I'm good, Jenn." I call out, lifting my hand in farewell. At last I'm good.

# CHAPTER SEVEN

The walk is long, especially in heels, but the cool evening air invigorates me. When I turn up the drive at eleven o'clock, my mother has the door open before I even get to it. "Why didn't you call a cab?" she snaps.

"I wanted to walk," I say, and breeze past her.

"You wanted to walk?"

"Yep." I turn back, give her a quick kiss on the side of the head, and turn toward the kitchen. "Any good leftovers?" I open the fridge door, letting the light surround me.

"Autumn, are you okay? Baby, what's going on?"

"I'm good, Mom." I look back at her and smile—a genuine smile. "Really good. I'm just hungry."

"There's spaghetti squash and garlic sauce. On the bottom left," says my mother, tension behind her words.

"Great." I open the Tupperware container. "Smells good."

My mother leans against the wall as I dump half of the contents onto a plate and pop it in the microwave. "It's good to see you have your appetite back."

"Yeah," I say. "It is."

Mom's shoulders slump forward, her eyes have large bags beneath them. I'm sorry to see her that way but know my recent decision will help her get her life back too. I smile and take a seat at the island, waiting for my food to be ready.

"Can you tell me what's going on, please?"

"I hung out with Jenn. I walked home—it was a nice night—and now I'm hungry."

"I talked to Jenn."

"Oh?" The microwave beeps and I stand to get my food. "You made the sauce out of cauliflower, didn't you? Nice."

"She said at first it seemed like you were doing really well. and then you started talking about pretending you never knew Matt, said you were leaving. What did she mean?"

"I am doing really well. Is there any salad?"

"What about the rest of it?"

"Mom." I set my plate down. "I got up today before noon. I showered. I dressed. I took care of…things that needed to be taken care of. I went out. I thought this was all what you wanted. Why are you questioning me?"

"I don't know, Autumn," her voice wavers, "I—"

"Matt's gone. And that's been really hard, but it's like you've been saying, like those books have been saying, I can't just let it be hard forever. I can't just constantly live my life with his shadow over every thought, every choice, every moment, can I?"

"No, well—"

"And so I'm not going to do that anymore." I take a bite. "This is really good!" I chew and swallow. "I'm going to move on with my life. I'm going to start doing things. And I'm not going to let his memory hold me back."

"Well, that's good, but—"

"I don't want you to mention him to me anymore," I say, my voice firm. "I'd like to be able to ask that of everyone, but I know that's not possible. I can't expect everyone else to act as if they never knew Matt. But I can."

"Autumn, I don't think that's what the books meant. I don't think—"

"I'm going away." I say. "I'll look into booking trips

tomorrow. I think it'll probably be Europe…you know I've always wanted that." I grin. "But Asia could be good too. Or South America, maybe."

"Autumn." My mother sits down across from me. "I think it's good. Great, that you're thinking of making plans, that you're excited. But I don't know that you're thinking clearly. I don't know that you're ready yet to—"

"Mom," I snap, then soften my tone. "With all due respect, it's not really about what you think. I'm twenty-eight." I look away from her. "And I've been under your hair long enough. This is what I'm doing. Be happy for me." I fight to keep my voice steady. "Just be happy for me," it cracks, "support me. Okay?"

She nods again. She's giving that same smile she's been giving me for weeks. "Okay, Autumn. Okay." She turns to leave, then looks back. "Your hair looks really nice, Sweetie."

❧

THE NEXT MORNING I wake up early, ready, and motivated. I wake up with purpose. I reject any thoughts that try to destroy this feeling. I style my new hair, which takes much longer than I expect. It's tricky and frustrating, but such a small, insignificant problem—who cares? Eventually I settle with good enough. When it comes to my face, I stand and scrutinize. Large dark crescents sit under my eyes, my skin has lost the lustre it once held, the scar…is there, and there's nothing I can do about it. Everything else will fix itself now that I'll be sleeping better and eating the way I should. It's all good.

When I enter the kitchen, both my parents eye me like I'm a time-bomb, just ticking away. I smile, say good morning, thank my mother for the scrambled eggs she's left on the stove for me, and sit down.

"Your mother says you're going away?"

"Yep."

"This is sudden."

"I suppose."

Dad rubs his hand across his stubble. "When do you think you'll be going?"

"As soon as I can."

"And you don't know where?"

"Not yet. I've got the whole world to choose from though." I get up and pour myself a cup of tea. "I really am still leaning toward Europe…we'll see."

"Mm-hmm."

"So, you tried twitter yet?" I ask.

"Twitter? Oh, uh, no, I haven't."

I sit back down with my tea. "You'll figure it out."

My parents keep silent as I eat my meal. Underneath my smiley demeanour I'm so anxious to get away from this tension, this pressure, this reminder that something is wrong, it almost itches. I'm not stupid; I know going away won't completely erase all thoughts of Matt from my mind, but it'll help. It'll be better. It has to be better. When I finally finish, I stand to leave the room. "Oh," I say, casually turning back, "I sorted all the stuff in the sewing room yesterday in piles. I marked them. If you're still willing, I'll take you up on your offer to handle the cards, and if you could just deposit all the money into my account, that'd be great."

I don't wait for a response. I know Mom will do it, and that's one more problem that's behind me. I still need to figure out the apartment lease, but that will come next. I go upstairs, open my laptop, and start exploring my options. After about an hour, my head is spinning with the possibilities. Feelings of defeat creep over me, but defeat isn't one of my options. It's never been an option for me. Yes, there were those few months in University but, overall, my life is defined by success. My life is defined by forward motion, forward movement.

Despite the allure of the articles I've read on climbing to the heights of Machu Picchu, or exploring the Australian outback, I know the most about Europe. I spent months planning our…my trip there. Throughout high school I scrap-booked possibilities. In University, I researched the most interesting locales and tips and tricks for the backpacking enthusiast. In the past year I'd put almost as much energy into planning the perfect trip as I put into that other perfect thing I'll no longer speak of.

So I decide—Europe it is, but not London. Not England. For me, that locale is going to stay trapped away, forgotten, like all the other things I'm hiding away. I find a good price on a flight to Italy that leaves in two days. It's perfect, the land of my ancestors, so I book it. The moment I click 'confirm' it's as if a heavy cloak rises off me and I'm suddenly lighter. I'm ready. I decide not to book any additional flights. I won't stick to a solid plan or schedule. I no longer have a three-month restriction. I can stay as long as I like in any spot. I can find work. I can visit one country or ten. If I decide to, I don't ever have to come back.

My parents stand shocked when I tell them the news. They try to dissuade me. They tell me to give it a few weeks. "Get an apartment first," says Mom. "Go back to work and then, once you're settled and stable, take off on this adventure."

"That makes no sense." I give her arm a friendly squeeze. "That kind of logic is entirely illogical. Right now is when I'm free. Right now is when this will work."

They stare at me. Mom opens her mouth as if to say something more, but what can she say? I'm right. My father holds me tightly.

My mother cries. "I'm not ready for this." She wrings her hands. "It's too sudden."

"Life is sudden," I say, and her tears increase.

She calls Daniel and tells him to come over for dinner

the next night. She invites Jennifer and Billy too, without asking me. "Autumn," she says, as I walk toward the stairs. "What about anyone else, is there anybody else you'd like here to see you off?"

"No. We're good. I don't want to make a big thing of it."

"But it is a big thing."

"We're good, Mom. Thanks."

"What about Mike and Carol? I'll give them a call. They'll want to see—"

"Mom, no."

"But Autumn, you haven't seen them since the funeral. They want to see you. They want to talk to you."

"I don't want to see them."

"They are your parents-in-law and—"

"They were my parents-in-law," I pause, "and now they're not."

"Autumn." She tilts her head down, giving me this look like I've just tried to kill a puppy.

"I can't, okay. I'm sorry. I just can't."

She purses her lips, shakes her head, turns to leave.

"Just give me a break," I say to her retreating figure.

She stops but doesn't turn around. "Autumn, that's all we've been giving you."

A gross feeling settles in my gut. Why can't she understand? I don't want people coming because I don't want anyone mentioning Matt. It still hurts. Is it so unreasonable to want to get away from the constant reminders? His parents would be the worst reminder of all.

I spend the two days before my trip organizing as much as I can, deciding what to pack—not hard, considering all the stuff from my last journey is right here—and I go see the apartment manager. The worst task. But it goes better than I would have thought. The manager is understanding. He tries to convince me it's still a great place for one, but I'm not having any of it, and he concedes. I sign some papers and, with the promise that I'll send a death certificate, don't even lose my deposit. It seems people are sympathetic when speaking with a scarred widow, especially when she starts crying in their office. Not planned, but effective.

❧

WHEN THE EVENING before my voyage arrives, I think to myself—get through this dinner, get through this night, and then you can embrace the life you've set out to live. I feel some guilt for thinking this way—that I need to 'get through' a dinner with the people I love most, but they're not what I need right now. I have no idea when I'll be able to have them back in my life, when that will be healthy, but I'll deal with that problem when I have to. For now, I'm taking one step at a time, and this first step is what I'm focused on.

At the sound of voices, I come down from my room, smiling and ready. My smile fades when I see Eloise, Tracey, and Allison standing in the front foyer with Jennifer and my mother, all with furrowed brows, frowns, or pained expressions. I quickly put the smile back on and head over to them.

"Autumn!" They say in a chorus and rush toward me. They paste their smiles on, and I can imagine the discussion I interrupted—talk about my 'transformation,' about wanting no mention of Matt, or of the misery I'm clearly still in.

"Your hair looks awesome," says Allison. "Very chic."

"That's exactly what I thought." I flip the longer side up and give my head a little shake. I can't help wondering if it was Mom or Jenn who invited them tonight.

"And your arm," says Eloise. "It looks great. It's hard to believe you're bionic now."

I nod. "It'll make my travelling a little more interesting."

"Oh yes," says Tracey. "It's so exciting. You're so brave. Just taking off on your own like that." She hesitates here, as if she expects me to react badly, to break down in tears or something. It's not an unfounded fear. "You'll have such an amazing time," she continues. "I just know it."

Jennifer stays behind the girls. Her stance tells me she's battling disapproval and the desire to show support. I want her to support me. I want her to know I'm making the right choice for me. It doesn't matter though, not really. I know I should be doing this. That's what's important.

Eloise steps closer. She rubs her hand along my arm. Her dark eyes and even darker lashes blink slowly. "This will be good for you." She gives my arm a squeeze. "I'm sure of it. The trip can be an homage to you and Matt, to what you had planned together, as well as a chance for you to create your own path, to light out on your own."

I smile at her, thinking, *apparently you didn't get the memo.*

"That's what I plan to do," I say, not wanting to make her feel bad. "Light out on my own." We all smile at each other. "Come in." I motion them toward the living room. "I'm sure Mom will have something ready for us to nibble on before dinner."

I'm right. A tray of veggies and dip sits on the coffee table. We sit and I spend what energy I have directing the conversation. I prompt Tracey to tell me all about her new position at a high school and how she's thinking of getting her master's on the side so she can teach advanced courses. Allison updates me briefly on the club, tells a funny story about a new client, and says she's considering training for a fitness competition. Eloise tells us about her latest promotion as a Public Relations Consultant and how she now gets to travel to conferences with the firm's partners in Japan, Korea, and the UK. Next week she'll be in Tokyo. She's just telling us about how excited she is to see that city when Daniel walks in with his new lady, Mallory.

Mallory's nervous, almost skittish, and I wonder if it has

more to do with meeting Daniel's newly widowed sister or if it's simply the general nervousness of meeting a significant other's family for the first time. Daniel shows her off proudly, and I can see why. She's just as sweet as Jennifer said, and a small part of me is sad I won't be here to get to know her as the relationship progresses. Daniel doesn't bring just anyone home to dinner.

Billy arrives a few minutes later, sauntering in with an expression I can't read. We sit around the table and everyone does a fantastic job of not mentioning the elephant in the room. Despite that, I feel him and the gaping hole he's supposed to be filling so strongly it's all I can do not to scream. His memory is in every smile someone sends my way, every redirected conversation, every breath. I talk about my plans when people ask me—what I have planned anyway—and brush off the concern from my parents when I tell the rest of the group that no, I don't know where I'm going beyond Italy, or even where in Italy I'll be after my flight lands, and no, I have no idea how long I'll be gone for. It could be a few months. It could be a few years.

Daniel and all the girls try to act like this is cool, like it's great, like it's exciting, and the worst part is I know if I'd been planning this several years ago, before I met Matt, their excitement would have been sincere. Now concern leaks behind every word and smile, so much so that a small part of me wonders if their worry is legitimate.

But I don't have time for worries and concerns. I'm leaving tomorrow and that can't be changed now. I'll say goodbye at the end of the night—goodbye to these people and, hopefully, goodbye to so much of the pain and sadness and regret that never leaves my side.

"Why are you doing this? Really?" says Billy.

"What do you mean?" I glance at him, but don't keep his gaze. "To explore, to travel, to fulfil this lifelong dream." He's about to speak again when Eloise cuts him off.

"What are you most looking forward to?" She grins. "What is most exciting?"

I'm stumped for a moment. "I don't know," I say. "Just seeing new things I guess, meeting new people." The real answer? Getting away from everything and everyone at home that drips of memories of Matt.

She nods. "Travelling changes you. I saw it when I first moved to this country, and I've seen it so many times since—when I've gone home to visit relatives, on my post University excursion. But travelling alone, and with no agenda?" She grins again. "Now that's another story. You'll be a different person when you get back, Autumn."

I nod. "Here's hoping." Somehow in my rush to plan, I forgot Eloise spent a year backpacking with some friends after University. She did South East Asia though. I imagine it would have been an even more intense culture shock.

"Well, not too different," says Mom.

"Just enough," adds Daniel, and I'm sure we all sense how awkward the conversation has become.

I notice during dessert that Jennifer is the only one who turns it down and wonder if it's to make up for the indulging I basically forced her into two nights ago. She's definitely put on a few pounds in the past months—maybe as many as I've lost. Matt's death must be hard for her too, especially so soon after the death of her mother. I should make some time to find out, but I dismiss the thought. I don't have time for it right now and, honestly, I'm not confident I'd be much help, anyway.

The girls ask if I'd like to head out somewhere for a drink—it's a Friday after all—but I decline, feigning tiredness. It's nice that they're all friends now, when I'm the one who brought them together. I smile as I watch them putting on their coats, wondering when I'll see them again. Still, I'm relieved when the hugs are over and they all walk down the driveway and into the night.

Billy leaves just after them. Daniel lingers a little longer.

While Mom is talking with Mallory, he ushers me out to the back porch.

"We're worried, Autumn."

"Don't be."

He sighs and leans against the railing. "It just seems really fast."

"It's slow," I say, making my voice light. "I was almost supposed to be back from my backpacking trip, and here I am just getting started." He stares at me with that big brother look, letting me know he is not impressed. "Daniel," I say. "Really, I'll be fine. This is a good thing."

He pushes his hair back. "I don't know what you're going through and I won't pretend to." He takes a step toward me, puts his hand on my shoulder, and immediately I have the urge to shrug it off, step away. "But when things ended with Janine, I felt like my world imploded and I wanted to get away from everything and everyone that reminded me of her, but that's not what I needed. What I needed was the support from my friends and my family. That's what got me through." He takes another deep breath and I'm terrified he might start crying. I'm not strong enough to handle his tears. "I'm worried that's what you're trying to do. That you're just trying to—"

"I'm not." I move his hand away gently. "I'm moving forward. That's good, Danny. It's positive. Really."

"Autumn, don't do this."

"I have to."

"No, you don't. What you need is to stay here."

My throat tightens with a mix of anger, fear, and burning pain. "I have to."

"You don't, Autumn. I know you think…but it's not going to work, okay? This isn't really what you want, this—"

"What I want?" The words spew out of my mouth. "What I want is Matt to be standing here beside me. What I want is for him never to have died, for just one stupid second in the history of the world to have played out differently. But it didn't, and there's nothing I can do about that. Nothing! The only thing I can do is try to let go of it all, to move on, and the only way I can move on is to let go of him. To just, I don't know, try to erase him as much as I can. I can't do that here. I just can't." I'm shaking and Daniel wraps his arms around me.

"Be safe, okay, Sis?" I nod into his chest, my head crushed against him. "And just…I don't know. Keep in touch."

After a few moments he lets go of me and we stand there, awkwardly.

"I'm sorry." I wipe my arm across my face roughly, wiping away the tears.

"No," he says. "I should take off." He steps away from me. "But hey," his smile is slight, "what do you think of Mallory?"

"She's great." I say. "Really sweet."

"Yeah." He looks down, looking shy—an expression I'm not used to on him. He looks up again. "I like her a lot."

"She likes you too. I can tell."

"I think so." He nods a little too vigorously. "I hope so. I wish—"

"I know." I don't actually know what Daniel was going to say, but fear it had something to do with wishing Matt were here to meet Mallory, and I don't want to hear that. "I'm going to stay out for a few minutes," I whisper.

"Sure."

While he goes back into the house, I turn around and lean on the railing, looking across the yard—the old willow under which Matt and I shared a stolen kiss the first time I brought him home to meet my family, the lawn where we'd played flag football with all of our closest friends at the rehearsal dinner, this deck where he'd taken the time to get to know the people I loved. I think of them too, of all the people who showed up tonight and all the ones who weren't invited. Who knows when I'll see them again? I close my eyes and breathe in the faint scent of a BBQ that must be going on up the street. I open my eyes to gaze at my rings, sparkling in the porch light. Biting my lip, I slowly slide each one off of my finger and curl them in my fist. I'm saying goodbye to Matt—for good.

# CHAPTER EIGHT

A cacophony of noises surrounds me when I step out of the airport in Italy. It's thrilling. Everyone is moving fast and talking faster. For a moment, I wonder if I should have learned Italian but quickly pick out numerous English voices in the crowd. All I have is a hiking backpack and a purse, so when I see a driver on a moped waiting in the taxi line-up I head straight over. He smiles at me, winks, and calls me 'Bella' as he asks where I'm headed. I show him the name of my hostel—written on a notepad—and we're off.

The wind whips around us and I cling to him as he maneuvers through the overcrowded streets. This city is like nothing I've ever seen. High end cars zoom past dinged up and rusty beaters, bicycles, and an array of motorcycles and mopeds. Most amazing is what's off the street. New shiny buildings stand beside crumbled down ruins. And these aren't your typical old and run-down buildings, though I see those as well, these ruins are ancient, characterized by toppled over stone that's been fighting gravity for centuries. I don't know much about Roman history, but my guess is I'm taking in sites as old as the Colosseum. And that's when it hits me. I'm here. I'm in Rome. I'm going to see the Colosseum! I squeal as my driver weaves between two cars so tightly we're only inches from scraping them both.

When he pulls to a stop in front of a cement building with brown and green peeling paint, I question him, show him the writing again in my notebook, then choose to believe his chorus of "Si's," hoping he knows more than I do. I pass over the money, unsure of whether it's reasonable or not, and stand in front of the hostel, thinking the pictures on the website were definitely false advertising. It doesn't matter though. If it's as bad inside as it is outside, I'll stay here one night and then be on my way. I'm free. I can do what I want.

I venture in and breathe a sigh of relief—the interior's not bad at all. Despite my bravado, I've never actually roughed it. I've camped, yes, but that's an entirely different scenario than what I feared might await me here. The man at the desk looks gruff at first glance, but as soon as he smiles I feel at ease. He's pudgy, though not fat, and has a dark black moustache that reminds me of my father when I was a child. Jenn used to say my father looked like Luigi and though I couldn't see it in him, this man bears the resemblance. Two big rings of sweat drench his shirt, enhancing a smell that reminds me of Parmesan cheese. He looks my name up in the logbook and confirms that the booking went through. When he asks how long I'll be staying, I shrug. He wipes his hand through the air like he's wiping away worries. "You're free!" He kisses his fingers to the air in a way that makes me smile as I wonder how many other stereotypes I'll see throughout this journey.

He takes me on a tour of the place, showing me where I can come down for breakfast—fruit and pastries, tea and milk; the activity room—two old couches and an array of chairs with a small box television, coffee table, an assortment of books, and three ancient looking computers; and then the communal showers. Thankfully, they're at least separated by gender. We wind up a tight, dark staircase to get to the dormitories, the steps creaking the whole way. At the end of the hall behind two massive wooden doors is my room. He pushes one door in—it has to be at least eight feet tall—and smiles proudly as he holds his arm out, letting me survey the space. Several bunk beds line the wall and a row of singles sits in the centre. Throughout the room little lockboxes perch beside each bed, not even big enough to fit my backpack. "It's nice, yes?" he says, smiling broadly as he waves his hand toward some flowers in little glass vases on several of the lock boxes. "We have strict rules here." He grins. "No cavorting. For that you get private room."

I nod back. "Mm-hmm"

"We use no curfew, but you stay out very late you come in very quiet. Yes?"

"Yes."

"I get many complaints on you, you find new place to stay." I nod again and he puts his hand on my shoulder gently, like an uncle would. "But I think with you we have no problem."

I look around the room again and notice although most of the beds are made and have several items on them—one, a man sleeping in his boxers—folded sheets and a pillow sit in the centre of three of the beds. "Where am I?"

"Anywhere you want," he says. "Just pick one."

I scan my options. He leans in close and whispers in my ear. "You take the one way over in the corner. Quiet for you. Not so many people go past."

I nod then head over to the bed he's referencing. I set my things down and take a deep breath as he waves grandiosely and heads for the door. "Oh," he does a little half bow, "if you need me, my name is Mario."

He closes the door and I can't help but laugh, then quickly cover my mouth when I remember my sleeping roommate. I guess I was thinking of the wrong brother.

After making my bed, I look at the clock and realize it's just past noon. I still have a whole day ahead of me. For the first time since I've arrived, my excitement about this journey starts to waver. I have no idea what to do next. I didn't even bother bringing the lists of specific things I'd planned on my previous trip. I remember a number of them, but have no clue where anything is in relation to where I am. I also didn't take the time to switch my phone service over internationally, so it's no better to me than a watch. Welcome to life without Google Maps. I consider going down to the computers in the common area to find out what's nearby, but the whole purpose of this trip is adventure, so adventure is what I'll pursue.

After securing a few valuables in the lockbox, I make my way back down the rickety steps and out into the sunshine. The street I'm on is not all that busy, more of an alley really, and the three to four-storey buildings block my view of any notable landmarks. I turn left and within minutes am in a large piazza. A fountain dominates the centre of it, and people sit on benches and at tables throughout the square. I smile as it hits me again—I'm in Italy. I'm in a whole other country. A whole other world. Nothing looks like this back home. I debate stopping at one of the cafés and taking a seat at a cute little table but I'm more hungry for exploration.

I cross the piazza and turn up another slim alleyway that, after a block or two, takes me to another, smaller square. Only two people sit in this one. An old man, hunched over, legs crossed, with a book in his hand and glasses propped on the tip of his nose, and a young girl eating some kind of pastry topped with whipped cream. I walk by and the man nods at me. The girl is oblivious of my presence, her eyes large as she daintily rips off piece after piece of the pastry. The bakery must be nearby; a sweet and warm scent fills the air.

Around the next corner I find myself in what looks to be a shady part of town. The building fronts are worse than that of my hostel. Black mold grows along the cement of the walls. I quicken my pace and hike up a thin but steep set of steps. When I get to the top, the scene changes completely. An amazing and somewhat familiar smell dances in the air. My stomach growls. Scanning the area, I pick out the source—a pizza cart. Young people fill the scene, sitting on benches, lounging on the lawn, coming in and out of a massive building with wide steps leading up to the doors. It must be a university. I give into my hunger and line up for a slice of pizza. It's much thinner than what I'm used to, with barely any cheese but it doesn't seem to need it. The rich flavours of garlic, olive oil, and basil are intoxicating. After the first slice I head back for another and eat it on the lawn, just a few feet from a group of students in a heated debate. Again, I wish I'd thought to take some time to learn Italian. Once I've finished my meal, I prop up my purse like a pillow and lie back in the grass, my legs crossed, my soul relaxed. It occurs to me that I didn't contact my parents to let them know I've arrived safely. But it's okay. If something were wrong, I'd contact them. They should know that. The whole point of this trip is to get away. They'll need to get used to the fact that my emails and calls will be sporadic.

I don't know how much time has passed, but after probably an hour of lying there, completely oblivious to anything but the moment, I get up, give one last look to the busy people around me, and walk toward another set of stairs leading down. I enter another dark and sketchy alley and head toward the shards of light at the end. I turn the corner and gasp.

There in front of me, just at the bottom of another hill, lies the Colosseum. It's like nothing I've ever seen before. Not only is it massive, but it has a majesty that seems to quietly say, *I've been here lifetimes before you, I'll be here lifetimes after…*and there's something humbling about that. I walk closer, stepping down the hill until I'm probably only twenty to forty metres away. The closer I get, the more overwhelming it becomes. It seems criminal that something so beautiful, so intricately designed, was the site of such horrors. Although much of the detail has weathered away, the time and focus that was put into the monument is still obvious. It's a testament to both the best and worst of mankind. I debate for a moment whether I actually want to go inside and sit in the seats people sat as they watched mind numbing atrocities for fun, to walk the floors where blood poured out as a spectacle. I decide I'll regret it if I don't and make my way to an entrance.

As I walk through the interior, a surprising hush surrounds the grounds. Plenty of people fill the arena, but they've all brought their voices down a bit, presumably out of an innate sense that this is hallowed ground. When I'm about a quarter of the way in, that sense is torn apart by a group of young teenagers who are anything but quiet. I hurry my way through; the contrast of their liveliness to the memory of death that fills these walls is a little too much. I can't help thinking of Matt, of the fact that this was one of the places on our list, that I should be walking through here with my hand in his, that he, like all the souls who lost their lives on the ground below me, is no more. That's not what I'm here for though. I can't think these thoughts. So, as I make my way past the exit, I push them away.

Outside the sky darkens, and within moments rain pours down. Running to a canopy of trees not far away, I realize an umbrella would have been a smart thing to pack. Matt had had one, so I didn't bo…I shake the thought away and notice a woman touting an armful of umbrellas through a central part of the square, just down from what must be the Arch of Constantine. After taking a moment to stare in awe at the arch, I jog toward her.

"Don't do it!" A voice stops me. Clusters of people stand under other trees. A guy who looks maybe a year or two younger than me smiles and waves me over to the grouping of trees he's taken refuge under. "It'll be the most rubbish umbrella you've ever bought." He grins. "And if Rome is anything like the rest of Italy, this shower will pass in a few minutes."

"But—"

"Trust me." The grin deepens. "You can throw away your money if you like…" His voice trails off, and I find myself wanting to hear more of his strong British accent—a mix between the uppity Downton Abbey style drawl and a lower-class twang. His smile would put Beckham's to shame and is a little off kilter. He's fair-skinned, with something undefinable in his features—it could be some Spanish or Mediterranean ancestry, or maybe even a bit of African mixed in. His hair falls in lush waves around his face—waves that are just itching to curl. He hasn't shaved in several weeks. I catch my breath.

"He's right, you know," says a girl beside him. I pull my gaze away to look to her. "Those things are cheap. They'll break at the first sign of wind." She smiles. "I'm Emily and this is my brother, Jakob." As soon as she says it, I can see the resemblance. Her hair is just as thick and lustrous as his, but her curls have completely taken over and puff out around her face, a clip barely holding them back. Her eyes are dark, her skin is smooth, and her gap-toothed and subtle smile is completely disarming.

"I'm Autumn," I say, and we shake hands rather formally. As we do, I notice the faint scent of lavender.

"Are you alone?" she asks.

"Yes," I say, and suddenly feel exposed. "I'm backpacking."

"Us too," says Emily.

Jakob maintains his grin. "How long have you been at it?"

"A day," I stammer. "Just today. I arrived a couple of hours ago."

"Wow." Jakob nods and giving me a once over. "So, you're fresh."

"Don't mind him." Emily laughs. "We've been backpacking a few weeks now. We started at the tip—in Syracuse—and have been making our way up."

"We actually started in Tunisia," says Jakob.

"Well, we started at Syracuse in Italy." Emily faces him, her tone reminding me of the way Daniel and I sometimes challenge each other. She looks back at me. "We were in Tunisia for a couple of days and then took a boat across."

"Nice," I say, and wish I could have come up with something better.

"I'm guessing you haven't seen much of the city yet," says Jakob.

"No." I wave a hand behind me. "I just started exploring and happened upon the Colosseum. I had no idea where I even was until I saw it."

"Nice," he replies, and I feel less stupid. "Well, you're welcome to tag along with us as we explore this ancient city. If you want company, that is."

"You should," says Emily. "Do you speak Italian?"

"No."

"Well, it's not like you need it." She emphasizes the word need. "But we do and it's helpful, especially when it comes to paying for…just about anything. Or not getting scammed. Some people are fine, but a lot of locals try to take tourists for everything they've got."

"Yeah," I say, thinking company wouldn't be such a bad thing. "Sure. That'd be great."

"Brilliant," says Jakob. He raises his arm out and his eyes twinkle. "Well, would you look at that, the rain's let up."

I laugh and follow them back into the square.

As we head onto the sidewalk, it really is an ancient city we're walking by. Again, I'm struck by the contrast of it. To the right of me cars and motorcycles speed by, streetlamps lining the way, and to the left stand buildings that have occupied this space for a couple thousand years. Some are complete ruins, while others look as if they've been refurbished enough that they might be habitable. As we go along, Jakob spouts off facts about the areas we're passing—our own private tour guide. Emily looks at me at one point and rolls her eyes, but I'm loving it. When we get to a less busy area, he runs over to a fenced off section with exceptionally ruined ruins at the bottom of a gully. He leans over the railing. "We're looking at the Imperial Forums," he says. "Not to be confused with the more talked about Roman Forum."

"Oh, really?" Emily gives me a wink.

"The earliest of the forums were built around 46 BC. The latest around 113 AD."

"Around," says Emily.

"Well, we can't be absolutely sure. Records could be somewhat inaccurate." Jakob glances over at us; I smile back. "They were basically city centres. We're standing where everything important went down. Politics, Religious events. Trade."

"So what forum is this?"

"Uh," he takes look around, hesitates, "I'm not sure. Augustus maybe." He shrugs. "They're all connected. It was actually due to a ruler named Domitian who built the Transitional—"

"Okay, okay." Emily holds up her hands. "It's grand, it's really interesting. But let's just enjoy it."

Part of me wants to speak up for Jakob, but I don't want to create any tension. Their chatter is a good distraction from my own thoughts; it'd be nice to stay with them for as long as possible.

After touring the streets for another hour, then visiting a museum, Emily clutches her stomach and insists we find a café. When we walk up to it, quaint is the first word that comes to mind. Vines with white blossoms trail along the trellis and huge, colourfully blooming pots line the entrance. The scent is intoxicating. Inside, strings of lights line the walls and a single yellow flower in a tiny vase adorns each table.

We sit down, and I let Jakob order a large pizza and wine for us. As we sip our drinks, waiting for the food, Emily leans back. "So, what brings you here?"

I shrug and try to remain casual, saying as much truth as I'm comfortable with. "I'm between jobs and I've always wanted to see Europe. I had some money saved up and so, here I am."

"Brilliant," says Jakob. "And why Rome?"

"Oh." I laugh. "It was just the cheapest flight I found. Plus, my family emigrated from Italy."

"So, you're one of us then," says Jakob.

"Oh, well, it's a couple of generations back. My father wasn't even sure of the town, just that it's somewhere in the north."

"And are you going to find out? Visit it?" asks Emily.

"Probably not. Painful history, I guess." Emily nods. "I'll probably be in Europe for a few months at least though," I say. "This trip is more about that. I want to visit several countries. I may even stay in Europe long term, try to find a job. I don't really have anything holding me down at home."

"You don't have a man?" Jakob asks.

Emily whips her head toward him. "Jakob!"

"Or are you running away from one?" He raises an eyebrow as Emily punches him in the arm. "Your hand," he says. "You've got a tan line."

I look down, where the rings sat until just yesterday. I'd been fidgeting with the empty feeling on my finger all day. It's not surprising he noticed. I shrug. "Something like that."

"Well, this is the place to forget." He holds up his glass. "To new beginnings."

Emily looks over at me and smiles in a way that says, you'll get through this and my brother's an idiot. She raises her glass and I lift mine too. "To new beginnings."

# CHAPTER NINE

L azy with good food and wine, we walk the city, enjoying the cool evening air.

"Autumn," says Jakob. "We're going to this rave tonight. You should join us."

"Rave?" I question, picturing a bunch of drunk and high university kids in an abandoned lot. "No, I think I'll pass."

"You don't like to dance?" asks Emily.

"Sure, I love to dance. It's just—"

"Oh," says Jakob. "A club. We're going to a dance club. It's different across the water," he says, turning to Emily.

"Oh, right," says Emily. "In American movies a rave is quite illicit, right?"

"So, it's just a nightclub?" I ask.

"Just a nightclub, the focus is on the music, some drinks not, uh, other forms of entertainment," says Jakob.

Our hostels are only a couple of blocks away from each other and we agree to meet again in two hours. They pick me up right on time. We enter what looks like a regular restaurant and weave through the tables until we reach a slim corridor toward the back. Jakob exchanges a few words and a handshake with a guy who looks like he was born to work security. It seems Jakob knows the magic word, since we pass through a door and down a dark staircase. Emily trips on the stairs and grasps my arm for balance. "Sorry," she breathes. "It's these new heels." She gestures down to a pair of strappy shoes. "I'm still getting used to them."

"No problem. They're nice. So," I wave my arm, "how'd he find out about this?"

"Jakob has his connections," she whispers. When the door opens, we walk into a dark massive room with rock walls, lit by multi-coloured strobe lights. The music is some kind of European jungle-techno and loud enough that I feel the bass bouncing through my chest. Jakob passes three slips of paper to a woman at a booth and I try to yell over the music, asking how much it is. He waves my question away and shouts something unintelligible.

We weave through the crowd to a bar at the far side of the room. "You want a drink?" He mouths. I nod then watch as he motions for the bartender to come close enough to speak into her ear. He's so smooth, at first it's hard to believe this is the same guy who was spouting off facts about ancient Roman architecture a few hours earlier. But there was confidence there too. He passes Emily and me this green drink in a vial that reminds me of lab class and raises it in the air. Emily and I raise our vials and then I down the drink in one swallow. It's tart and potent and almost immediately I can feel my body warming. "What is this?"

"Absinthe."

"What?" My eyes go wide.

He laughs. "It's basically a vodka lime tonic. I wouldn't throw absinthe upon you without your consent."

I nod, chuckle, and wonder if I know what I'm getting myself into. I just downed a drink from strangers without even asking what it was. I don't actually know anything about these people…yet I trust them. We head to the dance floor and it's not exactly my type of music, but I give into it anyway. The repetitive beat sinks inside me as my body takes over, letting my mind go free. As the hours pass, I have more drinks than I probably should—but what does it matter? The men are tall and lean and dance around me, but with Jakob nearby none seem to try their chances at getting too close. Just as I'm thinking this, a hand gently rests on my hip, an arm slowly wraps around my waist, pulling me close, just as Matt used to. I imagine Matt, my back so tight against his chest I can almost feel his heart beat. I'm turned around, toward the man behind me, and our bodies move in sync. It feels so natural, so right, and I revel in it until my flesh betrays how wrong it is.

This man's smell is nothing like Matt's. His arms don't feel the same. I haven't even looked at his face, but of course it's not Matt's I'll see. He turns me back around and silent tears start sliding down my cheeks. This is not what I want. A hand grasps mine and I look up to see Jakob. He pulls me away and we squeeze through the crowd and into another corridor, through a door, and up a different set of stairs. When we're far enough away from the music that he doesn't have to yell, he puts his hands on my shoulders. "Are you okay?"

I shrug, not wanting to look up and have him see my tears, though I'm sure he already has.

"Was he hurting you?"

"No, no." I shake my head vigorously and finally look.

"Did he touch—"

"No. Nothing like that."

He smiles then. It's tender. He nods, rubs my shoulders gently, and it makes me want to start my crying anew. "You want to go back to your hostel?"

I let out a puff of air, thankful. "Yeah."

"You wait here, okay? I'll go get Emily." I nod and watch him leave, then lean against the wall, the cold rock soothing my steaming back. My head is spinning. I close my eyes and try to breathe, try to forget. It followed me here. He followed me here. I take deep breaths and will the tears to stop. It was stupid to think…but this has got to be better. "It will get better," I speak into the dank corridor. But somehow I know it won't, not like this—living like Matt was never this huge part of me. He's ingrained in me. He'll keep popping up.

I sigh and turn my head to the wall, letting my forehead rest against the cool rock. Even if I can't forget him, I still can't keep holding onto this aching love every day. After every break-up there's a time of mourning. A time when any man's touch brings back the previous one's. And then those feelings fade, the love fades and, in essence, I forget the person who once meant so much…or at least how much he meant. My voice whispers, breaking the silence in the stone-cold stairwell. "You need to forget. Please, forget." I wipe my eyes and put on a smile as the door bursts open.

Emily grins, sweaty and breathless. "What a party!" She laughs. "Whoo! Good call though." She swipes her hand along my shoulder as she passes by. It's shaking with energy. "I don't know how much more of it my body could have handled. I'm positively legless. Bed shall be good!" Jakob comes up behind me and places a hand on my back, gives me a smile and a nod to let me know I should go ahead.

"Yes," I breathe. "Awesome party. Quite the introduction to Rome."

"You've got that right." Emily pushes open the door at the top of the stairs and steps into the night. It's cool. It's dark. It's wonderful. And with Emily and Jakob standing beside me, I feel less alone.

We make our way down the street and, much to my surprise, it's only marginally less busy than it was earlier in the night. Cars still whip down the winding roads. "Is it always like this?"

"Like what?" asks Jakob.

"So alive!"

"But, of course." He laughs. "This is Rome." We wait at a crosswalk, other night revellers crowding around us, then enter the street, trying our best not to be jostled by the throng. When we make it across, the crowd thins out and Emily gasps.

"What is it?" Jakob grabs her elbow.

"My pouch."

"What?"

"My pouch. It was in my purse. It's—".

"Shit. Pickpockets." Jakob scans the crowds, then takes off back across the street toward a group of women. Emily runs after him, then screams, falling face first across the road. I run to her.

"My heel." She winces in pain.

"What?" I look down to see the heel of her shoe wedged in a storm grate. I yank on her foot while she tries to undo the buckle, her hands shaking. It's not budging so I push her hands aside and start undoing the buckle myself. We're near a sharp turn in the road and when the light changes cars will whip around that corner. The ones already at the light will see us but…

"Damn," I yell, as traffic starts to move. The clamps are tight and with the angle of her foot putting pressure on the straps I can't seem to get enough leverage to loosen it. The first wave of traffic works its way around us, but I can hear more coming in the distance. "Try to get up."

"What?" Emily's voice shakes almost as bad as her hands.

"Stand!" I yell, trying to work the clasp that still won't give. But it won't. I can hear the pickup truck barrelling toward us before it comes into view. I turn from her and run a few steps back the way we came.

"Autumn", she screams, the lights of the truck acting as a spotlight on her terrified face. I bolt back toward her, throwing my body into her side as the truck swerves and zips by us, honking madly.

We land in a heap just by the curb, then scramble to the sidewalk where Emily flings her arms around me. We're both shaking now.

"That was close," I breathe.

Jakob walks toward us, and I can see he's just finished a run. The pouch dangles in his hand. He steps closer, a strange look on his face, then drops beside us and pries Emily's arms off of me. "Are you okay?" He grasps her shoulders.

"Yes." She wraps her arms around him, tears streaming down her face. He looks at me over her shoulder. "What about you? Are you? I saw. I thought you were just leaving her there and then——"

"I'm okay." I smile. "Emily though, are you sure? You kind of broke both of our falls. Sorry about——"

"Yeah." She laughs, the tears slowing. "I should be right miffed at you. Next time you save my life try to do it a bit more gently."

"Are you okay though? Are you sure?" asks Jakob as she draws away from him.

"I'll be bruised." She leans forward and grasps her ankle. She twists her foot back and forth. "I don't think it's sprained, maybe just a bit of a twist." As she lifts her leg, the now broken heel dangles off her shoe. "So much for these."

I laugh and can feel my pulse settling. I hadn't even realized it was racing. "Beware the strappy sandal."

"Yeah." Emily glances to Jakob's lap. "You got it?"

He grins. "I got it."

"My ID, my meds." She starts to cry all over again. "If you hadn't——"

"It's okay," he says. "I did. It's okay. And you're okay."

Emily nods. "I was so worried about the pouch and instead I almost——"

"It's okay." Jakob takes one of her arms "Let's get you up." He braces her, while I rise myself, still a little shaky.

"Thank you." Emily hugs me again. Leaning on Jakob's shoulder, she manages to undo both clasps and slip her ruined heels off. "Not everyone would have done that."

"Sure they would have." I shrug. "And the truck was swerving, anyway."

"I don't know." Emily smiles, then steps aside as Jakob hugs me.

"Really, thank you, if you hadn't…I don't even want to think of it." He shakes his head, as if shaking away the possibility.

"Well, look at you," I say, "dashing after the thieves like that."

"Yeah," he laughs awkwardly, "a group of young women all at least four inches shorter and fifty pounds less than me."

"Still," I say. "It was brave and quick. Quick-witted even, that you knew who to go for."

"Okay, okay, enough." He winks. "We're both heroes."

"And what does that make me?" says Emily.

"In need of better footwear." He wraps an arm around her as we make our way back across the street. Emily clasps my hand and squeezes, then links her arm in mine.

When we reach my hostel, Emily hugs me again. "You want to tour with us again tomorrow?"

"Yeah." Jakob. grins. "The woman who saved my sister's life? I think maybe we better hold on to you for a while."

"Sure," I laugh. "That'd be great."

WE MEET UP THE NEXT day, and the next, and before I know it I'm sitting on a bus with them on the way to Florence and, several days later, Milan. We've met a few other people along the way but I'm the only one they've clung to like this…or perhaps it's me who has clung to them. Either way, something about that first night brought us together in a way I imagine doesn't usually happen.

Through snippets of conversation I learn that this is a grad trip for them—Emily has just finished her undergrad in Science and Jakob his master's in business administration, although he majored in History for his undergrad. When I asked about the switch, he just shrugged and smiled. "My family needed me."

The two are from London and he'll be going back there at the end of the trip to take over the family business. Emily's not sure what's next for her. They have a younger sister too, who's still in high school. Their family immigrated to England when Jakob was just a baby. Their Italian mother met their Swedish father when he was picking grapes in her family's vineyard.

They talk to each other casually, and with an intimacy that seems almost abnormal for a brother and sister, but not in a creepy way, so I assume it's just a cultural thing. I've let a few tidbits drop about my past as well. They know I took Kinesiology, I'm a trainer, and I grew up in Nova Scotia. They haven't pried deeper. Neither one has asked about the scars on my face or arm or why I set the alarms off in more than one museum. Neither of them has mentioned the fading tan line again. But sometimes they look at me as if they're waiting for me to tell my secrets. There's no point. I'm determined for that part of my life to remain a mystery.

# CHAPTER TEN

The rocking motion of the bus to Milan lulls me into sleep and Emily has to rouse me when it stops. We step off and I immediately feel something different about this city that's designed as a spider web. It has a pulse. The bus drops us off near the centre of the web and, apparently, the centre of its energy. The younger women in Italy have all seemed particularly in touch with fashion, but here it's as if they're ready for the runway. More than that though, the people seem ready for change. We walk down Via Agnello and I've never seen so many bikes or mopeds in one place. Over a hundred line the thin little street in every colour, size, and shape. It's like a motorcycle emporium. "Matt would have loved this," I laugh, before realizing my words.

"Who's Matt?" asks Emily.

"Oh." I smile back, but it's forced. "Just a friend." We continue down the street as I try to keep myself composed. It's the first time I've ever let anything like that slip. Despite my attempts at unawareness, at forgetting, I've never forgotten.

It's nearing dusk when we walk into a massive square full of people who dress more like us. Soft yellow light glows through stone windows, making me feel miniature—like we're inside a model of the town, with candles lighting our way.

"We're meeting Dominic at the Cathedral," says Jakob. "It's close." I'm a little nervous to meet their cousin. I don't know why. That's what I wanted, to get to know local people, but I've never been this transient in my life and I've liked it. Something about meeting a person who is settled here, about being welcomed into a family home, gives me pins and needles. We trek along, and all too soon we're at the Cathedral, the Duomo Di Milano. To say it is breathtaking seems trite, but it actually takes my breath away. I gasp when I see it. We've seen beautiful buildings. We've seen monumental buildings but nothing like this. A dream couldn't be more captivating. I'm in awe and humbled by the mastery that went into it, the countless hours and days and hundreds of lives that must have been devoted to this one structure. It's hard not to tear up.

"Nice, isn't it?" says Jakob. "I really enjoy this one." I just nod. "Dominic!" He calls to a guy sitting on the steps of the cathedral. The man stands. He's all ease and sophistication. Clean shaven, slightly shaggy hair, and a smile I can see the family resemblance in.

"Ciao," he says. "Ah, Bella." He steps past Jakob, straight for Emily, and cups her face in his hands, kissing the air beside each of her cheeks and then hugging her tightly. He steps away and gives Jakob a hearty hug then talks to them in speedy Italian. I pick up the odd word here and there but not much. Jakob stops him after a minute.

"English." He gestures to me. "This is Autumn, who I told you about."

"Ah, yes," says Dominic, and though his accent is strong, I can tell even in those words that English won't be a problem for him. "Autumn, welcome. I am Dominic Lombardi." He does a little flourish of a bow and gives me the two air kisses but leaves my face untouched. "Milan is marvellous, yes?"

"I love it." I say, and then laugh. "Well, I've only seen a bit, but I love what I've seen."

"This is my favourite spot." He spreads his arm theatrically. "It is a testament to all we are." I nod in response. "But come." He waves his arm in a motion to follow this time. Today we see Milan and then tomorrow to Nonno and Nonna. They can not wait to see you two." He smiles at me. "And you too, Autumn. They very much want to meet this Canadian girl."

We put our packs in a local locker facility and commence our tour. For the most part, it's Dominic who tells us about Milan. He walks along with a casual swagger and gives us a tour of the city with the familiarity of someone showing a friend their childhood home. It shocks me the things he knows. I couldn't give someone a tour of my city like this, and it's not even his city, not really. Although he went to school in Milan, he grew up in a village in the countryside. Despite Dominic's knowledge though, it's Jakob who adds in extra historical facts and tidbits of information. At one point they disagree on who built a certain building and why and get into a heated debate about it that quickly transitions into Italian. After several moments, however, Dominic laughs and claps Jakob on the shoulder. "I will let him win." He winks at me. "He is the one with the big degree after all of it"

We walk for several hours, until the night has fully set, and then Dominic takes us to a quaint little restaurant. He seems to know most of the people there, including the owners. He keeps forgetting to speak English at the table since whenever anyone else walks by to say hello, they do so in Italian. He apologizes profusely whenever he realizes it and seems to try to make up for it by asking me lots of questions about my experience of Italy.

"You didn't see enough of Milan," he says to me. "But you can come back again after you see Rocca di Giorgi. It is an entirely different type of beauty." He smiles proudly. "It is my home."

We stay in a hotel that night and it's nice enough that I imagine Dominic must have some money. The next morning we hop on a train and, despite the weeks we've been here, my eyes still can't take in enough of the rolling and lush Italian countryside. When we get to our destination Dominic leads us through the train station, and then to the parking lot where he points out his car—a classic looking convertible. We drive through hills and valleys, with vineyards and large open spaces on either side of us. The area is less modern than most of the Italy I've seen, and the stone buildings are much simpler. "It is like a fairy tale, yes?" He glances back at Emily and me.

"It's this blurry memory for me," says Emily. "I'm not sure I even really knew this was where this land, these images, came from."

"When were you here last?" he asks.

"When I was five, I think. That's right, Jakob?"

"Yeah, seems right."

"Well, Rocca di Giorgi welcomes you," says Dominic. "You are home."

Emily grins, and as I look over at her, I see a look I haven't seen before. It's expectant and hopeful and somewhat sad. She glances at me and her smile softens. "I'm glad we could bring this new friend, too."

We drive down a lane through a massive vineyard and up a hill until we approach a large but modest looking house. Modest in that it doesn't have the intricacies of the architecture I'm used to seeing in the cities. It's a farmhouse, but not like any I've ever seen. Dominic pulls into the driveway and hops out of the car without opening the door. "Here we are," he says. "Mi casa es su casa." He gives me a wink.

"Oh, come on," says Jakob. "She's not clueless."

"Well," laughs Dominic. "The sentiment is true."

I grab my bag and follow the others into the house. A short, round woman shuffles toward us. She lifts her hands and speaks so fast I can't pick up any of it except to know she's speaking excited words of love. Her full apron is more colourful patches than anything else and her hair is tied back with a scarf, equally colourful, which makes me wonder if the patches are intentional, not fixes. Her whole face turns into one huge wrinkle when she smiles, which she's doing a lot. She grasps Emily to her and kisses her then pushes her away, looks at her, says some more words, and pulls her to her again, squeezing Emily as if she might disappear if she's not held tightly. She hugs Jakob, then ruffles his hair, cups her hand to his scruff and shakes it. The tone she uses makes me think, 'tut tut.' Then she's back over at Emily again and she starts crying. She holds her tight, pushes her away, and pulls her back in again. It's overwhelming but beautiful. An old man, tall, lean, and sturdy looking, but with a hunch, comes into the room. At seeing him, the grandmother settles down. He says a few words then hugs and kisses both Jakob and Emily, looking at them with such tenderness it's almost painful. He throws his hands up in the air and then clasps them together again and holds them to his chest. He tilts his head and gazes at his family, kisses his fingers, and makes some kind of pronouncement. It's at this moment that he looks over at me, saying something I'm hopeless to make out.

"English, Nonno," says Dominic. I've been standing away from the group, in the shadow by the door. He waves me over. "This is Autumn. She is friends to Emily and Jakob. She is our guest."

The man makes his way over to me, and I hurry my steps so he has less distance to travel.

"Welcome to my home," he says. "Welcome to Rocca di Giorgi."

He embraces me boisterously then pulls away. His expression changes. "A sadness." He touches my face, right along the scar. "A shame, a mar to such beauty. It is new?"

I nod, not knowing how else to respond.

He nods too. "Your face is not yet used to it." He raises one shoulder, almost a shrug, then sighs, smiles. "But it'll help you grow a different kind of beauty, a deeper beauty, no?"

I look at him, my mouth slightly open.

"Nonno," says Dominic. "Now we show these ladies our home. You are the master of the house. You must do it."

He leans in close to my face. "You call me Nonno too." A smile full of delight and welcome crosses his face, wiping away the previous moment's concern. "If Emily and Jakob brought you here, that means you are family now."

My mouth is still agape; I close it then smile back. The old woman takes my arm and leads me behind her husband on a tour through the house.

As I suspected, it's their vineyard, and the land has been in their family for generations. The home is rustic and lived in. Everything has a place, and I wonder if this picture or that vase has sat where it's sitting since before I was born. An energy permeates the house, despite the age; it's an energy that radiates from the inhabitants as well, and that radiates from Jakob the longer we're here. Something is different about Emily in this house though, and not necessarily for the better. She seems less carefree, less…light. It's as if a sombreness has taken over her and I want to ask her about it but am not ready for the possibility that she'll ask me the source of my quiet moments, the source of the scar her grandfather brought up—the first person to since I arrived in this country. So I keep quiet.

When Emily and Jakob told me they were coming to visit their family and invited me along they said they didn't know how long they'd be there, maybe a few days, maybe a few weeks, but I was welcome to stay as long as I wanted or continue on my own.

I was uncertain when they made this offer, wondering if I should decline in case they were just being polite. Although part of me wasn't sure about being in a home again, another part wanted it. I told myself I'd come for the experience but make sure I didn't stay long enough to overstay my welcome. Shortly after the tour, cousins and neighbours pour onto the property with such casualness and ease I wonder if overstaying my welcome would even be a possibility. The home seems meant for everyone. The air fills with unrestrained laughter and conversation as we sit in the back garden. Delicious scents waft out toward us through the kitchen windows. By the time dinner is ready near thirty people have gathered around the long wooden table on the back porch and at various smaller tables and benches throughout the courtyard. A string of twinkle lights adds a festive air to what is clearly a joyous occasion for everyone present. Pointing at the lights, Dominic leans over to me, "The fairy tale," then goes back to his conversation with who, from the way they interact, I'm guessing is either another cousin or a childhood friend.

Despite the fact that pretty much all of the conversations are in Italian, someone always seems willing and eager to speak to me in English or to translate the gist of whatever conversation is going on. I've been hugged and kissed more times than I can count, but for the most part people's interest is focused on Jakob and Emily. I feel welcome though, and whole.

When we sit down to eat, Nonno stands at the end of the large table and raises his arms to silence the group. When he begins his speech, Elena, a young, shy looking girl with straight blond hair, fair skin, and light blue eyes, translates for me.

"Today is a joyous day," he says with a smile. "Today what has been lost to us across the sea has returned again." Loud cheers and assents erupt and, with a patient smile, he motions for silence. "Our Jakob was here just four years ago." His smile is full of love. "But our Emily," he turns his gaze to her, "has not been here in over fifteen years." He clasps his hands to his heart again, like he did when we first arrived. "A lifetime for her. My joy could only be more complete if my daughter were here with her children, to share in our joy and to add to it." Many people nod and some look down. A few cross themselves. "But we are thankful for what we do have. The love we share," he motions, encompassing everyone present in his sweep, "and the memories of all the ones who can no longer be here to share our joy with us. We know they share it still." He looks at me now, and so do most of the other faces. "I also want to welcome our other guest, Autumn Caparelli. While you are here, my child, you are our family. Here you are safe, here you are welcome, here you are loved." Heat rises up my face and I smile awkwardly. The man beside me grasps my shoulder and squeezes it. "And now," says Nonno, raising his hands again. "We eat."

# CHAPTER ELEVEN

The dinner is more of an event than a meal and I see it as my first real introduction to Italian life. The wine flows, and the courses flow along with it. Relaxation seems to float through the air like fog, settling over us as the hours pile up. The volume dims as the evening progresses and speech and movement become more languid, though I wouldn't say anyone is drunk. They're at peace. I notice, though, with the exception of Emily and Jakob, those who speak with me or translate do so a little more slowly, with a little more thought behind each word.

A group of old men referred to as the Zios, which I learn is the Italian term for uncle, sit chatting in a corner of the yard. One motions to a boy who's probably pushing seventeen and draws him over to the group. He speaks to him softly, then waves him away again. The boy returns with a violin and, after some discussion, lifts it to his chin. He starts slowly—the sound that emerges seeming impossible from someone so young. It's painful and sweet. After a verse or two the man who called him starts singing in a deep resounding voice. Several of the others join in. It's the most hauntingly beautiful thing I've ever heard. I feel immersed in it and all that pain, all that sorrow and anger and sadness that I've done my best to push deep within me, rises to the surface as the song lifts to a crescendo. I keep my eyes attached to the first Zio, whose eyes are shut, and watch as his face carries the weight of all the sorrow I've felt in my heart these past weeks.

When the song draws to a close and the last note on the violin dies away, leaving only a hush where once there was muted conversation, Dominic leans over to me. He wipes the stream of tears from my cheek, grazing my scar as he does so. He smiles then places the same hand on my chest, just above my shirt collar. "It touches you," he says. "Here."

I answer with the slightest of nods.

"Good." He leans back again in his chair, one leg casually crossed over the other. "This is what Italia is for."

I close my eyes and hold on to the ache brimming inside me, but only for a moment, and then I hide it all away again.

People disperse around two in the morning. Mothers carry their small children in their arms and fathers lead the older ones along. There are more rounds of hugs and kisses and, this time, I'm included in the affection. When I follow Emily up the stairs, she turns to me with a sleepy smile. "Are you sure you don't mind sharing a bed?

"It's perfectly fine," I tell her.

"Okay." She spritzes her pillow with lavender. "It helps me sleep deeply. Just give me a pinch if I kick."

In the bathroom I stand in front of the mirror. This is the first time I've stood and looked since before I came to Italy. I've become adept at naturally washing my hands without glancing up. I brush my teeth with the sink behind me and only turn to spit. I haven't been wearing much makeup in my travels so that isn't an issue. I place my hand where Nonno held his earlier, where Dominic wiped my tears away. People used to tell me I should go into modelling and I knew I was often considered the most attractive girl in the room. I thought I hadn't let it get to my head. I thought I believed it didn't matter. I smile for the mirror. The scar crunches up, wrinkling the skin around it. It's not hideous. Definitely not. I can say that objectively, but I'll certainly never be asked about modelling again. I quickly wash my face and return to the bedroom.

Emily is already asleep and, as I crawl in beside her, I realize it's the first time in over four months that I've had another body beside me in bed. He used to wrap his arms around me at the start of the night. He held on so tightly, but as he eased into sleep, he would loosen that grip, roll over, and then somewhere through the night I would wake up with my arms around him. I scooch over to the edge of the bed. I used to teach my clients about muscle memory— how important it was to build that up, how once you've developed it the memory can stay for years. I don't want my muscles' memories to give Emily a shock in the middle of the night.

THE WINDOW IS RAISED, and when I open my eyes only a few hours later, I watch the curtains blow gently in the breeze. It's a sight that may never seem commonplace to me again. It brings me back to the curtains I watched on the day I learned my world would never be the same. Faint light is just starting to enter the room. I tiptoe out of bed and pull on some clothes, shivering in the cool of the morning. Emily rolls over in bed and I halt my movements until she's settled again. The door squeaks as I open it and I cringe and look back, but she's unmoved. When I get downstairs the quiet and empty rooms seem hollow after being so filled last night. A noise draws me to the backyard. Nonna is there, sitting in a chair, humming, and looking out to the fields. The sunrise is full of purples and blues on the horizon, muted by the morning mist. I sit down beside her and see that she's rolling some sort of meat into ping-pong sized dough balls pinched together like Hershey's Kisses. She looks over at me, her lips pursed in a contented peaceful smile, then says something that sounds welcoming. She goes back to her rolling and her gazing. After we sit there like that for a while, her humming while she works, and me beside her, I try to ask if I can help. "Soccoroso?" I say and make a rolling action with my hands. She looks at me like I'm crazy then chuckles.

"No, no," she says. "No."

I sit back and look at the fields again. I can see the grapes from the closest vines, plump and ready for picking.

"It's more complicated than it looks." Dominic comes toward us. He kisses his grandmother on the temple, and she cups his face in her hand without looking up at him, pats it. Dominic then pulls up a chair beside me. "It takes practise and training to get them just right. But stay here awhile, watch her, and maybe by the time you leave she'll let you lend a hand."

"Oh," I say.

"You are up early. Your bed was not comfortable. You couldn't sleep." He says these as statements.

"No. I slept just fine."

"Then you like the morning."

"I guess." I smile over at him and then look back to the sun reaching over the most distant hills of the vineyards. "Who wouldn't like this?"

"It is beautiful."

"You can say that again."

"It is beautiful."

"Oh, I meant—"

"I know what you meant." He looks at me with that half grin I've become used to seeing on Jakob. "It is a joke."

"Yeah," I can feel my cheeks turning red. "Of course, I—"

"You think the Italians cannot joke. We can joke."

"No, I—"

"I am still joking now."

I laugh out loud then cover my mouth, afraid of waking the others.

"Autumn."

"Yes."

"I am going for a run now. You will come with me."

"Is that a question or a command?" I tease.

"It is a question," he says. "A request."

"I don't know." I look toward the fields. "I don't really run anymore. I haven't been exercising in a long time."

"You are a trainer, no?"

"Yes."

"And you don't run?"

"Well, I'm not a trainer right now. I'm travelling. I'm on vacation."

He laughs. The sound is robust yet soft at the same time. "Autumn, there are two things we never take a vacation from—the soul and the body. I think you trained your soul some last night, yes?" He gives me a nudge. "Come with me. Train the body."

I almost say no, but then I don't. "Okay. When?"

"Now. While the day is still young. This is the best time to run."

I tiptoe back into the room, grab my running shoes, then change into some shorts. I'm about to tie my hair back in a ponytail—like I always would—when I remember there's only one side to tie. Some clips rest on the dresser so I pin the longer side back as well as I can. Dominic is waiting for me with an eager smile when I get back downstairs. We start out and for the first few minutes I feel a little out of breath. Dominic has a fast pace, but as my blood starts pumping speed comes back to me and I push ahead of him. He laughs at this and brings our strides in sync. We settle into an easy rhythm and I take in the scene around me. Leaving the road, we turn up a path that follows the vineyard on one side and a stream on the other. We push ourselves as we head up a hill into the sunrise. This definitely rivals any run I'd be doing back home. When we reach the hill's summit, Dominic motions for me to turn and follow a path into the woods. We run into a clearing, then slow to a stop in front of another stone house that makes the Lombardi's look small. "What is this?" I ask.

"Just a place I enjoy." He walks closer to the building. "It is abandoned now."

"Why?"

"Politics." He shrugs and stands in front of a large wooden door that looks like it would have been a back entrance. "The story is a long and frustrating one." He pulls open the door and motions to me. "But come and see."

"It's just open like that?" I take a few steps closer. "Isn't this trespassing?"

He laughs at me, like I'm a nervous little girl. "No one is present to care. We will not do any harm."

"Will it do harm to us?" The bricks of a structure next to the building remind me of a Jenga tower ready to topple over.

"You will be safe," he says. "Just speak softly. Do not touch the walls." He winks but I'm not so sure he's joking and as I tentatively step into the building, glancing up at the uneven stone above me, it hits me—I don't want to die. I don't want to not exist. I'd been trying to live my life, I'd been telling myself I have things to live for, but until this moment I'm not sure I really felt it. In those first few weeks after…I just didn't want *to be* anymore. He *wasn't*, and so why should I be? It wasn't him who I didn't want to exist, not really. It was me, and by saying he never existed, I was saying the part of me that loved him didn't either. The thought makes my racing pulse race faster. I do love him though, that part hasn't died. But I want it to.

# CHAPTER TWELVE

I brush cobwebs off my arm, shivering at their sticky cling, and step into a dark room. I can't just forget Matt. I can't pretend he never existed. That's stupid. It really is. But maybe I can let go of the part of me that can't let go. I still love him just as much as I ever did. That's what I need to forget, to let go of—how much I love him. If I let go of that, maybe I can finally let go of all this pain. It still means I need to not think of him—a feat that seems impossible.

Just as my eyes adjust to the darkness, Dominic opens the shutters on a window across the room, making me squint. I open my eyes against that shard of light and look around the space. A dainty teacup and saucer sit on a handmade wooden table. Cast iron skillets rest on a cast iron oven. Children's clothes hang on a line by the window. Despite the gaping holes, I can make out several girls' dresses of varying sizes. "They had three daughters," he says and walks into another room. This one is grander, and the furniture looks more modern, though still older than me. "Nonno knew them," he says, and walks by a row of paintings so dusty the colours are hardly colours anymore.

"And everything was just abandoned? I don't get it. What happened to—"

"Nonno wouldn't tell me when I was a boy," he says, walking through the room like it's a museum, careful not to touch a thing. "So I made up my own story. I said that the littlest girl, Bella, made a wish that her family could live with the stars. Then one night a fairy came and asked Bella if she was sure. Bella said she was, so the fairy gathered her family and took them away and everyone was so happy and so thankful to Bella because now they would live up in the sky and be together for always. They held their hands and closed their eyes and were transformed." He stops, smiles at me, and I can almost see that hopeful boy looking out through his features. "The real story is much more sad."

I take several steps toward him. "Come now," he says, the smile returning to his face. "This is what I wanted to show you." He takes my hand and leads me up an open staircase. The steps seem precarious and again I get that feeling deep inside that reminds me life is precious. When we reach the landing, he pulls down a door, letting a stepladder drop. I follow him into what must have been the family's attic. He carefully walks across the floor, avoiding rotting beams, never loosening his grasp on me, and I follow in his footsteps. He opens the shutters on another wooden window and looks back at me, his face full of pride, then moves to the side so I can get an unobstructed view. He rests his hands on my shoulders. "This is my favourite sight in all of Italy. It is the legacy of my family."

The vista before me is incredible, rows and rows of grape trees, the sun lighting them up like a spotlight. "These are all yours."

"Si."

"It's beautiful." I turn. "Thank you for showing me."

He nods and there's that little boy again, shy this time. He lets one hand trail down the length of my arm then takes my hand again to lead me back out safely.

"Do you want to sit for a while?" he asks as we stand outside, his hand trailing down to my hip. "Enjoy the rest of the sunrise?"

"We should finish our run...and eat!"

"Of course." Dominic stands tall and is back to his casually confident self. "We'll be finishing the last of the harvest in the next week or so," he says as we run back. "Will you stay? It is a special and festive time. We have many workers and, for the final days of each year's crop, many family and neighbours join. You may pick too."

"Well—"

"It is not like dumplings," he says. "Even you can do it."

I laugh as we make our way to the house and before we can even see the building the smell of bacon and fresh bread welcomes us.

Emily and Jakob sit at the kitchen table and, after a quick shower, I join them. I'm told Dominic has gone to check on the harvest workers and will be back soon. "So, they're doing it right now?" I ask.

"Oh yeah," says Jakob. "They would have been going at it for several hours by now. It's best to start before the sun comes up. They usually break throughout the mid-afternoon and then go back at it again."

"And will you two be picking?"

"We'll help out," says Jakob. "The last few days the whole neighbourhood usually gets involved. At that point it's more of a social thing. We can make a difference, but we're nowhere near as fast as the workers."

"And we wouldn't want to take away too much from their income," says Emily. "A lot of families really rely on harvest season."

"That too," says Jakob.

"You'll like it," says Emily. "I mean you don't have to join us. But—"

"No, I'll do it." I sit at the table with a full plate. "When will I ever get the opportunity again?"

"That's the spirit." Nonno bursts into the room. He cups both the heads of Emily and Jakob and gives them a kiss then cups and kisses mine as well. He sits with a flourish that lets me see where Dominic gets his flare from. "You must embrace life. Embrace every new experience." He grins like a mischievous little boy. "And right now I must embrace this pig." He piles an obscene amount of bacon on his plate then adds eggs, bread, and fried onions. "So," he continues. "What is it you young ones will do today?"

"Dominic and I were thinking we'd show these two more of the fields, initiate them into the whole harvesting practice and then show them some of our old haunts. Some of the town," says Jakob.

"Buono, buono. Does that suit you?" he asks of Emily.

"Yes, Nonno." She smiles at him, and again I feel as if I'm missing something.

When Dominic returns, we sit and drink tea and chat as he eats his breakfast, then the four of us set out. We start in one of the rows that comes up to the backyard and continue walking onward as Dominic tells Emily and me about the vineyards and the harvesting practice. I'm half listening and half blown away by the fact that I can't even see the workers yet and all of the vines around me are heavy with clusters of grapes. I don't know how far the rows on either side of me go but I can tell it's far. It doesn't seem possible that all of this will be picked within the next few weeks. And then, as I see the multitude of bodies and the speed at which they pick—though never seeming rushed—it becomes more believable. "All these people work for you?"

Dominic turns to me. "Yes."

"That's…a lot of people."

"It is a business," he says. "We must have workers."

"Oh, I know," I say, feeling embarrassed. "Never mind. I just meant it's impressive."

"Yes." He smiles and his chest rises just slightly. "It is most impressive."

People of every age and walk of life tend to the rows. I don't know what I had expected—though I suppose I'd barely thought of what to expect—but it wasn't this. To my left a boy no more than seven hustles by me with a pail of water. "Where do they all come from?"

"They are from everywhere," says Dominic. "They

are…" he waves his hand, searching for a word, and then speaks something in Italian.

"Migrant workers," says Jakob.

"Yes." Dominic smiles. "We have migrant workers who travel from across the continent and pick. People from the community—even Americans. Richard, Rachel," he calls out, an arm upraised. Two people wave back to me. One looks to be of Filipino descent and the other is blond and blue eyed. They wave back. "These are what we call our picking interns. There is a program. We fly them here, we pay for them to stay during the harvest, and then we deduct those expenses from their pay. But afterward they are in Italy and they have enough money to travel for several weeks before returning home. It is a pleasant system." He leans into me and gives a wink. "Though they are not always quite as good workers as they should be." He continues walking. "Those two are focused though. We will invite them back."

I nod and follow along as Dominic takes us through the rows. He talks to most of the workers in Italian with occasional switches to French, Spanish, and English. For the most part, I observe silently. Emily translates for me at first, but I tell her it's not necessary. I enjoy watching quietly. When we get to the end of the unpicked rows Dominic spreads his arms. "I will show you the town now, if it is your wish." Emily and I both nod. Jakob is several paces behind. We turn to watch him talking to a little boy, though yelling may be a more accurate description. The boy yells back, with attitude at first, then his tone softens when Dominic walks up beside Jakob. Fear passes over his expression. Jakob continues to talk at him, his arms gesturing with emotion. "What's happening?" I ask Emily. "Is everything okay?"

"It," Emily seems embarrassed now, her lips pursed, "it's not his business." She sighs. "But he's trying to do what's right."

The issue seems to be resolving but I ask anyway. "Can you tell me? What is it?"

"It's the boy." Frustration leaks from Emily's voice. "His mother was asking for help—For water and to take a message to the boy's father. The boy was being rude. He told her off and Jakob stopped him. He's been lecturing him." She shrugs. "It's not his place. He thinks it is, but…" She stops when Jakob and Dominic return.

"I'm sorry, I…" Jakob runs his hands through his shaggy hair. "It just drives me crazy. That disrespect. The kid—"

"Emily explained," I say.

"I had to say something. He doesn't know—"

"He's just a boy," says Emily softly. "A child."

Jakob turns to her; his look is pointed and says more than they are. "Well, now he knows that's not okay."

"Maybe," says Emily. "Or maybe now he feels more cause for rebellion."

"Let us go to the village." Dominic smiles and puts one arm around each cousin. "It is a beautiful day for taking walks down memory lane, yes?"

"Yes," says Emily. As Dominic's arm drops, she grasps his hand and squeezes it before letting go. They fall into step and Jakob walks beside me.

"It must have been weird to see me just blow up at a kid like that."

I smile and shrug. "It was a bit shocking."

"Sorry. I just can't stand that. If you'd heard the way he was talking to his mom…"

"I'm sure you had your reasons. You don't have to defend them to me. Seriously."

"Yeah." He kicks a piece of wood in the path. "I probably scared the crap out of that kid though."

"He didn't look too scared," I say. "Well, not until Dominic came along at least."

He shrugs. "It's Italy. People are used to taking care of other people's kids here. The boy's probably used to it. That would not have flown in England. It hasn't." He looks away, as if he's seeing something I can't. "I remember when I was a rotten little kid here. It wasn't just Nonno and Nonna who were kicking me in the butt. The whole village seemed to think I was their responsibility." He laughs.

"So, you were here as a child?"

"Yeah, I lived here for a while. Almost a year."

"And what a year it was!" Dominic yells back to them. "We had some big adventures."

"Misadventures is more like it." Jakob laughs, and it seems whatever was burdening him lifts, letting the strong, easygoing guy I'm getting to know emerge.

"You remember Zio Niccolo's sow?" asks Dominic.

Jakob almost chokes with laughter. "Like I could ever forget."

"It was a beautiful, beautiful thing, ladies," says Dominic. "My Jakob here, he decided he wanted to be a cowboy, but he was too much afraid to get on a horse. And so he decided he was to practise on Zio…our Uncle's cow. No. Sow." Dominic is cracking up already, and it seems to be affecting his ability to speak English. "Jakob, I cannot," he says.

"So, yeah, I decide I'm going to practise on the sow, and I get into the pen, real stealth-like. I tiptoe through the muck, thinking I'm on this grand adventure. I've got a rope in case I need to lasso the thing and a cowboy hat on my head that's so big I can barely see. I crawl up on the sow and it just sits there. I didn't need to creep at all. It couldn't care less. I'm feeling embarrassed now, and frustrated because there's Dominic and this pretty little girl—what was her name?"

"Camilla."

"Yes, there's Dominic and Camilla staring at me and I want to impress them both. So, I drive my heels into this big old sow and again nothing. I start slapping the thing and yelling every cowboy type word I can think of and the thing acts as if I'm nothing more than a fly perched on its back."

"He is making such a…a ruckus," says Dominic, "that it alerts Zio Niccolo."

"He comes racing out of the house with his pants half down and one boot on." Jakob stops, and his face brightens before he bends over laughing. "Oh, wow. I didn't clue in before, but he must have been having some afternoon delight."

"But yes!" says Dominic. He laughs through several words in Italian. Jakob laughs harder and Emily rolls her eyes.

"So, he comes barrelling out, his arms waving in the air like a madman, and he's headed straight toward me. It's at that moment the sow looks up and suddenly realizes I'm on her. She takes off like there's a firecracker up her ass and—"

"Right through the fence," says Dominic. "Right through it."

"And I go sailing."

"He was all but mud and muck," says Dominic, adding a few more Italian words.

"I thought I'd never be able to look Camilla in the face again." Jakob rubs a hand along the side of his face, his grin sheepish.

"But you were." Dominic punches Jakob's arm. "I do believe she was so scared for you, so concerned for your wellbeing, you managed to take her first kiss."

Jakob chuckles. "I may have finagled it out of her. It will be the kiss upon which all others will be judged and found wanting." He raises his arm and says this in a tone that makes me think he's quoting something.

"It was Zio Niccolo you really needed to be concerned about," says Dominic. "I do not know if, to this day, I have seen him this angry."

Jakob puts his hand to his head and slumps his shoulders. "I know." He laughs. "He was furious. He came and picked me up by the arm and marched me all the way to

Nonno. He said that I was a bad apple then lectured Nonno that he needed to learn how to take care of his charges and said if Nonno didn't he'd take me away from him and teach me some discipline."

Jakob shakes his head. "Well, Nonno supported his brother's words that I needed discipline, feeding his self-righteousness. And then as soon as Zio Niccolo left, Nonno started laughing. He dusted me off and asked if I had gone for a good ride." Jakob stops now. He smiles—it's sweet and tender. "He told me I wasn't a bad apple or a bad boy. He said I was a good boy and I would grow up to be a good man and he was sure I meant no harm when I got on that sow, that I was only trying to have an adventure and adventures were good but I also needed to respect other people's property.

"He told me I would work to repair the fence and any other damage I had caused." Jakob looks away, talking more to himself now than to us. "He said he understood I was angry and scared a lot of the time and that was okay. I was going through a hard and confusing time that no boy should have to go through. He said that Zio was right, I needed discipline, but that he was not the one to discipline me. He said all my life I will have opportunities to do bad things, or things that others will perceive as bad, and I need to weigh my choices and my actions."

Jakob focuses back on us and shakes his head slightly. "He said I must learn to discipline myself for that is the only discipline that matters. And that he knew I would learn this and grow up to be a man that made my family proud but, more importantly, a man who was proud of himself." We're all silent for a moment when Jakob stops—his words seem to have affected Emily and Dominic more than me, and I wonder what difficult time Nonno was referring to. Jakob wipes a tear out of his eye.

"I did not know this is what he said," says Dominic. He switches to Italian.

"It was meant for me," says Jakob. "That day changed my life. I went home shortly after. You remember."

"Yes." Dominic nods, his brow furrowed. "I remember."

"Anyway," says Jakob, and I can see he's trying to shrug the moment off. "I couldn't go home until I'd fixed that fence. It was good though. Taught me a thing or two about how to use my hands. And I learned another lesson—despite what you may think, a pig can not be used as a substitute for a horse."

"A good lesson." Dominic claps Jakob on the shoulder. "Now, Emily, Autumn—here is downtown Rocca di Giorgi!"

# CHAPTER THIRTEEN

Downtown is definitely not the right word. Rocca di Giorgi is so small I wouldn't even call it a village. About five buildings line the road. The whole scene could fit on a postcard—a very picturesque one—and, like the rest of Italy, the street is a mix of the old and the new. A coffee shop advertises free Wi-Fi beside a butcher shop and chickens peck their way through the backyard of a bakery where a Fiat sits in the driveway. We run into several people who were at the Lombardi's that first night and Dominic seems to know just about everyone else, not that there are many people around to know. When he and Jakob run into a man who seems to have been a boy Jakob used to know, Emily pulls me to the café for a cup of tea.

"You sure you don't want to stay with them? I don't mind the Italian."

"No," says Emily. "I'm happy to sit down for a while. This will be nicer." She's out of breath, though we've only been strolling along.

The café seems more like a converted living room than a coffee shop, cozy and quaint. "So, you said you haven't been here since you were five?" I ask. "Why is that?"

"My father is quite protective of me. The last time I was here I came with my mother. Now that she's gone he doesn't come back here, and he didn't want me to come without him."

"But he's okay with it now?"

"I'm twenty-one now," she says. "He doesn't really have a choice."

I nod. "Have you travelled many other places?"

"It's hard for our Papa to be away from the restaurant for too long so I've never left Europe. I've been to all the countries nearby."

"All the countries nearby." I laugh. "That could be a lot."

"I suppose," she says. "It's different for us. It doesn't feel like travelling. Not in the same way. I mean it is, but..." Her face lights up. "I want to do what you've done. I want to travel far away. All on my own. I want to go to the Americas and Australia and Asia and meet people I wouldn't know existed if I hadn't."

"So, do that," I say. "What's stopping you?"

She's hesitant. "I need to be near my family."

"You can be as near as you want," I say. "I'm pretty sure the internet is in all those places. You can Skype and email and be more connected than they'd even want."

"No, it's different." She shakes her head. "They need me there. The business. My grandfather—he's getting older. And I need them."

"Okay," I say, hesitant to push. "If you say so. But, you know, if those are your dreams..."

"I have other dreams too," she says, "dreams I can fulfil at home."

"Like what?"

"I don't know." She laughs self-deprecatingly. "I want to be someone important. I can be someone important at home by being a support to my family and maybe work as a counsellor or in a school. I can help people make their lives better."

"Yeah," I say, feeling uncomfortable with the way she says this, as if it's rehearsed. "That all sounds great."

"It will be great," she says. And I don't know which of us she's trying to convince. "But what about you? What are your dreams?"

"This was one of my dreams." I look around me, my arms outspread. "I always wanted to come to Europe, to visit small villages and big cities, to meet new people, explore different cultures."

"And here you are, doing it."

I nod and laugh. "Here I am, doing it."

"And are you happy?"

I watch her watching me. "Sure I am. It's been awesome. It's been more than I could have imagined. I mean meeting you and Jakob, and then coming to be with your family, I couldn't have planned that."

"I mean has this made you happier. Like really happier than you were back home?"

"I don't know." She stares at me and I don't know what she's getting at. "It's complicated."

"I don't know either." She laughs. "Never mind. I just…sometimes I hold on to that dream, you know? And I'm happy with my life. I have a wonderful life. I'm blessed to be living it. I've just always wondered how different it would be to live somewhere completely new…to follow those dreams. I don't know how you were back home and I can see you're having a good time but," she looks down at her cup of tea, "maybe where we are doesn't have a whole lot to do with general contentment, you know? Maybe it's more about how we choose to look at our lives. Maybe I could get everything I've ever thought I wanted and at the end of the day it won't have made that much difference."

She sips slowly and seems sad as she does. "Maybe there are things back home that could have done for you what all these experiences have done. Maybe there are things back home for me too."

She stops and I'm not sure if she's done, if she's waiting for me to say something, so eventually I do. "Maybe."

She shrugs, smiles the peaceful smile I've come to know. "All I asked you for was a cup of tea. Not these types of hypotheticals."

"I've always thought hypotheticals go well with tea."

It's that genuine laugh again. A full one. "They do!" She sits back. "Maybe we all already have enough and it's the act of wanting more that makes us dissatisfied."

"What are you getting at, Emily?"

"I don't know. I'm just musing." I can see she's fighting a tear. "I'm sorry. I guess I'm feeling a little mopey today. And a little contemplative. I'll snap out of it."

"You don't have to. I just—"

"No. I'm snapped." She perks her head up and does this cute little nose scrunched smile. "But my tea is pretty much done. Another cup or should we grab the boys?"

"Whatever you like."

"The boys." She takes a final sip of her tea then stands.

⁓

AFTER A FEW MORE DAYS of exploring neighbouring villages and towns—actual ones—Jakob, Emily, and I decide we're ready to join the harvest. Dominic says we can start whenever we want and end whenever we want. We don't need to view this as real work but if we don't, we shouldn't interact too much with the regular pickers as it may lower morale. I tell him no, I want to get the full experience, and Jakob and Emily agree. We wake up three hours before the sunrise, when the coldness of the morning air feels like an assault. It hits me, tightening my skin, and after the first hour of picking with numb fingers, I doubt I'm cut out for this. I curl my fingers into my hands then uncurl them again and again, trying to let warm blood flow and relieve the cramping.

It doesn't take long before I'm noticeably behind the people I started with. Even Emily and Jakob are several plants ahead of me. I decide I have to be capable of doing more, doing better, seeing as I have the same raw materials as everyone else but, despite my efforts, when we break at mid-day I'm further behind and have less grapes than the others.

"And how was your first morning of harvest?" asks Dominic.

"Exhausting." I flex my aching fingers. "I don't know how people do this day after day."

"This is how it is," he says. "This is how it has been for generations. It is a joy." I'm sceptical and my face must say it. "Okay, it is not always a joy. It can be quite exhausting, as you say. It is hard work. But it is good work. I have worked the vineyards for years and years as a growing boy. Now I most of the time oversee, but I remember. We are proud of the tradition. We are proud of our wine. We can not have one without the other, and so we pick."

This makes sense, of course, and I realize it's been over five months since I've worked at anything I'm proud of— anything at all, really.

After lunch Dominic takes Jakob to the nearest town for some business meeting and Emily says she's going to call her father and grandfather in England. Deciding to head back out to the vineyard, I grab an English-speaking child and ask him to come with me. I've scoped out one of the fastest pickers there and have the boy explain to the middle-aged woman that I want to learn from her. She laughs, and he translates that it would take many years. I tell her I want to get better at least, and she looks like the best person to learn from. She appraises me, tilting her head back and forth, then has the boy tell me to watch.

So I watch, and at first I can't quite make sense of anything she's doing that is so different from me. But, as I watch closer and longer, I see her specific method. She doesn't waste a movement but works in an efficient pattern. She's focused but at ease. She shows me a few tricks, corrects some of my movements, but mostly just ignores me and lets me pick beside her, quickly finishing my sections before we move onto the next plant.

The next day I'm still behind Emily and Jakob but not by nearly as much. I seem to be doing better than some of the younger pickers. By the day after that I'm just on pace with the two, and by the third I've surpassed them, and it feels good. This whole experience feels good. I've always been a morning person, but the sunrises here make me eager to get out of bed. I pick in anticipation of the rich colours that, each day, seem more beautiful than the last. The morning break always corresponds with the sun's journey above the horizon, allowing us to rest and enjoy a piece of it. It's our reward for the morning's frigid work.

On the third day, shortly after this break, Dominic stops as he's passing through my row.

"You do not need to work so hard. For you it is only an experience. Not a real job."

"I want to." I brush a strand of sweat soaked hair off of my forehead. "I want to do the best I can. Like you said, it's something to be proud of."

"So maybe I should be paying you?"

"How about room and board?"

"Ahh," he laughs. "To you the room and board is free."

"Then consider the view payment enough." I gesture toward the sun.

He smiles. "You have true passion." He looks at me in a way that makes me somewhat uncomfortable. "You are surprising to me." He continues up the aisle and I continue picking. I'm surprising to myself too, and it feels good. For some reason, I'm able to go to another place when I pick, a place with purpose, a place that makes me feel more like the me I remember.

When the harvest is almost through, neighbours and

family come for the last day—just as Dominic said they would. More than picking, the people in the fields laugh, talk, and dance, which is just fine, since all the grapes for the winery are already being shipped. I'm told today's harvest is for the family wine.

"What do you mean, family wine?" I ask Jakob. "They make different wine?"

"They make traditional wine," he says. "Not through the winery, but in the old way. That's what we've been drinking all this time and…" He grins and shakes his hair with a laugh. "Nah, I won't tell you any more. You'll see." He pats his hand on my shoulder and saunters away. I watch him, his broad shoulders, his lean figure, and feel a yearning I haven't felt in weeks. I noticed inklings of flirtation that first afternoon we met, but ever since Jakob noticed my tan lines he's treated me more like a sister than anything else. At times, when he smiles like he just did though, I wonder if I could come to love again.

When the grapes have all been picked, the real party begins. Even the children steal drinks here and there and all the hired workers join the festivities. Nonna, tipsier than I've ever seen her, calls me into the kitchen. She rambles to me in Italian, at least it sounds like rambling, and eventually Emily comes in and translates for me.

"She says today is the day you shall learn dumplings. She says anyone who has picked like you've picked must have the fingers for dumplings."

It's tricky, and mine clearly don't look as good as hers— or Emily's for that matter—but Nonna seems happy with them. She seems happy with everything and everyone, her squat little frame bouncing around like a schoolgirl's. The kitchen and the dining room and the back porch are full of food and full of people and as much as we're busy preparing dishes, others keep bringing more from their homes. No one will care about my dumplings. Eventually, Nonna seems finished with making new dishes and ushers Emily and me out of the kitchen. She takes off her apron and disappears.

When I get to the backyard almost twice as many people as before fill the space. The young girl who translated for me the first night, Elena, sidles up beside me and says hello. Moments later, several other young girls join her, giggling and ribbing each other and saying English phrases to me. Clearly, they're nowhere as far along in their abilities as Elena is, so they get her to ask me questions. One asks me about the scar and, as I'm stammering, Nonno raises his arms and says something to get everyone's attention. The music stops, and a hush falls over the crowd.

Nonna steps out behind Nonno, wearing a white dress that lets me see the beautiful, lithe woman she must have been. As I look around, I notice many of the women are in dresses. They're old fashioned—loose and flowing. "It is time for the...squishing." Elena translates. "Of the grapes...Sorry, I don't know exactly how to— Abriana...that's Nonna...will begin." Nonna walks up to a big vat in the middle of the courtyard. She takes off her sandals and glides up the steps like a princess on her way to coronation. When she reaches the top, she hikes her skirt and takes a step into the vat. A chorus begins—fiddles, tambourines, a guitar—and Nonna stomps. I can't help but laugh out loud, and others are too, from the joy of the view. It's as if her whole body is smiling, and I can't believe this little woman who shuffles around the house is moving like she is.

Nonno makes another announcement, and the music dims but doesn't stop. "It's you," says Elena. "He's saying you are to come."

"No." I shake my head, still holding in my chuckles from watching Nonna. "Not me."

"Yes, you." Elena pushes me forward and I notice Emily is getting pushed toward the vat as well. She looks at me and laughs, looking nervous but excited.

"Come, come," says Nonno, motioning to us. "It is time

for your initiation."

"I've done it before," says Emily. "Let Autumn go."

"You will both go." His voice bellows. "You can not remember." Nonna waves us in, stomping vigorously, and Nonno reaches out a hand to help Emily up and over the edge. I take off my shoes and follow behind her then squeal at the sensation while trying to keep upright. The cold, squishy grapes slither through my toes and splash against my ankles. The three of us stomp for several minutes, trying to keep our balance, and then Nonno must be welcoming the children because several scamper up the steps and hop in with us.

Nonna says something and motions that she wants to get out, so Emily and I help her. When I get to the bottom of the steps, a lady points to a water bucket off to the side and I clean up. I'm still laughing when Dominic comes up beside me.

"Now you are really Italian."

I smile up at his proud grin while trying to get grape peel out from between my toes. "I don't know about that." The girls from my earlier posse come up to me, speaking quickly.

"Here." Dominic reaches out a hand to me and says something to the girls. They pout. I ignore my sticky legs and follow Dominic to a path to the left of the house, my hand held firmly in his.

"What are we doing? Isn't this the way to the old outhouse?"

"Yes," he says, a glimmer in his eye. "And more."

"And more, oh really?" The wine I've had today makes me giggly. "Well, do tell."

"I will show." He leads me past the outhouse and down a barely visible foot trail. The music grows dim until I'm not even sure I hear it anymore.

"What is this?"

"An old pool," he says, "I thought you could clean yourself here. This is really traditional style." It's more than a pool. Statues covered in vines surround the area and an old stone bench sheltered by a Gazebo sits at the entrance to the rock-rimmed pool. The air smells crisp and cool. I step forward, awed. "My great-great-grandfather built it," he says, "for my grandmother. Tellings say she thanked him here, and that is how Nonno's father came to be."

"I can see that." I walk by the stone bench and trail my fingers along the smooth, hard back. "It's so beautiful."

"I thought you would enjoy it." He takes several steps toward me and rubs his fingers along my arm. They're cold and I pull back. "Does it make you happy?"

"Yeah." I walk away from him and into the Gazebo. I can't believe how incredible this all is. And it was just hidden here, so close to the house. I dip my foot in the ice-cold water. "And this is clean?"

"It is well water. It is not dangerous."

I sit and let my feet dangle in the pool, splashing them and feeling young. Dominic sits beside me and dips his feet as well.

"Here." He picks a clump of grape guts out of my hair. "Thanks." I laugh. It feels good. Life feels good. He lets his hand linger on my neck, and his face softens—I know that look. He leans toward me as I pull back, then look up at the sound of a holler. Three boys rush through the trees. They burst out into the clearing, one of them swinging something red in the air like it's booty. They pass by us and a moment later a topless Jakob comes rushing out behind them. "It's a war." He's laughing so hard he can hardly breathe. "Help me vanquish them!"

I jump to my feet and run off after them. Within minutes Jakob and I have tackled the boys. Jakob holds his shirt above him and uses it as a taunt to the jumping boys. Dominic is nowhere to be seen. Jakob claims himself victor then leads us back to the house where the boys run off, something else catching their interest.

Jakob wraps his arm around my shoulder, panting. "I

think I need to go on those runs with you and Dominic," he says. "I am clearly out of shape."

"Oh, you're all right." I laugh.

"Are you kidding?" He turns to me and slips his shirt on. "I'm a sweaty mess and look at you. Not even out of breath."

"Okay, maybe you do need to go on those runs." I twist my face and jokingly appraise him, secretly glad his shirt is back on. He doesn't look out of shape, not at all. "Tomorrow morning, now that the pickings are done, we'll start first thing."

"First thing," he moans, that smile making my stomach flutter. "But I was going to sleep in."

"Almost first thing, then. Just before daybreak."

His eyes widen and he laughs. "Deal." He puts out his hand and I grasp it—the deal struck. Our hands linger in each other's grasp a moment longer than necessary. "I need more sustenance." He drops my hand and heads to one of the large tables. I watch as he fills a glass of wine, my hand over my abdomen, feeling as if I've just committed an act of betrayal.

"And maybe some food too." I step in line behind him.

After eating, it's time to dance again. Old and young swing and skip to the sound of fiddles and a hand drum. Hours pass and as people wind down, the music does too. I'm sitting on a bench watching a handful of couples sway to the languorous beat when Dominic extends his hand. I shake my head, exhausted, but one of the Andrev's cousins pushes me forward. Dominic pulls me close, his hand on the small of my back pressing me into him and sways my body back and forth against his. We're pressed so tight to each other the side of my forehead rests against his cheek. He sings in Italian, his voice deep and low beside my ear. I want to pull away but know it would look odd. I'd cause offence for nothing. Because this really is nothing. People are in each other's arms all around us. His thumb massages the small of my back. It's been so long since I've been touched like that, I feel something awake inside me that I'd let sleep.

But I don't want this, and certainly not with Dominic. Not with anyone. When the tune ends, just before another begins, I extricate myself from his arms. "Another?" he whispers softly.

"I'm about to collapse." I let every ounce of tiredness show on my face.

"I'll hold you up."

Jakob walks by with an Afghan he takes to Emily and a girl she's cuddled up with. "That's what I need," I say, and join Emily and the girl on a pile of pillows against the back of the house, cuddling in beside them. Dominic watches us for a moment then goes inside. "About that run…" I smile at Jakob.

"Another day."

I nod and let the soothing caress of the music settle over me, the only caress I'll welcome today.

# CHAPTER FOURTEEN

Despite the abundance of food at the party, the next morning we have a hearty breakfast. As we're finishing, Dominic says he has to travel to a town a few hours away to finalize winery contracts. Jakob and Emily go with him to visit some other cousins. It's been too long since I connected to the people back home, so I let them leave without me. The thought of making those connections, however, and opening the messages I know await me, makes me nervous. A couple of days after arriving in Rome I'd sent a quick note back to my mom's frantic message, telling her I was okay, was loving Rome, and had met a backpacking brother and sister who'd taken me under their wing. I'd also told her it was hard to get access to internet and what I did have access to was mind numbingly slow so she shouldn't expect to hear from me often. I left every other message in my inbox unopened. I just hadn't felt ready. I still don't feel quite ready. And why should I? I'm nearly thirty years old. There's no need to be in constant touch. My grandmother told me that when she was young and living far from her family, it could take two to three months for a letter to arrive. There was none of this instant communication. People were more independent. That's what I am now. Independent. It's just me. But still, after last night, after being around all that love and friendship, I miss my mother. I miss all of them.

I've been at the Lombardi's home for almost two weeks

now—in Italy for over four. It's time. When I open the laptop Dominic told me I could borrow and sign into my email I'm surprised by the number of waiting messages. I enter my sent folder and am reminded that the one message I sent to Mom was over a month ago. It's selfish. I go back to the inbox and see the names—Daniel, Jenn, Eloise, Tracey, my old boss, some of Matt's friends, his parents, my father, even my ex-Uncle Richard, and, of course, my mother. Six emails sit from her. It's not just selfish. It's cruel.

Usually it's hard to find a spot to be alone in this house for more than five minutes. I use that as my excuse, my justification, but I know it's weak and I have no excuse now. Dominic, Emily, and Jakob will be gone all day. Nonno is taking his afternoon nap and Nonna looked busy enough in the kitchen to stay there for hours, which is good. I have a lot of writing to do. I open my mother's oldest email first. It's casual and newsy. She's happy I'm having such a good time. She's glad I've met nice people. She understands I'm busy and it's hard, but she asks me to make sure I contact them at least once a week. The next letter is a little less casual, a little more eager to hear from me. As the letters progress, so does her intensity. By the final one she sounds completely frantic with worry. She's angry, spouting off how I could be dead and saying this is ridiculous, how could I just desert my family? Don't I even care? And if nothing's wrong with me, what if something had happened to one of them? It's dated four days ago, and she says if I haven't written back in one week, she's calling the authorities. At first it makes me angry, but when I think of the call she must have received several months ago, I can't really blame her.

I compose a quick message, apologizing and saying it's just been really busy, then tell her I'm still having a wonderful time and am now staying with Emily and Jakob's relatives. I ask about her and the family and give her the number at the Lombardi's, letting her know I'll be here at least a few more days and if there's an emergency she can call.

When I'm done, I read the other messages. They're filled with glazed over concern and tidbits of my loved ones' lives. They're also filled with hopes and dreams for me and my travels. Some of them say how much they miss me. Others say they hope I'm finding what I'm looking for. A few ask when I'll be coming home. Tracey asks if I don't plan on coming home at all, and if I have been swept off of my feet by a beautiful Italian man. I cringe. It's too soon for her to say that. But then I think of those moments with Dominic by the pool and on the dance floor and feel guilty. But I shouldn't feel guilty. I didn't do anything. He didn't do anything. And even if we had, I'm a single woman. That's all. That's it. That's how it's going to be from now on out. I stare at the screen. If I don't want to spend the rest of my life alone, I'll have to be ready for a relationship one day. Not that I am alone, not right now anyway. I'm surrounded by wonderful people who shower me with affection, who know nothing of the life I once lived, which allows me to live whatever kind of life I want. But despite how much I want to believe it isn't, I know life at the Lombardi's is a temporary thing.

Drawing my attention back to the task at hand, I realize it would take hours to write back each person individually, so I compose a newsletter type message filled with the excitement I know they're all hoping for. I close the letter by saying it could be weeks to a month before another update comes their way and then take the time to write one to two-line responses to individual messages. At the end of it I realize almost three hours have passed and, deciding Nonno had the right idea, close the laptop, head to bed, and crawl under the covers. Several hours later I wake up to Emily standing over me.

"Autumn," she whispers. She's been crying.

"What is it?" I sit up and rub the sleep out of my eyes.

"Our trip is over."

"What?"

"Jakob and I. We have to go back now. To London."

I swing my legs over the edge of the bed and motion for her to sit down. "Tell me what happened. Is everything okay?"

She looks away from me but sits. "It's family stuff. Our grandfather, he's not doing so well. He has…a condition. It's taken a turn for the worse. Our father needs Jakob back to take over more of the business and me to care for Farfar." She turns to me now, smiles through renewed tears. "It's been a good trip though. A trip to last a lifetime."

"Yeah," I say. "It's been good. But your grandfather. Will he get better? Maybe you can finish the journey then."

She laughs. "Our grandfather's not going to get better. Only worse until…" One of her hands shakes and she rests her other hand on top of it, holding them firmly in her lap. "And there's not likely going to be any trips again for me either. Not like this anyway."

"I'm sorry, Emily." I sit there for a moment, not sure whether to put my arm over her shoulder. At last I do, and she leans into me. "When will you have to leave?"

"Jakob's looking at flights now." She turns to me. "Dominic though, and Nonno, they say you're welcome to stay, or you could even come with us." She squeezes my hand. "We stomped grapes together. You're family now."

My throat tightens. "You would need time, wouldn't you? With your family? This will be a hard time."

She looks at her hands, nods. "Maybe a few weeks. But once Jakob gets things organized and settled, we'd love to have you." She smiles. "You've been thinking about staying in Europe awhile, haven't you? England would be a good place to do it. No worry about the language and you could even work for the family for a time, then set up your studio business once you're ready." She lets out a soft chuckle.

"Being fit is becoming all the rage in Jolly Old England."

I squeeze her hand back. "We can figure that out later. What can I do for you now? How can I help?"

"I don't know," she says, looking lost.

"Do you need help packing?"

"I guess, but it's not hard. We brought so little."

"I'll help anyway." I stand and open the drawer holding her clothes then grab her backpack, haul it over to the bed, and start rolling and transferring. I can feel her eyes on me and turn to look at her.

"I'm not ready to go yet," she says, sadness in her voice. She stares at the floor for a moment then shakes her head and stands up, a look of resolve washing over her features. "But it's okay. It'll be good to be home too, to see Dad, and Amalia, and Farfar."

"Yeah," I say. "It'll be great. You'll see." But I understand her feelings. It was hard enough just writing home today. I don't know what I'd do if I were suddenly called back. "Go downstairs," I tell Emily, "be with your family. I'll handle the packing."

When I finish organizing Emily's belongings and head downstairs, the house is almost as full as that first night. A flurry of women talk and cook and laugh in the kitchen. I've picked up some more Italian in the past two weeks but with so many people speaking at once I can hardly make out a thing. Dominic comes toward me and puts his arm around my shoulders.

"It is sad, sad news," he says. "We do not want to see them go but we do not want to see you go either. What will you do, Autumn? Will you stay?"

"I don't know." Several eyes are upon me. "Maybe just a couple of days until I figure out what to do next."

Dominic speaks loudly, more to the room than to me. "Here you are welcome. Stay as long as your heart wishes." We sit down to dinner and the phone rings. A minute or two later Nonno enters the room and motions for me to follow him. I know from the look on his face it's not good. I pick up the receiver. "Hell—"

"Autumn? Is that really you?"

"Yeah Mom, it's—"

"Five weeks, Autumn. Five weeks." Her voice reveals she's been crying.

"I know Mom. I'm sorry, I—"

"You have no idea how worried we were. After Matt, after having to get that phone call and hear—"

"I'm okay, Mom. I—"

"This time you're okay. This time. But what about last time? What about next time? How am I supposed to know?"

I sigh. "I said I'm sorry."

She's silent on the other end.

"Mom?"

She whispers. "I was so scared, Autumn. I didn't know what to do."

"I didn't mean to—"

"Your father told me everything would be okay. He told me you just needed your time, your space...but I didn't know."

"I know Mom."

"Don't do it again."

"It's not always easy."

"One email a week. Preferably a call, but no less than one email a week."

I'm silent.

"Autumn." Her voice is sharp and I'm pulled between wanting to be enraged at her for demanding this of me—for treating me like a child—and wanting to crawl into a hole from the shame of putting her through this.

"Okay, Mom. One a week."

I can almost hear her relax through the phone. I picture the way her tensed shoulders will settle down, the crease in her forehead melting away. She takes a deep breath and I imagine her placing that smile on her face, the one she reserves for when Daniel or I have done something to piss her off or worry her, but she wants us to know she loves us anyway. "So, it sounds like there's a crowd there. A party. Who exactly is it you're staying with?"

"It's Jakob and Emily's grandparents. And their cousin lives here too. There's a big gathering tonight because Jakob and Emily have to cut their trip short and go back to England. Their other grandfather is sick."

"Oh." It's amazing how well you can know someone. I can see the way she purses her lips and draws her brow together as she makes this sound. "I'm so sorry to hear that. Will he be okay?"

"I'm not sure…it sounds like maybe not."

"Well, that's good of them. They must be good people…to do that for him."

"Yeah. They're really good people. They're great, Mom."

"I'm glad, Sweetie. I'm glad you found them. I hated to think of you over there all alone at a time like this."

I take several deep breaths, hoping she doesn't go on. "I chose to come here, Mom. I wanted to be alone."

"I know, but—"

"How's Dad?"

"He's good, Honey. He misses you. We both do."

"And Daniel?"

"He and Mallory have been over a few more times. I think it's getting quite serious." Excitement creeps into her voice. One of her babies is happy.

"That's great, Mom."

"She's so much better than that other one. What a little tramp!"

"Mom."

"Well, she was."

"Yeah, she was."

There's more silence and I'm about to say goodbye. "How are you really doing, Autumn? Really."

"I'm great Mom. You don't have to worry about me at all, okay? I'm great."

"But—"

"I'm having such a great time and Italy is so beautiful. The Lombardi's have been so welcoming and—"

"What are you going to do now that those two are leaving?"

"I'm not sure. Maybe Venice? Maybe travel through France. They offered for me to come see them in England in a few weeks—"

"You're not going to come home soon? It sounds like doing all that would take a while and…are you sure you want to go back to England? So soon, I mean."

My thoughts are right where hers are, but I try to pretend they're not, to push them away. "They said they might have a job for me. Emily mentioned London was a great place to set up a studio—"

"You can't possibly be thinking of moving there? Autumn, that's—"

"I don't know, Mom." I pause. "I really should go though. It's their last night and all…"

She's quiet again. I know she wants to say more. "Okay. You have a good night, Autumn. I love you."

"I love you too, Mom."

"Thank the Lombardi's for me. Okay, Sweetie?"

"I will."

"And once a week. You promised."

"Okay. Bye."

"Bye, Honey."

She won't hang up first. She never does. I hold the phone to my ear for just a moment longer than I need to and then set it down.

# CHAPTER FIFTEEN

Yet again we don't bother going to bed. We talk into the night and then through it. It's not until around six in the morning that people start dispersing, wilted and sad. It seems more like they've been at a funeral than a goodbye party. I ask Nonno about this and he smiles at me, like I'm simple. "We celebrate life, we celebrate the tie we share, but we also know that life can stop at any moment and so we must have moments of sadness too, moments to mourn the fact that life is so fleeting, that we may never all be on the same ground again. It's a balance." I don't respond to his words, knowing how true they are, but not wanting to think of them. He pats my shoulder and moves to hug one of his brothers goodbye.

At seven, I grab my pack as Jakob and Emily say goodbye to Nonna and Nonno. I come back to tears and heartfelt whispered words. Nonna, especially, clings to Emily like she may never see her again, like she's incredibly precious. I suppose this really is possible, even likely. Nonna's not getting any younger. It's embarrassing to be standing here. Despite what they say, I'm an outsider witnessing intensely intimate family moments. Jakob and Emily go up to get their bags and now that they're done with their grandchildren, Nonno and Nonna come over to me. "Are you sure my dear?" says Nonno. "You are welcome to stay. Stay as long as you will. Walk the fields, fatten up—you need more of this. Enjoy life."

"I'll never forget your kindness." I accept the hand that Nonna holds out to me. "And I hope I can visit again one day." I smile. "But I think I should move on. I've still got a whole big world to see, and a whole big Italy."

Dominic translates and Nonna tuts at my words. "You can see the whole world in one house," Dominic translates back for her. "Our house is like this." She says some other things and Dominic argues with her. Nonno laughs. "She says you should find a good man," says Dominic, "settle down. She says your youth will not last forever and home and family is the ultimate good a woman can have…despite what society tells you."

"That is not all she said," says Nonno, giving Dominic an elbow in the ribs. It's the first time I've seen Dominic embarrassed and the first time he's given anything but looks of love toward his grandparents.

"Did she say something about you?" I ask. "You're not too young either. You should be finding a home and family too, no?" I grin at using his style against him.

"Something is near to what you say," he says as Jakob and Emily return. I've noticed that his English is always a little less solid when he's been speaking or even translating Italian—the night of drink and no sleep probably also plays a role. Another flurry of hugs and kisses erupts then we pile into the convertible. With the sun just coming up over the horizon I ask Dominic if he can take the back road around the house so I can watch the light over the vineyard once more. "It is in your soul now," he says. "This is good."

I smile and lean back against the plush leather as we drive slowly by. Soaking it all in, I wonder if I'll ever be in a place this beautiful again. Each morning for the briefest of moments when I gazed at the rolling hills, the rows and rows of vines in the rising sun, the pain I'm so used to carrying always seemed lighter.

Once we're back to the main road, Dominic floors the gas and we fly away. A cold, twisting feeling settles in my stomach—this is where my real journey begins. I only had about three hours alone when I got off the flight in Italy. I set myself up to have this great soul-enriching adventure, I saw myself as so brave, but after meeting Emily and Jakob I didn't have to be. I won't admit it to anyone, but I can't deny it from myself, I'm scared. As much as I've experienced since I came, as much as I've had moments of happiness, it's all been somewhat of an act. I've lied to them all, just as I've been lying to myself. Without people around to distract me from my lies, without someone there to believe the reality I've created, I'm afraid I won't be able to fool myself any longer.

When we get to the airport, I say my goodbyes to Jakob and Emily. "Just promise you'll come." Emily rubs her hands on my arms and gives them a squeeze. "You can't visit Europe and not see London."

I smile at her, feeling the full force of all my lies hard against my chest. "It just wasn't part of my plan."

"And neither was meeting up with us and spending two weeks on our family's vineyard, but look how that turned out," says Jakob. "You can't tell me you didn't have an amazing time."

"I did." I turn to him. "And I'm so glad I met you both. I wouldn't have changed a minute of it." I look back to Emily. "I'll think about England, I will. And the offer means so much to me. I'm just not ready to promise it."

"But—"

"She has her reasons." Jakob cuts Emily off. "She's not ready to tell us, but I'm pretty sure she has her reasons." He gives me an understanding look and follows it with a grin. He knows I've been holding back...and he's not pushing. "Either way," he says, "keep in touch."

"That I can promise." I smile back. "I need to hear how things are going with the business. And I hope things are as good as they can be with your grandfather. I know it'll be hard."

"We'll make do." Jakob wraps his arm around Emily's shoulders. "That's why we have family."

I nod. We have one last round of quick hugs then Dominic and I watch as the two head into the terminal. When they're out of sight, Dominic turns to me with a broad smile and his characteristic arm flourish. "And now on to our day of Milan!"

"First stop the train station?" I say. "I want to make sure I have everything figured out with my ticket—and I should be able to book my first night's stay there too, right?"

"Yes," he says, looking disappointed. "But I really think you should stay longer in Milan. This city deserves much more than you're giving it."

"I know. It's a big change, travelling on my own and all, and I just really want to start it all anew. Jump in. Somehow it's less scary that way."

"Okay, okay." He motions for me to follow him. "Then we will make this last day count. That is right, yes? Make it count."

"Yeah, that's right."

Dominic isn't kidding. He packs so much into the day that by the end of it everything is a blur. Rather than really seeing Milan, I feel as if I've sat at a train window and watched it speed by, only I know that's not the case because my feet ache. Despite my protests that I'm fine in a hostel, Dominic insists that while I'm on his clock, I will have a nice room. When we get to the hotel, he talks to the concierge who replies in such rapid Italian I have no hope of understanding anything. We're each handed a key and Dominic places his hand on my back, motioning for me to head toward the elevators. I look at the room number and press the corresponding floor. We get off and I head down the correct hallway. He follows me along. When I stop at my door, he does too. "Where's your room?" I ask.

He looks at me like I've asked a weird question. "Here. This is our room."

"Oh, right." I shrug, feeling a little prudish and embarrassed. It was silly of me to assume he'd spring for separate rooms, just because he was willing to pay. After all, I would have likely been sharing a room with men in the hostel. I slide open the key and push in the door. In the centre of the expansive room is a lavishly dressed Queen-sized bed. I take a few steps in and look around, suddenly wondering if I've lost my ability to read a man's signals or if I'm just missing something. "Is this a mistake?" I ask. "Were we meant to get two doubles or…" I notice a daybed against the far wall. "I can take—"

"No, this is our bed for us." He walks into the room and tosses his overnight bag on the daybed. "At last we have some privacy. Is it not wonderful?"

"It's a really nice room." I speak slowly. "But I don't know that—"

"Autumn," he steps toward me, "from the moment I saw you I knew that we would have to experience each other." He cups my face. "Your beauty, the voluptuous energy I see in you, just bursting under the surface, just rearing to get free." He draws his hands down to my waist and I push them away.

"I'm not planning to experience anything."

He laughs. It's cocky, as he often is, but this time the tone is unnerving. "A woman like you must have much experience of love. What is a tour of Italy without a little romance?"

"This is not romantic." My pulse races and my skin warms. "What made you think I was interested? What made you think—?"

"I see." He slides his fingers down the side of my unscarred cheek. "I feel it in your eyes. You are a woman starved for love. I could feel it as we danc—"

"Yeah, well, not your love," I snap, then soften my voice. "I'm sorry. I don't just—"

He looks hurt and confused. "But the other day…by the

pool. We would have then if we did not get interrupted, no?"

"No!" I say. He looks as shocked and hurt as I am that he thought I wanted this.

"Is it…" he hesitates, "does your scar make you nervous? Do you think you are no longer desirable? I see past this. Nothing can mar your beauty."

"No," I yell. "Shit, why would you—?"

"Autumn," he takes a step back and raises his hands in defence, "I did not mean to offend you. I…this is a biggest surprise to me. I am shamed. You were a guest of my grandfather and—"

"It's okay." I step toward him, then stop a few feet away, not wanting to give him the wrong idea. "I'm not angry. I just…it was a misunderstanding, okay? Just a misunderstanding. No harm done."

He offers a wavering smile. "Your body, it is…it is wondrous, Autumn. It is a hidden island just waiting to be discovered. You must forgive me. I do not want you to think unkind of my family."

"I don't," I say, and at the sight of him standing there, all eagerness and embarrassment mixed with male virility, a small part of me wants to go along with his offer, lose myself in him the way he clearly wants to get lost in me. And why shouldn't I? I'm supposed to be living as if I never knew Matt, as if I'm completely free in the world. But I can't. My lies, even to myself, don't run that deep. I'm not ready.

"I'm sorry," I say. "I'm sorry if I said or did anything to mislead you. I didn't plan on it."

"No, no." He waves his hand, takes a step toward me so we're less than a foot apart. My skin tingles with the thought of touch, but I hold on to my resolve. Even if I ever am ready, I wouldn't want it to be like this—when it would mean nothing, when I'm leaving the next morning probably never to see this man again. "We are still friends?" he asks.

"Yes, yes. We're still friends."

He looks around the room now, the virility slipping away, the embarrassment taking over, and the fact that he's five years younger than me has never seemed more evident. "What will we do about the room?"

"I can take the day bed. That's no problem."

"No, no." His chest rises. This is his opportunity to redeem himself in some small way, to be valiant. "I will take the day bed. The queen is meant for you."

I laugh then, and all at once feel surprisingly tender toward him. "Come here," I say, and wrap my arms around him. He returns the hug quickly then pulls away.

"You may use the bathroom first." He motions toward it with a grandiose gesture. "Take as long as you like. Enjoy the jacuzzi."

"You're sure?"

"Yes. It should be a beautiful relaxation for you."

"Thank you." I take a few steps toward the bathroom then look back as I hear him settle on the daybed and turn on the TV.

I let the water run and undress. My reflection is much as it was—a little less toned, but still undeniably appealing. It's my face that usually turns me away from the mirror, but for the first time since the accident I feel able to look past it, to see again the beauty Dominic spoke of. I smile and watch the skin crinkle around my scar. My face falls. But it's not hideous. I'm not hideous—and still desirable.

# CHAPTER SIXTEEN

The next morning I say goodbye to Dominic and board a train to Venice. It feels altogether too real. I've never actually travelled alone before. There was always someone to join me or someone I was going to see. I didn't have this feeling when I hopped on a plane to Italy about five weeks ago, perhaps I was too determined and eager to just get away—too anxious to prove everyone wrong. This time I'm not really proving anything to anyone, just myself.

I touch my face to the raised and slightly puckered skin. I've always had my face to help me through new situations. The 'freemaker,' my college friends used to call it. Fair or not, most humans feel more comfortable around and are more likely to go out of their way to help attractive people. I know this from firsthand experience. And now, from time to time, I experience the other side, the way some turn from me, try to avoid my gaze. I know I'm not hideous, but even Dominic, who knows me, mentioned that he was able to see past my disfigurement, indicating, whether he meant to or not, that it was distasteful enough that he needed to see past it. This thought kept me awake for hours last night. Not even my scar could hide my beauty, he'd said, or something like that. Well, as his grandfather also commented on first seeing me, it's marred it. I feel vain even thinking these thoughts: vain, self-absorbed, and ridiculous. I always used to tell my clients that it's health and who we are inside that's important. We work out not to have the perfect figure or the sexiest muscles but to live our lives as well as we can, to not let our bodies hold us back. In that sense, my scar doesn't hold me back from anything.

And I'm alive. I'm alive and I have no right to be anything but grateful. But if I have no right, what does that say? If I'm grateful I'm alive does that mean in some small way I'm grateful it was him and not me? I let my gaze and my attention focus on some boys playing soccer in the field outside my window. I watch until they become so tiny I'm no longer sure I see them.

When the train stops, I'm shocked to realize I'm already in Venice. I assumed I'd have to take a boat to get to the islands. I shouldn't have though, since Dominic suggested I book a hostel near the station, advice I didn't listen to. Upon exiting the station, the first thing I notice is the smell. It's not overpowering, as I've heard some people say, but I imagine that's because I'm here in early fall not the middle of summer like a friend once warned against, but still, this faint mix of sewer and exhaust is not pleasant and though a breeze gives me a reprieve, it's not a scent I imagine anyone could grow to like, even if it's one they could easily come to ignore.

According to the guidebook my hostel is about a five-minute water taxi away but I've been looking forward to travelling the canals so much that I hire a gondola instead. The sun is low in the sky and I have a feeling this more authentic introduction to the city at dusk is a sight I'll remember forever. It's worth the splurge. When I step in the boat it rocks gently and, along with his hand, the oarsman offers me an easy gap-toothed smile. His ease wanes as I negotiate a price Dominic suggested was reasonable—I'm sure when he saw me he guessed he'd be getting the American tourist price, but I won't budge.

The whole city seems to have a relaxed air to it. Nothing's moving too fast, and the things that are don't feel like it. The oarsman tells me we're on the Grand Canal and points out the Grand Hotel proudly, saying this is where I should stay. It's nice, but I'm more interested in the green dome building with tall pillars just past it. And then, up ahead, another structure catches my eye. Human statues of varying poses adorn the walls, and the whole building has a dark and sombre air, almost as if it's a mausoleum right amid all the bustle. Something about it makes me shiver. The purple light, stretching across the sky, fits perfectly with the overall atmosphere. As we travel along, the buildings become more flat-faced and square in an array of creams and salmon. We turn down what is basically an alley, although we're still on the water, and something about this delights me. It's scummy looking and the walls are falling apart. If it were in another city, I'd expect to find a drug dealer lurking around the corner or the homeless finding shelter where they can, but I suppose that can't happen here.

The oarsman stops at some steps and tells me we've arrived. When I get off the boat I walk down another little alley—paved this time—with brick walls covered in what looks like some sort of ivy. Potted plants line the way and brick and mortar crumble out of the walls. I pass a large pile of garbage and then turn the corner to see my hostel. Like the other buildings, the stucco has broken off in clumps to reveal crumbling brick underneath. Bars cover the windows with clusters of pink and red window-box flowers behind them—presumably an effort to add some cheer to the dank surroundings. This is obviously not the nicest part of town. I'm surprised. Based on the price I expected something better, but then I've heard Venice is a pricey place to visit. I don't have specific plans but doubt I'll stay in the city long. Two girls who look to be in their early twenties come out of the building. I beam as they pass by. One barely acknowledges me, so wrapped up in whatever story she's telling, the other gives me a quick glance then averts her eyes. Before she does, I see in them the look I used to have for older women who I could tell used to be beautiful. She sees in me the fleeting nature of her own beauty. I thought it would be years before I'd receive that look.

Once I'm in my room and settled, I consider going to explore the city on foot but stay seated on the bed. All I feel is tired—this fatigue is deep and full of all the things I've been hiding from. But it's too hard to keep up the facade and, for the first time since that nightclub in Rome, I allow myself to let go, to stop lying. I cry for Matt. I cry so hard my throat hurts and my eyes burn and then, when I'm so exhausted I can hardly see straight, I put it all away again and slip under the covers before any of my nine dorm mates have the opportunity to return and try to introduce themselves.

In the morning I keep to myself, afraid of receiving more looks like the one last night, afraid that whoever came in the room just minutes after I laid down would have seen my red and wet face. Three people get ready near me. Two girls and a guy who look to be in their mid-twenties. One of the girls smiles over at me, her dimples deepening. I offer the slightest of smiles back.

"I'm Lacey," she says, and perches on the edge of my bed. "You just arrived, right? This bed was empty yesterday."

"Yeah."

"So, are you travelling alone?"

"Yeah," I say, standing and straightening my sheets. She stands as well, to get out of my way.

"Been there done that." She motions to the other girl and waves her over. This is Kat. Kat…what's your name?"

"I'm Autumn." I shake both of their hands.

"You're welcome to join us today if you want. Kat's been here before, so she has a pretty good grasp on the city."

"It's okay." I try to look thankful. And I am. "I think I'll venture out on my own today."

"That's cool," says Lacey. "Maybe we'll see you around. As you'll find, this place really isn't all that big."

"Okay, maybe I'll see you. Thanks." Gathering my toiletries, I step out into the hall. Just over twenty minutes later I'm ready to go. One thing about this new hair, it's quick. I start my day at St. Mark's Square. Almost as soon as I get out of the tight alleys and onto a main street I feel as if I'm in a completely different city from the one I walked in last night. People crowd every corner of it. No, actually, tourists crowd every corner of it. In places, I have to slow my pace, the streets are so thick with us. Where tourists don't stand, vendors gather, eager to sell all the Venice paraphernalia imaginable. And pigeons. Lots and lots of pigeons. Making my way through the throng, I feel small and expendable in this sea of people. As I near the main square, despite my disbelief that it's possible, the intensity increases.

I approach from the outside and weave my way through. The square is massive and adds to my feeling of insignificance. Standing in the centre, where the ground is slick and reflective, I turn in a full circle, taking it all in. Hundreds of people surround me but I'm not sure I've ever felt so alone. I try to reject the feeling, telling myself I'm on the adventure of a lifetime—I'm happy, this is wonderful— but I don't believe me. Maybe it's from hearing Mom's voice the other night. Maybe it's from saying goodbye to Jakob and Emily. Maybe it's from allowing myself to indulge in memories of how things used to be. All I know for sure is I have to get away from here.

I run from the square and step into a museum just next to the Basilica then pay my fees and walk the halls. The rooms are grand and ornate and filled with paintings of death and destruction. My eyes scan vision after vision of bodies piled on each other like fallen leaves in a burn heap. I want to scream. I want to curse life and curse mankind and curse whatever presence decided to put us here to suffer like this. For generations and generations this is what we've had to deal with. Pointless, sickening, unfair death. The proof surrounds me. Matt was one of the best guys I've ever known. He was sweet and funny and considerate and sexy as hell. The only guy I'd ever been with who saw me for me, who cared more about treating me well and knowing me and cherishing what we had than about showing me off to his friends. And he gets thirty years. Thirty. It's ridiculous.

Desperate to get away from the paintings, I step into the museum's courtyard. It's smaller than the square, with fewer people. I can handle this. I lean on a pillar and try to make my breath calm. At least no tears have betrayed me this time. I need to not feel like this anymore—like I'm about to be crushed from the inside out. I can't just keep standing here and I've already paid for my ticket, so I go back into the museum and, thankfully, the rooms I enter are less graphic. I'm bored of it though, and before I've seen the whole thing I leave and make my way to the water. An overpriced hat saves me from the glaring sun, and I find a place to sit just out of the streams of foot traffic. I watch the people trailing by for several hours, thinking how really this is no different than what I was doing in my old room at my parent's house. I might as well be staring at a wall. But then one of the people stares back, because of course this isn't a wall. "Autumn? Hey, I thought that was you." It's Lacey, Kat just a step behind her. The guy with them is haggling with a street vendor a few feet away.

"Hey."

"So, what are you up to here?"

"Oh." I try to smile easily. "Just people watching. Relaxing."

"Nice," says Lacey. "You hungry? We were just about to get some food. Wanna join us?"

I've been ignoring growls for a while now. "Sure." As I stand, the guy comes over.

"This is Matt," says Lacey.

Perfect. I smile and shake his hand, trying not to let the pain at that name show on my face. "I'm Autumn."

Lying in bed later that night I realize, despite the dagger that drove into my gut every time this Matt's name was used, the three hours I spent with Lacey, Kat, and Matt were better than any of the hours before I joined them. This whole being alone thing doesn't seem to work for me. With people, I have someone to hold up the facade for—pretending I'm all right. And I even believe it a lot of the time. With Jakob, Emily, and the Lombardi's life seemed normal, the pain that overwhelms me now was this weak background emotion for hours, even days, at a time. As much as I never want to see London again it's only one little spot that scares me. The three backpackers from today are heading the way I've just come, so tagging along with them isn't an option, not that I want to anyway. What I want is people I've already started to love. I'll take the train in—I won't even have to see the airport—and I'll avoid the stretch of highway and the area surrounding the hospital as much as I can. I'm not even sure I'd recognize the highway. No matter what, it's better than home. At home he's everywhere.

I roll over in bed, feeling calmed by these thoughts. Jakob and Emily need their time to settle into life back home, so I'll work my way through France for the next week or two and then join them again. Concrete plans have always worked well for me, step-by-step goals. It's how I help my clients focus and how I focus best. If I make a plan for myself and follow through, if I'm focused and committed to that plan, I can work my way back to being okay. The first step is to email Jakob and Emily and let them know I'm coming. The second is to chart out the specific places I want to see in France and how long I will stay in each city. No more of this aimless wandering around. And while I explore, I will be vivacious. I will be energetic. I will engage with everyone I meet. The third step is to get to

London, get set up in a job at the restaurant, find a place to live and, when I feel settled enough, start working on a business plan for a fitness studio. It's a big step, a multifaceted one, but I can do it. I can create a new life. I can be excited about every point in the process and I can succeed. This life I'm planning will become so meaningful for me, so real and fulfilling, that one day I will be able to return home again, and on that day I'll be fine.

# CHAPTER SEVENTEEN

I wake to the sound of other travellers moving around and speaking softly. Before I open my eyes, the resolutions of the previous night float into my consciousness. Eager to start following my plan, I get dressed quickly and go down to the lobby to email Jakob and Emily. The computer in the hostel is so unbelievably slow that this takes me over a half hour. If I want to do my planning and bookings for France online, I'll be here all day and at four euros for every half hour that's not a great plan. Remembering that the Piazza San Marco has a grand library, I grab my things and make my way through the crowds. Today I hardly notice the throngs of tourists, the racing and frustrated locals, or the mangy pigeons. I'm on a mission.

The library distracts me from that mission for a few minutes—it's unlike any library I've ever seen. It should be a museum, almost overly ornate, and I wonder how anyone is supposed to get any work done with such stimulation.

As I leave the main corridor and explore some of the stacks, I wonder what Jenn would think of this place. For the past couple of years she's worked as a writer and has expressed thoughts here and there of transitioning to novel writing. She studied literature in University and used to hide behind the pages of a book in our high school's halls. She'd love it here. So would Eloise, also an avid reader. As I think of them, I get this scraping feeling in the back of my throat, like my own voice is itching to tell me something about the path I'm on. I quickly shake off the feeling and find a spot to sit, my guidebook on one side and my notebook on the other.

Discovering all there is to see and do in France takes up my whole morning. I approach the task methodically, the way I would have set up my process for an in-depth lab experiment back in University. I label and I group and by the time I'm done I'm looking at a full two-and-a-half week plan detailing everything from where I will sleep, to the best places to eat, to potential second and third place backup scenarios in case I meet people along the way who alter my plans. I don't want to be anal about this, after all. It is still an adventure. It's just an organized one.

Pride surges through me as I look at what I've put together. It feels good to have direction. I dug down to a part of me I haven't let flourish in months—a part Matt used to love. Before I can redirect it, my mind drifts back to one of our first dates. We'd been friends for several months at that point, so there wasn't that awkwardness and tension I often felt in the first couple of weeks of seeing someone. I knew he wasn't interested in me just for my body or trying to get into my pants. He hadn't even tried. After our first run together, we sat on a bench sharing a bottle of water.

'You're really fast,' he'd said, grinning at me and trying to pretend he wasn't trying to catch his breath.

'Oh, really?' I'd said coyly. 'Were you pushing it? That was just a casual jog for me.'

'Sure.' He took a big swig of the drink and handed it to me. 'I wouldn't even be surprised. So, what made you get into training?'

'I don't know.' I hesitated, unsure whether to give him my typical answer, which emphasized my belief in the importance of health and fitness and wanting to see people's lives transformed, or to go deeper with my response. Looking at his smile, I knew. 'I don't tell this to a lot of people.' I stopped the shaking in my voice, choosing to trust him with my geekier side. 'It really started from my science and kinesiology classes in undergrad. I started learning about the body. It's this amazing machine. I got really into my courses, asked for extra projects, I even watched past videos of Olympic athletes and studied and compared their training methods. The physical progress humans have made in just the past several decades is incredible. I became obsessed with it, with how to see people improve in ways they would have never imagined—and often with less energy and overall effort than they were using before. I got insanely into setting up training plans so that all the processes of the body could work in sync. I used members of our school's sports teams as guinea pigs and they loved the results they were seeing. It was just incredible, and I felt incredible and…' I stopped then and realized Matt was staring at me, his expression unreadable. I've lost him, I thought, he expected and wanted the simple, obvious answer.

Then he smiled. 'That's the sexiest thing I've ever heard.' With those words I'd started to fall in love.

I take a deep breath and blink back the one tear threatening to escape. That scratching, uncomfortable feeling is back, and for a brief second I wonder again if I'm making the right decision in trying to forget our love, in trying to imagine all the memories, like that one, are no more important than the insignificant and almost forgotten moments with the men before him. But I have no choice. With an exhalation, I pick up my books and head to a computer to book my ticket out of here and all the days and nights that will get me back to Jakob and Emily. Once back at the hostel, I pack up my things, telling myself it'll get easier. It has to. I'm twenty-eight years old. I knew Matt for less than ten percent of my life. It has to get easier.

FOR THE NEXT TWO weeks I feel as if another person is living my life. On the surface it's amazing. I see such wondrous sites. I meet incredible people. I store up memories I'll have for a lifetime. I laugh. But there's always that other self inside of me, cowering beneath the shell I've built. At time's I feel as if my whole time in France is nothing but a school trip—I take note of what I should take note of, I experience the things I am expected to experience, as if I must for the post class report. Only this isn't a school trip. There is no report to be written. This is my life, and I'm barely present for it.

As nervous as I am when the two weeks end and I board the shuttle to London, I feel relief too. There's something about Emily and Jakob that I know will make things easier, help me forget about that self I can't reveal. It's not even just that their presence helps me pretend, they know me— the parts of me I'm choosing to reveal, anyway.

When I get out of the train station, I look for the right exit to reach the underground. "Autumn."

I turn and there he is, though it takes me a second to realize it. He's clean shaven, his hair is shorter, trimmed into more of a wave than a fight to curl, and he's looking sharp in a dress shirt and slacks. Despite these changes, there is still that smile. Those eyes. "Jakob!" I run two or three steps into his waiting arms and, as he squeezes me, it feels like home.

"We've missed you, girl." He takes my pack from me. "I wondered if maybe in all your travelling you'd find another brother and sister to shack up with—forget all about us."

"Impossible." I loop my arm around his middle.

"And how was France? All you hoped and desired?"

"It was great, really great."

He looks at me for a moment. "Not as good as Italy?"

"I'm not sure that anything could be."

"Such the flatterer." He leads me to his car and opens the door. A row of London cabs brings back a flash of memory and I turn my face away with a deep breath, annoyed at how silly I'm being. They're just cabs, and it's not even as if it's the same terminal. That was the airport. "It might have been faster for you to take the tube," he says as he buckles up. "But I wanted to come get you."

"Doesn't matter the speed. This is better."

"We're about an hour and a half away with traffic," he says. "I'll have to head back to work after I drop you off, but Emily's at home. She's excited to see you."

"That's great." I grip my leg as he pulls onto the highway. "I'm excited to see her too." I clench my thighs. It's not even the same highway. I know this.

"Are you okay?" At the sound of his voice, I realize minutes have passed. I look down and see my knuckles are white. I release my hands and breath at the same time and smile over at him.

"Yeah, I'm fine."

"Just quiet?"

"Highways make me nervous."

He nods, and I can see on his face he's thinking about asking more. "An accident?"

"Yeah," the word sighs out of me.

"The scar?"

I repeat my previous answer. He nods again, his lips pursed, his eyes on the road. He squeezes my knee gently then returns his hand to the steering wheel. "I'll do my best to keep you safe."

"Thanks," I say, battling to not let my eyes water. Maybe things won't be as easy with Jakob and Emily as I thought, but still, it'll be better than home. He's not going to ask any more questions. I'm not going to give any more answers.

As I start to relax I notice that, although they are definitely different, my surroundings seem more like any city back home than anywhere in France or Italy did. It's nice to be able to read all the signs I see, rather than the odd mix of English and either Italian or French that have become familiar. "So tell me more. What is it exactly that you do at the restaurant?" I ask.

"I manage things. I hire staff. I do scheduling. I oversee orders. I was handling all the invoicing too, but I've finally convinced my father to source that out. It just takes so much time. It doesn't make sense for me to be tied up with it—or him, for that matter."

"And so he was doing all of this stuff before?"

"Most of it. They started out as just a little place—ma and pop style, you know?" His lips upturn just slightly. "It was Mum's dream. Nonna taught her well. She'd been to several Italian restaurants here and thought she could do just as good, if not better." He stops, and I can tell he's lost in his memories. I give him a few moments.

"And so it just grew from there?"

He glances over. "Yeah, pretty much. Mum and Dad got a small little following. After several years it grew, so their three-table restaurant just wasn't cutting it. They interviewed for some other chefs—ended up bringing over a friend of Mum's from Rocca di Giorgi. They got a bigger place…things got hard for a while after Mum got sick. And then…well, Mum's friend—Lia—she's a great cook too. You'll meet her.

"Dad didn't want to let Mum's dream die away as well…He was never a trained businessman, but he learned as he went. He became a jack of all trades and it wore him out." Jakob stops as he concentrates on switching lanes and taking an exit. "I want to have him back off slowly. It's hard for him to let go. But at the same time, I don't want to take over his role. It's not focused, and it's so draining the way he does everything. I'll find other hands to handle the things I don't excel in and focus on the things I do."

"That sounds like a plan."

"Yeah." He grins, and I see the adventurous boy behind the enterprising man who has been taking his place. "It is. My dream is to have the restaurant basically run itself, to have people in place who know what they're doing and don't have to ask me about every little thing. I always want to be a part of it, but I want to be the visionary. I also want time away from it to be with family. When it comes down to it that's who all the work is for, right? I don't think my dad always got that. Our grandfather spent more time raising us than he did."

"I'm excited to see the place. And to meet them."

"Emily will bring you there for dinner tonight. If you're not sick of Italian food, that is."

"Never."

When we exit the highway, he drives through a neighbourhood with rows and rows of brick duplexes broken up by a middle school with children playing in the yard. We go a little further and Jakob pulls into the driveway of a stand-alone house with gables and brick siding. Plenty of trees shade the house and shelter a lush garden in front. "This is home," he says, and hops out of the car. He has my bag before I'm even out of my seat and motions me toward the front door. "Just be quiet at first." He slips his key in the lock. "Our grandfather may be sleeping."

I nod and follow him inside. The house looks cozy and lived in, but tidy. A whiff of cooking food makes my stomach grumble. "Oh, sorry" says Jakob. "I didn't even think to ask if you were hungry. Clearly you are."

"Oh, just now," I say.

"Well, it smells like Emily has something on the go." He sets my bag down and I follow him through the living room. He pushes open a door at the back of the house and peeks his head around. I hear some shuffling and then see Emily's sweet smile as the door is pulled open.

"I'm so glad you made it." She hugs me tightly. "When we left last time I really wasn't sure if we'd see you again."

"I made it," I say, and see an old man in a wheelchair sitting by a window. He's looking at us, an open but droopy smile on his face.

"Come meet Farfar," says Emily. "We're just finishing his lunch but say hello first, then Jakob can show you the place."

I step into the room and toward the man. His hands are cramped over and various parts of his body twitch and tremor. I've never been good with old people. Both sets of my grandparents died before I was old enough to remember them well and I've avoided other interactions. Just like the faces of women who had once been beautiful, the sight of the elderly always reminded me of what I had to lose. It seems somewhat less important now. I touch my scar without realizing it and continue my walk to the window.

"Farfar, this is Autumn. She's the one who'll be staying with us for a bit. Autumn, this is our grandfather." There's love in Emily's voice. Pride. And something else I can't quite figure out.

"Hello." I reach my hand out to his offered one. His smile increases and it makes my discomfort worse. His tongue wags freely and his cramped hand is hard to grasp.

"We...we...welcome to our home, Autumn," he says. "It is a p...pleasure." He's trying to hold my hand firmly but the pressure wavers. He shakes his arm and then releases me. "I am J...Ja...Jakob. The first." He manages a wink. "But you can call me Farfar. That's what ev...everyone else does around here."

Something in his eyes disarms me and my initial discomfort melts away. "It's nice to meet you, Farfar," I say.

"You go with J...Jakob. My eating mann...erisms are a little messy. We don't want to sc...scare you off the first day."

"I'm sure I'd be fine," I say, but take a step back.

Jakob leans in and kisses his grandfather on the temple, "Afternoon, Farfar," then motions for me to follow him. He shows me the rest of the main floor before leading me upstairs. "My room," he says. "I just moved back in actually—to help with things. It's a little weird to be back in the room I grew up in after what…four years away? And that's Emily's room." He points to the closed door. "My father's." He takes me to the end of the hall and up another short set of stairs with a small hall and two doors. "And yours." He pushes open the first door. "A study and guest room. Don't worry though. There's another reading room downstairs. This is yours while you're here."

"Thank you," I say. "I like it." The room is dark with a slanted ceiling. A four-posted canopy bed rests against the far wall beside a set of drawers and a desk and chair sit in the corner. I set my bags down on a comfy looking but old-fashioned lounge chair. Three of the walls are covered in dark wood panelling and the fourth is all shelving—full of weathered and interesting looking books. The room smells like wood and old paper.

"Our mum was a big reader," says Jakob. "She used to love being up here."

"I can see why."

"Anyway," he says, "I don't come up here a lot, but I hope you like it."

"I do."

"Good." He tosses his head and I can tell he's not used to this new haircut. "I have to get back to the restaurant, but you can settle in here, head downstairs, get something to eat. Whatever you like. Emily should be done with Farfar soon. Just make this your home, all right?"

"Yeah, don't worry about me."

He touches his arm to my shoulder and grins. "Yeah, you can take care of yourself."

"For sure."

"Oh," he says just before stepping out of the room, "the other door is Amalia's room. She'll be home from school in a few hours. She's very excited to meet you. She's always wanted to go to Canada. Big Emily of New Moon fan."

"Not Anne?"

Jakob laughs. "Not as much. Anyway, don't let her shyness fool you."

"Okay." I laugh, having forgotten about their younger sister. I move my pack to the desk chair as Jakob dashes down the steps. After two weeks of living out of this bag, I could use a drawer. I open the top drawer of the dresser to find it full. I smile at the contents and pull out what looks like a baby's christening gown. The stitching is delicate and careful, perhaps Jakob and Emily's mother made it. I pick up other items. A blanket. A few onesies. Three sets of shoes. The next drawer is full as well. It's different though. A photo book lies on top. I flip to the first page and see who I guess are Mr. and Mrs. Andrev holding a baby in their arms, pride shining on their faces. The woman is beautiful and there's something of Emily in her smile, her flowing hair. The man is handsome. He looks a bit nervous. I flip the pages to see more pictures, realizing the baby must be Jakob, then close it, suddenly wondering if I'm prying. I don't know that I'd want someone looking through my memories like this.

I shut the drawer and try the third. This and the one below it are empty. They're deep and have plenty of room for all of my clothes. When I'm done unpacking, I head down to the living room. Emily and Farfar sit while she reads a book out loud. She sets it down and looks up at me when I enter the room. "Did you get a little rest?"

"I was just unpacking," I say and notice the same woman from the album in a picture above the fireplace. She's older this time and is holding a new baby in her arms with a young Jakob and Emily beside her. I guess not all of their memories are hidden away.

"Did you have enough room for all your things? I could always move some stuff around."

"No, it's fine. Perfect."

"Good." Emily stands. "Jakob said you were probably hungry. Follow me." I nod to Farfar and walk past him to the kitchen. "So, tell me about France."

"I don't know," I say. "It was good."

"Just good?"

"It's a bit of a blur to be honest." I lean against the counter and watch as Emily takes a bowl out of the cupboard.

"Beef stew. Is that fine?"

"Great."

"Did you go to a ton of places or something? See everything too fast to get a good feel for any of it?"

"Maybe. Yeah. Basically. But you've been, right? I'm not sure how much I could tell you."

"I've been to the main spots. But still, everyone sees things differently, right? I don't know how you would have seen it." She smiles over at me and something about her seems older than when we last met.

"Yeah." I take the bowl from her. "That's true, I guess."

"It is." She leans against the counter as well. "What would you like to drink?"

"Do you have tea?"

"Do we have tea?" Emily laughs and grabs a kettle. She loops the handle over the faucet while it fills. "I probably should have thought to mention Farfar to you. That must have been a bit of a shock."

"No, it's fine." I say, uncertain of what I should say. "I mean I knew he wasn't doing well."

She nods, her arms wrapped around her middle. "He's gotten a lot worse. Fast. It was a shock coming home for us too."

Again, I'm not sure what to say. I purse my lips and smile, letting her know I'm listening.

"I'm glad though, that they called us back, that I can help him. It's good to be needed." She takes the kettle off of the faucet. It shakes in her hand. She secures the cover and places the kettle on the stove. "I wanted to be a doctor. That was my plan. I gave that dream up last year. But staying home with Farfar—it means I'm still helping. I'm thinking of taking a home care course too…for after. I think I'd like that."

"Why'd you give up trying to be a doctor?"

"I wanted to be a surgeon," she says. I notice her hand tremble. She draws it back to her middle then looks down at it before looking back up at me. "I have early onset."

"Oh," I breathe. "I didn't realize. I didn't know."

She waves her hand as if brushing away my words. "It's not obvious yet. Not to someone who isn't familiar with the symptoms."

"But you could still be a doctor, couldn't you? I mean you could even be into research, right? Maybe you could find the cure."

"Maybe." She looks toward the window. "But I've watched my grandfather's," she pauses, "progression since I was a child. He even has some dementia now. They're not positive whether it's the disease or just old age but…" her voice trails off. "They have medication to help. Medications that are helping me too. But I don't know. I started so young. He didn't get symptoms until his late fifties. So for me, who knows? I just don't want to spend what time I have with my head in books. It's better to be here, with Farfar and my family, doing something I can see the benefit of every day. Helping them."

Again, I don't know what to say. I want to tell her she could do more, she shouldn't give up. But who am I to say anything? A whirring sound enters the room and I turn to see Farfar roll into the kitchen, his hand pressed against a little remote on his wheelchair that reminds me of an Atari controller.

"Emily," he says firmly. "Don't stay home f…f…f…from school for me. You can do g…g…great things."

"Oh." Emily flushes red. "I didn't know you could hear us, Farfar."

"My d…di…dis…disease doesn't affect my ears," he says with a jovial tone, and behind his smile I imagine the man he once was—like Jakob. "You go back to school."

"Farfar," she removes the kettle as it starts to whistle, "it's not for you. It's for me. I want to be here with you. And I want to do something tangible with my life. There's nothing wrong with that."

"Yes. B…but, you can not lose hope. I've told you before. As long as t…the…there is life, there is hope. As long as there is hope, there is l…li…life. You may never get like me. You must believe."

Emily walks to her grandfather and clasps his hand in hers. She's clearly fighting tears and, I'm guessing, the urge to say something more. "I know Farfar, I know. Trust me. This is what I want to do with my life. I want to take care of you, like you took care of all of us, okay? Trust me." She nods at him, kisses his hand. "This is where I want to be."

He jerkily pulls her hand to his cheek. "I don't know about you, my little rose." He says the words so clearly it shocks me. "I don't know."

Emily steps away from him and looks at me. "Black, green, or herbal?"

"Black." The word almost falls out of my mouth.

"And Farfar, do you want tea?"

"G…G…G…G…Green."

# CHAPTER EIGHTEEN

Emily and Farfar stay with me as I eat my stew, then we all move back to the living room. It's surprising how quickly I grow used to Farfar's mannerisms, the way he stutters through his words, the sudden jerk of a hand or a leg that startled me at first. His life and his spirit are bigger than these things. He clearly likes to talk and within minutes has me laughing at various tales from his youth and humorous instances his disease has gotten him into. The more he speaks, the deeper he is in a story, the less pronounced his stutter seems to be.

"It was e…e…early on," he says, telling a new story. "I was at some big business meeting. Some to-do. Black tie, a veritable affair. I could still hide my little shakes most of the time. My wife, Emily's Farmor, had left this world about a year earlier and I was thinking it might be time for me to get back out there. Have some fun." He gives a jerky wink and Emily smiles at him, looking embarrassed, which I'm sure is what he wants. "And so I walked up to the handsomest woman in the place. She was tall and firm—with hips that looked like they were made to sway. In a red dress, her hair done up in a pompadour, her lips just as red and rosy as the dress that hugged her. When I tapped her on the shoulder, she turned with a slow smile. A smile that could have stopped the war. And just as her eyes focused fully on mine, my hand gave a royal twitch, flinging my champagne directly in her face. She hollered. And what could I say as the droplets poured down her face, creating rivulets of that perfectly placed makeup?" He giggles now, and we're giggling with him. "Anyone would have thought I meant to throw my drink in her face! Her scream gathered a crowd of eyes. So I did what any self-respecting man would do. I proclaimed, 'You know what that's for,' and stormed out of the place like an indignant past lover."

Tears squeeze out of his eyes and he chuckles before continuing. "Needless to say, the business contacts I had hoped to make that evening did not get made and, thankfully, I never saw the woman again. I didn't even know her name but I'm sure everyone around her was wondering what she'd done to provoke such wrath. And despite whatever defences she must have given, what proclamations that I was a madman, I'm sure there's still a part of her, wherever she may be, that wonders the same thing."

"You should have explained," says Emily. "The poor woman."

"You would think that." Farfar shakes his head. "You've said it before. But where would the fun be in that? You've got to laugh at life. And that has been a laugh for years to come. If she's the type of woman I imagined she was, I'm sure she's still telling that story and laughing too. In this case, the truth would have ruined the joke."

Emily smiles at him, and I suspect she said that simply because it's something she's said before, as he said—though I'm not sure she would have allowed the joke herself.

"That wasn't even the worst one," says Farfar. As he starts another story, my mind wanders. It's the words he said earlier—about life and hope, that I ponder. Clearly they're words Farfar believes himself. Even after knowing his eventual death sentence, he was eager to find new love. I'm not sure what it is I'm supposed to do with these words though. At least Farfar had a life with his wife, a family. I give myself a mental shake and try to focus back on his story. Laughs are what I need and want right now.

"So, what should we know about you?" asks Farfar several minutes later. "I know you're a t...traveller. I know you're from the big land across the sea. I know you've got a sm...smile that could crumble a man's heart. What else is there?"

I try not to laugh. Maybe I used to have that smile. "I don't know." I shrug. "What do you want to know?"

"Whatever you want to tell."

"I used to work as a personal trainer," I say. "I had dreams of having my own studio one day."

"Had dreams?"

"Well, I'm travelling now. I quit my job at the studio before coming to Europe. I don't know what my next step is, really."

"I'm trying to get her to start her studio in London," says Emily. "Don't you think that sounds like a good idea, Farfar?"

"It s...sss...sounds like a grand idea."

"It's possible." I smile. "My life is an open book."

"Hmmm." He nods and, behind the boyish glint, his eyes hold something more serious. "All of our lives are a book, one we only get to co-author. Some people think we can wipe the slates clean, but we never can. Not really. Our past shapes our story, to be sure. It can't be erased, but the blessing is it doesn't have to define the rest of the tale."

Emily smiles at me and gives a slight eye roll. "Farfar likes to impart his words of wisdom, his philosophizing of life. He should have been a poet."

"I have the right," he says, a false gruffness to his voice. "I've earned it."

His words prompt an odd twisty feeling in my stomach. Erasing Matt is essentially what I'm trying to do. "Anyway, I don't know what I'm going to do next. I don't have any real commitments at the moment. I'd like to get a job, take some time, figure out what I want, before jumping into anything too big."

He nods. "And what of your family?"

"I have a mom and a dad, a brother. Some cousins. Not a big family."

"What do they think of this travelling, and of starting a studio here?"

"They knew I always wanted to travel…I haven't talked to them about the studio yet."

"No?" His eyebrow rises unevenly.

"Well, as I said, I hardly know myself whether it's something I want to do."

"Mm-hmm." The sound of the front door opening and shoes being kicked off makes its way to our ears. Farfar looks toward the hall, a smile lighting his face. "Ahh, it is my gullunge, my sweet child."

"Amalia," says Emily.

A moment later a young girl in a school uniform walks into the room. She looks to be about thirteen or fourteen and is practically a miniature version of Emily—minus the gap-toothed smile. Lithe seems an accurate description. I'd be surprised if a strong gust of wind couldn't blow her over. She walks into the room hesitantly once she sees me and seems to appraise me with her eyes as she heads toward her grandfather. Slowly, a smile creeps its way onto her face, and I imagine that I've passed.

"Farfar." She bends for a kiss.

"What is the one thing?" he asks.

Amalia thinks for a moment. She bobs her head back and forth as if it's floating on her neck to the tune of a mellow song. "I was introduced to T.S. Eliot in my extra credit course." She tilts her head toward the far corner of the room, an enchanted smile on her face. "The yellow fog that rubs its back upon the window-panes,/ The yellow smoke that rubs its muzzle on the window-panes/ Licked its tongue onto the corners of the evening." She pauses. "Do I dare/ Disturb the universe?…I have measured out my life in coffee spoons." The smile turns wistful. "I think I'm in love."

"The Love Song of J. Alfred Prufrock," says Farfar. "A good place to start and Eliot is a lover I approve of. '"There will be time, there will be time/ To prepare a face to meet the faces that you meet.' That line got me through some tough years. 'And should we prepare a face to meet the faces that we meet?'" He smiles. "Or does it equate to measuring out our life in coffee spoons?"

Amalia glances at me. She seems embarrassed and I don't blame her. "I think it depends," she says.

"A safe answer, but a good answer." He squeezes her hand and then releases it. "This, my dear, is Autumn. Our house guest. Autumn, this is my Amalia." She nods at me and curls up on the couch beside her grandfather, her feet tucked under her.

"It's nice to meet you, Amalia."

"It's nice to meet you too."

"Autumn was just telling us about her dreams of starting a fitness studio. And maybe starting it in London. I was going to ask her, why London?"

"I don't know," I say. "Because I'm here. Because…it's not home."

"What's wrong with home?"

"Farfar, don't grill her," says Emily.

"I'm not grilling her, child. I'm trying to get to know her. I think London is a fine place to be. And I think starting a fitness studio is a grand idea. Now that there are all these office jobs, people need something to keep them moving. But it will be much harder here." He looks at me. "I'm sure you had clients back home, people who could vouch for you, who would probably leave their club to follow you. You'll have nothing here. What is the appeal?"

I'm silent for a moment. "The challenge. It's new. Completely new." This isn't a complete lie, but there's definitely more to the truth. Besides being away from all the memories of Matt, the idea of setting up a studio in England and potentially failing isn't nearly so scary as setting up one back home. It'd make sense if I fail here. Like Farfar said, I have no following, no devoted clients to rely on, no reputation. To succeed would be incredible. To fail…well, it wouldn't be that bad.

"I haven't decided or anything," I continue, "but I've never lived anywhere else before. Even my University was in the same town I grew up in. I mean, I haven't made any decisions yet or anything. It's just a very distant 'maybe' but away from home I have the chance to be whoever I want to be. Create my identity."

"Mm-hmm." He looks at me, then smiles. It's clear he's holding something back, and I have a feeling I should be thankful. "Well, then, all the best to you on this journey. We will help you and guide you whether you are a guest in our little city for a day or a year.

"Now…I think it is time for my nap. Must do what I can to keep that Footman at bay as long as possible." He winks at Amalia. She doesn't smile.

"I'll help you, Farfar," says Emily. "Amalia, why don't you take Autumn to the park. Let her stretch her legs, show her the neighbourhood. Then when you come back, you'll start your homework?"

Amalia uncurls herself slowly and stands. She nods at Emily and then looks toward me. "Do you want to come?"

"Sure, I'd love to." I stand and follow her to the front door. "I've never heard of T.S. Eliot," I say as we put our shoes on. "He's a poet?"

"Yeah. He's really complicated. My teacher says as we read more of him we won't understand a third of what he says, if that, but that it's not always necessary to understand."

"And you like him?"

She grins and does look like a girl somewhat in love. "He speaks to me."

"Oh, yeah?"

"My extra credit teacher speaks to me too," she says coyly. "He's dreamy. That doesn't hurt."

I laugh. "I don't imagine it would."

"Do you like poetry?"

"I haven't read much of it to be honest. I was always more into science. But it sounded interesting—the lines you and your grandfather were saying."

"It's like," Amalia pauses as she opens the gate and we head down the street, "science can help you understand all the intricate details of the body, how it works, but then poetry lets you understand the soul. The body," she takes a few steps, "does what it wants sometimes. It's unreliable. I mean it's good to know, it's important. But for me, I want to understand the soul."

"Seems a good plan."

"I like talking about this stuff with Farfar. Emily and Jakob do sometimes, but not so much. Farfar says my mom talked about it."

"So you two have that in common?"

"Yeah, I guess so. Are you close with your mom?"

"Not super close. We used to be, when I was growing up. Not as much anymore. She doesn't exactly know how to give me space."

She looks at me like I'm a bit of a quiz. "Is she mean?"

"No."

"Does she not understand you?"

"At times."

Amalia nods. We turn down a path and through a small patch of trees. "This is Wandle Park. It's a nice place to come read or lie in the sun on a hot day. Sometimes Jakob comes and plays Frisbee with his friends."

"It's nice."

"How long have you been travelling?"

"About two months now."

"Wow. And all by yourself?"

"Not really. I met Jakob and Emily my first day. I stayed with them for over a month—for a couple of the weeks we were with your family in Italy."

"Oh, Emily told me." Her face lights up. "I haven't been yet. Nonno and Dominic came here to visit once a few years ago. I guess Nonna came too a couple of times, but I was too young to remember. It was when my mother was sick." We walk a few more paces. "Emily said you got to stomp the grapes with her. Was it really fun?"

I chuckle. "Yeah, it was great. All squishy and cold and…not like anything I've felt before." Amalia smiles and I suddenly feel sorry for this little girl. Her eyes are too old. "I'm sure you'll get to do it one day."

"Oh, I will. When I'm older. I'm going to travel all over—like you are. Well, if I can. Emily says she won't be doing much more travelling."

"She doesn't know that. Not for sure."

"I guess." She's quiet and I can tell she's thinking. "Jakob is fine. There's nothing wrong with him. At least not yet. Had you ever met anyone with Parkinson's before?"

"No."

"My friends don't like coming to my house. Farfar makes them uncomfortable. It's kinda stupid really—of them I mean."

"Yeah."

"I prefer to spend most of my time alone anyway. So it's not a big deal."

"Reading?"

"Yeah, and just thinking. I come out here a lot and lie on the grass. Dream. Cloud watch. Do you ever do that?"

I think of Matt, his love of cloud stories, and my chest tightens a little. "I used to."

"I've come up with poems doing that."

"You write?"

"I try. So why don't you do it anymore?"

"I don't know." I hesitate. "I used to do it with

someone…not anymore.”

“Oh, I see.” We walk in silence for a few minutes. “Do you have any brothers and sisters?”

“One brother—and then a cousin who was kind of like a sister growing up. We spent a lot of time together.”

“Same as me then—kind of.”

“Kind of.” When we’ve finished the looped trail and are back to where we entered the park, Amalia heads to the street. “Does where you live in Canada get real winters? Lots of snow? I know not everywhere in Canada does. Not in Victoria. Not really. It’s a big deal if we get a couple of centimetres here.”

“Sometimes we get a few feet or more. Not often though.”

“I want to see that one day. There isn’t even anywhere we can sled here.” Amalia kicks a rock out of the path. It’d be more like mudding.”

“Oh, we get enough snow for that. At least a few times a winter. And drive an hour and there’s lots more.”

“Cool.” We approach the gate and Amalia turns to me. “I’ve got to do my homework. But you’re staying a few days, right?”

“At least, yeah.”

“Cool.”

I watch her go inside, grab her book bag, and head upstairs. Besides my grandparents’ deaths, which I hardly remember, Matt is the first real tragedy I’ve had, and it came close to destroying me. When it comes down to it, I’m still a wreck. It was hard losing Aunt Cynthia, yes, but I was so focused on Jenn it hardly affected me personally. This little girl has lost her mother, is watching her grandfather get closer to the grave each day, sees her sister following the same path, and lives with the fear that it’ll one day be her fate as well, and yet she seems more together than I feel inside. It doesn’t make sense.

I push these thoughts aside, trying not to wonder what

she has that I don't. It's been a good week since I've checked my email so I head to the computer, which is set up in a little room off of the library. A picture of the family rests in a frame on the desk—everyone except their mother. I smile and lift it up. They look happy. I sigh, wake the computer and open a browser. Less emails load than that first time and I scroll through the ones from my friends first. Most of them are just a few lines—some details of their lives, comments on that group email I sent from the Lombardi's. Rather than reply to everyone, I write another group email about my time in France and where I am now. It's easier that way. Some of them ask how I really am. A few tell me if I ever need to talk, they're just a phone call away. It's clear they all think I'm running.

I open the email from my mother next, relieved there's just one. She tries to write lightly, but I can imagine the tension behind each word. The worry. She asks me again if I've decided when I'm coming home. She tells me my father is finally figuring out that social media thing and, though he won't admit it, she thinks he kind of likes it. She says she's never seen Daniel so happy—that Mallory seems really good for him—and that Jenn came over for dinner the week before and brought Rajeev. She thinks they seem like a really sweet couple. She finishes by saying she loves me and misses me.

"I'm glad you're making yourself at home," says Emily. I look up, surprised to see her standing beside me. I didn't even hear her enter the room.

"Yeah, I hope that's okay." I swivel toward her.

"Absolutely." She takes a seat in the armchair across from the computer. "Keeping in touch with people back home?"

"Yeah, trying to."

"You miss them?"

"I don't know." I lean back, away from the desk so I can see her better. "I mean, yeah, sure, but it's nice to be away too."

She nods. "It's nice you can still keep in touch so easily."

"Yeah." I glance back at the screen. "Do you need the computer?"

"No, no." She stands. "I was just seeing what you were up to. Jakob suggested we go to dinner at the restaurant tonight. I was thinking we'd leave here in about three hours. That work for you?"

"Absolutely. Sounds good. I'll finish up here then maybe take a quick nap."

Emily smiles. She walks by me and pats her hand on my shoulder. Something in the touch reminds me of my mother, and suddenly I really do miss her. It's not like I saw her all the time back home anyway, sometimes two weeks would go by, but rarely more than that. Daniel and I went home for as many Sunday dinners as we could. It had been rare for more than a few days to go by without a call, especially in the months leading up to the wedding. I close my eyes before I start to type, thinking of her smile, of Dad's, of that feeling of home. It's the first time since this trip started that I've really let myself miss them. I was saving all my missing for Matt—as ridiculous as that sounds. I shake my head, open my eyes, and type her a cheery, excited letter full of the wonderful sights of France, Jakob and Emily's home, and finish by telling her about the restaurant I may get a job in. I say things are going really well and I miss them, but I'll be staying here for at least a few weeks, maybe more, then apologize for not getting in touch sooner—it's been nine days—but, I assure, I should be able to keep it to a week now that I'm in one place again. I choose not to give her the Andrev's house number. She'd call and try to convince me to come home.

When I finish, I copy over excerpts of the letter to the group one and then head upstairs for my nap. It feels nice to be in a room all to myself. It's been months. I set the alarm beside the bed for an hour and a half from now, enough time to shower before dinner, and am dead to the world almost instantly.

# CHAPTER NINETEEN

The Andrev's restaurant looks like it could have been transported directly from Italy. It has the same brick construction, with vines creeping up the walls and an interior lit by a mix of candles and twinkle lights. A vase filled with fresh flowers sits in the centre of each table. The scent of baking bread and garlic fills the air. It's busy, and light bursts of laughter join the clinking of silverware and quiet conversation that permeates the place. We're ushered to our table, one that Farfar's chair can easily manoeuvre to and, once we're seated for several minutes, Jakob makes his way over to us, a man several inches taller one step behind him. From the family photos and the family resemblance, I know it's Mr. Andrev. His eyes are friendly but tired; the creases around them seem like they've settled too soon. He grins when he sees me. "You must be Autumn." I stand as he grasps my hand in both of his and shakes it heartily. "My babies say you are a great friend."

"It's them who have been great friends to me," I say. "They kind of adopted me."

"Well," he releases my hand, "they wouldn't adopt anyone who wasn't deserving—and seeing as you're willing to dash in front of a truck to save a stranger, I'd say that's pretty deserving."

"It wasn't that impressive." I laugh self-consciously. "I was just—"

"Saving my daughter." He walks around to Farfar,

Amalia, and Emily, kissing each of them, then pulls up a chair. "What do you think of our little piece of paradise?"

"It's wonderful," I say.

"Jakob here has made it even better, while making my work less." He looks at Jakob and the pride is evident. "One day soon I may be able to lie back and enjoy a life of leisure while he takes the reins."

"That's the plan," says Jakob. "I have to head back, but I'll check in every now and then." With a smile, he leaves us.

"My goodness," their father laughs. "I didn't even introduce myself. And shame on you for not doing it." He turns to Emily, then back to me. "I am Stefan. Stefan Andrev."

"Hi," I say. "It's nice to meet you."

"Indeed. So Autumn, my children have told me a little, but tell me more. What exactly brings you here?"

"Well," I hate this question, hate the need to only tell partial truths, "I've always wanted to explore Europe. I came to a point in my life where I could and so…here I am."

"And London wasn't originally part of your plan?"

I take a breath. "Not on this trip, anyway."

"Well, it's good you changed your mind. It would be a sin to not see London. I'm not saying it's the best place to visit in Europe. But this city had much influence in shaping your part of the world."

"Absolutely," I say.

"Have you seen any of it yet?" I open my mouth to answer, but he cuts me off. "No, I suppose not. You've only been here a couple of hours! Not to worry. We'll make sure you get the royal tour."

"Oh, that's not necessary." I wave a hand. "I'm good at finding my own way around. I'm sure you're all busy."

"Nonsense," says Stefan. "You are my guest now." He sends a grin that is entirely different from Jakob's—minus the energy behind it—and waves over a waitress. "If you will, allow me to order for you? Just tonight?"

"Okay."

Yet again, it's wonderful to be part of a family atmosphere. This dynamic is different than the one at the Lombardi's, but just as full of love. Stefan is clearly the 'head' of the family, but the respect and compassion he shows to Farfar is almost staggering. Most of my experience of family relationships with the elderly comes from TV and movies—they definitely don't display this type of caring. It's unnerving to see how the media has warped my view, leading me to see older people as a burden, sometimes comically so, whereas this family sees Farfar as a treasure. The Lombardi's did too, but Nonno and Nonna were still so vigorous. Farfar's vigour solely remains in his mind.

Several hours later I'm so stuffed I feel as if I might burst…but I've loved every bite. Farfar, Emily, Amalia and I pile into the car we came in as Stefan kisses Amalia good night and heads back into the restaurant to help Jakob and the rest of the staff with closing.

"So what did you think?" asks Emily.

"What did I think?"

"Of the restaurant."

"What could I think?" I laugh. "It was fabulous. I don't think I'll need to eat for a week."

"Papa can get a little forceful," says Emily, as she pulls the car onto the street. "You are allowed to say no."

I groan. "I'll remember that next time." I look over to see Amalia falling asleep against the car window. "Will she be all right for school tomorrow?"

Emily glances back. "Yeah, she'll be fine. What do you want to do tomorrow?"

"I don't know. Look into earning my keep perhaps? Maybe talk to Jakob about that job at the restaurant he thought he could get me?"

"Oh, there's no rush for that. Be our guest for a couple of weeks first."

"No, I think I've taken enough advantage of your hospitality. I want to earn my own way. Besides, the money I allotted for travelling isn't going to last too much longer."

"Well, if you insist," says Emily. "You can talk to Jakob about it tomorrow. I'm sure he can find a place for you."

"I do," I say. It's part of the plan.

⁓

"YOU DON'T WANT TO take it easy for a few days?" Jakob stands across the room as I help Emily with breakfast the next morning. "Explore a bit?"

"I can explore on my days off," I say. "And I've been exploring for a couple of months now. I'm ready to work. I mean I understand if you don't have a position for me. I can always look elsewhere."

"No, no," says Jakob. "It's not that. I can find you a position. We'll just have to get you a travel employment visa. The Youth Mobility would probably be best. We've used that with Canadians before. Shouldn't be too hard. Papa knows some people."

"That's great. Thank you so much."

"So, have you waitressed before?"

"No. But I'm a fast learner—and coordinated."

"Well, maybe we could start you as a hostess. Let you learn the ropes before you start on tables. The tips are better waitressing, but it can be a surprisingly difficult job to master."

"Whatever you think." I hesitate and trail my hand to my face. "Are you sure hostess is the best spot for me though…the first thing people see?"

"I don't see why not," says Stefan as he enters the kitchen.

"Yeah, that's no problem," says Jakob.

I feel myself grinning. I can't remember the last time I

felt this excited about something. It doesn't even matter that it's not in my field, not what I ever thought I would do. It's what's going to get me on a new path. It's a chance at the life I'm determined to have.

In less than a week my visa is in place—I'm amazed at the speed but, as Jakob said, Stefan knows people. I've already gone into the restaurant several times to shadow both the current hostesses and some of the waitresses. I'm going to be able to do this. It's the same underlying concept as how I work with my clients—make people feel welcome, make them feel listened to, be attentive to their needs. All things I excel at.

Nerves tingle through me as I get ready for my first shift. I take a long time on my hair and apply makeup for the first time in weeks, the first time since the funeral to be exact—I think this like it's an abstract event, just THE funeral, and somehow that makes it manageable. My uniform fits well and I take an extra moment to make sure everything is adjusted just right. I pin back my hair, ensuring no strands slide down to my face. All of this attention to detail is to ward off this feeling that something is about to go very wrong. I have no reason to think it though. None at all. I'm smart, I'm capable, I'm determined. This will go well.

It does go well. And the next night and the next night but still I can't shake this feeling of, for lack of a better word, doom. But it's ridiculous. Everything is going well. I ease into life at the Andrev's just as well as I did with the Lombardi's. We all have breakfast together every morning then Emily and I take Farfar for a walk. In the afternoon I sometimes help Amalia with her science homework, or Emily helps her while I keep Farfar company. Shortly after that I head into work. I'm only getting five hour shifts right now but two times a week I go in early to practise waitressing during the slow hours. I've started looking at apartment ads. I don't really want to leave the Andrev's and rent is expensive in London, but I also can't keep living off of others' generosity.

"You can always pay rent," says Emily one day when she finds me in the den searching apartments online, "if it makes you feel better."

"Huh?" I swivel in the chair and face her.

"You can pay rent. Here. That way you could stay and not feel like you were…what did you say the other day? Mooching?"

"Oh."

"We have lots of space. It's nice having you here. I like the company. I mean Farfar's wonderful company but," she hides the shaking in her right hand by pressing it against her abdomen, a habit I'm becoming used to, "it's nice having you around."

"I like being around. But this is your family," I say. "I think it'd be good for me to be on my own again."

She nods. "Well, don't feel you have to rush, okay?" Her other hand trembles and she slips it into her pants pocket. "Seriously."

"Yeah, okay." I watch her for a moment, and she watches me. "How have you been doing?"

"I'm good."

"I mean—" I gesture to her hand.

"Oh," she pulls her hand out of her pocket, looks at it, like it's a foreign entity. "I'm lucky. The medicine they have me on, it helps a lot. A little twitching here and there. It's really not that big a deal."

"Good," I say. We both know she's lying.

"I'm really just focusing on Farfar. Trying to make him as comfortable and happy as possible. That's what really matters."

"You matter too."

"I know." Emily picks up a blanket from the armchair. She folds it then tosses it back down again. "You know my secrets," she says. "When do I get to know yours?" I look at her, place a question on my face. "I haven't forgotten the tan line. You didn't come to Europe simply to explore."

"Yeah," I exhale. "I'm just trying to start over, Emily. I don't want to bring up the past. That's all it is, right? The past. It's not my life anymore."

She looks at me then shrugs, smiles that disarming smile she has. "Well, okay. Just know if you ever want to remember that past with someone, I've got two listening ears. Sometimes, despite our best efforts, our past refuses to stay there. Sometimes it's good to hold it up again, you know?"

"Sure," I say.

"Anyway, I'll leave you to it," she says. "Let me know if you have any questions about certain neighbourhoods. There are some it's probably best to avoid."

"Thanks."

I shake Emily's words from my mind but I've lost my motivation to apartment hunt for the moment so I head to my emails instead. It's been about a week. I scroll to the oldest unread message and read a note from Jenn.

*Hey, you. I miss you. Come home already, please. Or at least call. I want to hear your voice. I have so much to tell you. And I need you to kick my butt into gear. I think at long last I could take you as my trainer—seriously. Rajeev is a crazy good cook, but he just doesn't seem to get the whole, 'I'm trying not to blow back up into a balloon thing.' But it's good. We all miss you. We think of you. We love you. Come home already.*

I smile at that and head to the next message. It's from Eloise.

*I'll be in London in two weeks! My firm has a massive conference going on and I'll be crazy tied up in meetings, but I finagled two extra days at the end of it. Those days are reserved for you. We're going to do it up, all right? So be available! I love you, my dear, I'm thinking of you. We all are.*

This makes me less happy. It'd be great to see Eloise,

sure, but I don't know that she'll follow the rules—I can't recall if she even knows about them, about my resolve. I don't think she does—unless Jenn or Mom have told her. But at the same time, I can't not see her, she's one of my best friends. If she brings him up, she brings him up. I'll just have to deal with it. It'd be best to make sure Jakob and Emily don't know about this friend though. I don't want her slipping up in front of them.

Oddly, there's no letter from my mom, but one from my dad.

*Autumn, I don't want to alarm you but there's been...well, your mom has had a stroke. We don't know how bad it is yet, but you better come home. And call. Call as soon as you can. Let us know what flight you get. Let us know if you need money to book it. Love you, Dad.*

I stare at the screen, not wanting the words to be real. Not believing them. It's ridiculous. My mom couldn't have had a stroke. She's fifty-seven. She's healthy. She's active. My father must be exaggerating. That's it. He's exaggerating. He just wants a way to get me home. My mom might have even put him up to it. She probably had a little scare—a heart palpitation or some such thing—and that gave them the idea. My mom is fine. She has to be.

# CHAPTER TWENTY

"Autumn."

I exit out the browser, swivel in my chair and see Amalia standing at the door. "Hi. How's it going?"

"Good. Are you busy?"

"Nope."

"I wanted to play Scrabble with Farfar, but Emily's not feeling too well and Jakob and Papa are going to be home late. Will you place the letters for him?"

"Sure." I push up from the chair and follow her out of the room. I feel shaky and brace myself against the door frame for a moment. She's fine. She's fine. She's fine. My mom is fine. "So, Scrabble," I say, my voice squeaking out. "I haven't played that in ages."

"Farfar is a champion," says Amalia.

"Oh, she gives me a run for my money every now and then," he says.

"You let me."

"Never." Farfar gives me that double wink of his. "Come sit beside me." I do. "And no helping me, agreed?" He nudges my arm with his elbow. "Unless you come up with something brilliant."

"No, no helping," says Amalia. I'm in somewhat of a daze as the game begins. I try to compartmentalize, to squish that little part of me that fears my father is telling the truth deep down inside me. I keep telling myself my mother is fine, that if it really was a big deal, they would have found some other way to contact me. I even start to feel angry. How could they try to manipulate me like that?

I smile when I'm supposed to smile. I place the tiles where I'm supposed to place them. I laugh when it's appropriate. After a time, I begin to believe my own actions and thoughts. My mother is fine. I'm fine. It's all fine.

"Good game, my dear," says Farfar, when he places his winning word.

"Mm-hmm," says Amalia.

"You'll beat me one day."

"I know." Amalia brightens. "Maybe next game."

"Maybe," says Farfar. "Can you get Emily, though? I think I'm ready for bed."

"Can I help you Farfar?" I ask. Amalia hesitates, waiting for his response.

"I wouldn't want to impose my frail old self on a pretty young thing like you."

"Emily's a pretty young thing," I say, "and it's no imposition. I'd like to."

"Well, if you insist. You go get ready for bed yourself then," he says to Amalia.

"Yes, Farfar."

I stand behind him and take hold of the chair. "Just tell me what I need to do."

"The bathroom first." He reaches up and pats my hand. "I used to be quite embarrassed about all of this," he says as I wheel him over. "But then I came to accept that if life is about love, what better joy is there than to care for another and to let yourself be cared for? Sometimes the latter is what's most difficult." He shakes his head. "But it can also be most enriching to your soul. Too many people don't let themselves be cared for. And there are many ways we can be crippled. Ways not as obvious as my jerking and twitching." I nod and maneuver the chair into the bathroom. He works to unbutton his pants and pull down the zipper. He's having trouble, and so I place my hand on his, look up at him. He nods, and rather than looking offended or indignant, as I fear, his eyes thank me. "Now, stay there," he says, "with your arms out, and let me put my weight on you as you help me up." I do as he says and try not to cringe for him as he struggles with his hands on the armrests and pushes himself off the chair. I catch his weight and it's even less than I anticipated. We shuffle over to the toilet and I help to ease him down. "This is becoming quite the ordeal," he says. "But at least I can handle this next part. When I can't, things will really change. We'll probably need a bed pan."

"But not yet," I say.

"Not yet." He smiles. "You can step out. I'll call you back in when I need you." I stand outside the door and hear him struggle. I wonder how difficult it is for him to get his pants down the rest of the way on his own, if that's something Emily usually does for him. When he calls me back in, I help him to his chair—he has managed to get his pants up enough that the important parts are covered. I do the zipper and button for him then wheel him to the sink to wash his hands. "Teeth." He grins, and I wonder if this energy is for me or for him. He points out his toothbrush and I apply the paste. "It's a much less messy ordeal if you don't mind doing it for me." Embarrassment hides behind his smiling tone.

"My pleasure." It's the first time I've ever brushed anyone's teeth. It's foreign and somewhat uncomfortable, but also precious—that's the best word I can think of to describe it.

"Now a warm cloth," Farfar says. "My favourite part."

I let the water run until it feels just right then dampen a facecloth and gently wipe all around his face and neck. When I'm going over his left cheek, he places his hand across mine. It's firm. I look into his eyes. "You're a good person, Autumn. A special girl. Don't let anyone ever tell you different, even yourself."

I chuckle, uncomfortable. "What's next?"

"To my room." We go through a similar routine as I help him from the chair to the bed. Together we get his shirt and pants off and he shows me where his pyjamas are. It takes a long time.

"I'm sure I'm not as good as Emily at this," I say as I'm buttoning up his nightshirt.

"You're doing just fine."

"Is there anything else?" I ask once he's lying in bed with the blanket under his chin.

"No b…b…bedtime story?" he asks, and I wonder if he's emphasizing the stutter on purpose. I notice it so rarely now. It's there, but…

"Sure." I glance for a book—there are many.

He laughs. "I'm just joking, my dear. You've done plenty. Shut off the light and the door and you're all done."

"Are you sure, I—"

"I'm sure."

"All right." I step toward the door and let my hand waver over the light switch. "Goodnight, Farfar."

"Goodnight, my dear. Until the sweet morning."

The corners of my lips lift. I realize I love this man. It's a funny realization. I hardly know him. But I do.

# CHAPTER TWENTY-ONE

The smile stays on my face as I make my way to the living room. It brightens at the site of Jakob and Stefan sipping tea, faces lit by a rolling fire. "Were you with Farfar?" asks Jakob.

"Yeah." I curl up on the couch across from him, enjoying the warmth.

"You don't have to do that. Where is Emily?"

"She wasn't feeling well. I wanted to help."

"You are something," says Stefan. "And how are you finding the hostessing?"

"It's good. I think it's good."

Stefan glances at me. Setting his tea down, he reclines his chair back, his head against the rest, and sinks into the plush cushioning. "We haven't had any complaints. Several compliments. And your waitressing shifts?"

"I think that's going well too. I really like being there. It's different from what I'm used to, but almost everyone seems in such a good mood, so ready to have an enjoyable time. It's contagious."

"That's the idea," says Jakob. "We want our little restaurant to be an oasis for people, an experience away from the responsibilities and burdens of their lives."

"My son," says Stefan, and in his wink I can see what Farfar's used to be before the Parkinson's. "He has such lofty aspirations. My goal was simply good food in a clean place."

Jakob shifts in his seat. "Well—"

"No, no," says Stefan, his eyes closed. "I think your way is the better way. I see a change already. I wish I'd had you as my partner years ago. I could have learned so much from you."

I watch Jakob. He nods at his father's words but can't hide what they really mean to him. "It's the schooling," he says, "it's what they—"

"It's you," says Stefan. "I've worked with other people in the past who had the same type of schooling. It's you, my boy." Stefan looks up for a moment. He smiles at his son and I feel as if I'm intruding. "I don't mention it enough, I'm sure I don't mention her enough, but your mother—she would have been really proud of you." He lays his head back down. "Really proud."

Jakob casts his gaze to the carpet, he nods, but his father can't see him anymore. The room is silent for several minutes and then Stefan expels a long breath of air and sits up. "I think it's time for me to go to bed. He stands and, when he passes the mantel, kisses his fingers then rests them against the picture of his wife—an action I've seen him do more than once.

"Are you okay?" I ask once Stefan is gone.

"Yeah, I'm fine," says Jakob. He grins and shakes his hair like he's shaking off his father's words. He stands and then looks at me. "He doesn't talk about her too much. I want her to be proud of me." He shrugs. "It's nice to know he thinks she would be."

"Why wouldn't she be proud of you?"

Jakob runs his hands through his hair, freeing the strands from the gel he coops them up with while at work. My throat catches. "We all have our secrets, Autumn. We all have things we're not so proud of."

I stare at him, wanting to know, wanting to know everything about him, but I'm not willing to offer up my secrets, so I keep my mouth shut.

"You want to go for a walk?"

"Yeah." I smile, shocked by the offer. "Sure."

"It's late, but—"

"I want to," I say. He offers his hand and I grasp it as he helps me up. It feels warm and firm and I hate that the moment I'm standing he lets go. We head to the front door and put our shoes on in silence. He pushes it open and I pass through under his arm, still in silence. We turn down the walkway, through the gate, and onto the sidewalk that leads us to the park. The shock of the cool evening air after the warm fire casts a chill through me and I try not to shiver, wishing I'd brought a sweater. The streetlamps cast our shadows to the side of us: they mingle. It's not until we're halfway down the trail that I put my hand on his shoulder. "Jakob. Are you okay?"

He turns to me. "Just reliving some things. Sorry I'm so quiet."

"It's okay. I don't mind the quiet."

"What about you?" he asks. "Are you okay?"

"Sure."

"So you're liking it here? And at the restaurant?"

"Yeah, a lot."

He sighs. "Emily mentioned you've been looking at flats? You're thinking of staying long term then?"

"Thinking of it."

"What about your family, your friends—are you going to go see them first?"

"I don't think so."

I want him to slip his arm around me, draw me close. I let my hand linger near his; they bump once or twice. He slides his hands in his pockets, and as he does this I suddenly feel slutty, which is ridiculous…I think.

He looks at me, then back at the path ahead of us. "I can't help feeling like you're running from something. I know it's none of my business."

I'm silent at first, considering. "It's just…it's not

anything that matters. Not now."

He makes a humming noise. Something in his tone makes me think he knows my hand didn't idly brush his and makes me wonder if he actually believes whatever I'm hiding no longer matters. Could the tan line still bother him? It's paranoid to think that, or maybe some part of me hopes it bothers him, hopes he cares. Not that I want anything anyway, not really. Not now. If only his smile weren't so cute, his chest so broad. It'd probably feel amazing to cuddle in against that chest.

As I imagine this, my memory takes me to a more concrete feeling—My head against Matt, his arms wrapped around me, his gentle kiss on my temple, his scent that felt like home. I take a deep breath and try to push it all from my mind. I tell myself he was just like any guy I've dated, any guy I thought maybe I'd loved, only to learn soon enough the love was fading. I don't love him anymore. I can't love him anymore. Which means, I'm free to love again. As I repeat these words inside my mind, I hear how stupid they sound. How weak. Of course he wasn't just some guy. He was Matt.

I take a breath and let it out again slowly. This is not the time to let my mind and heart go here, with Jakob standing beside me. But I can't ignore the truth. Matt wasn't any of the other guys I'd dated. Lust or like or boredom fuelled those relationships. My love for Matt was so real, so strong, that even all these months later, while yearning for Jakob's touch, I'm yearning for Matt's as well. I still love him as much as the day we wed. I just really don't want to.

Breathing again, I push thoughts of him away, like I always do. That's why I'm here, after all. That's why I'm not even calling my father to see how serious the supposed stroke really was. With this reminder, my chest tightens. I focus on breathing normally, an easy in out pattern. Whatever happened couldn't have been serious. My parents have the Lombardi's number. If it was serious, they'd call.

They'd make sure they got a hold of me in person, not rely on email, especially when they know I've been checking sporadically. They probably just want me back, but I'm not ready. As much as Matt haunts me here, home he's a constant companion—We were perfect, and our wedding was perfect, and our life would have been…as perfect as a life could have been. And that's all gone now, all stolen, leaving me nothing but these painful memories I wish would disappear.

I glance at Jakob as we round the corner. What would he think if he knew he was walking beside a widow right now—not a jilted woman, or whatever he imagines? What does he think? That my fiancé or husband left me? Cheated on me, maybe? It makes me sick to think he could think that's who Matt was. But maybe he thinks it was me, that I got scared and left, that I was the cheater. He could imagine something more simple, that we realized we weren't right for each other and decided to part ways. He could think anything.

"Should we head back?" asks Jakob.

"Sure." I can't help the shiver that trembles through me as a breeze passes by.

"Here," he says and has his blazer off before I can stop him.

"Thanks." I smile as he slips the coat around me, savouring that brief moment when his hands trace down my arms.

"Thanks for the walk," he says as he pushes open the gate. We head up the pathway, go through the door, and take off our shoes. I bump into him while balancing on one foot and he braces me. Smiles. "See you tomorrow."

"Yeah." I follow him up the stairs. He turns down the hall and into his room without a look back. I continue up the next flight and enter mine.

❧

Whatever had gotten into Jakob, he's back to his normal self in the morning, teasing Amalia, trading quips with Farfar, and talking about some new plans for advertising with Stefan. But I can't help it, I see him differently now. Something has changed and I'm not sure I like it. Emily stays in bed. Whatever was bothering her last night is apparently still an issue, and so Amalia and I prepare pancakes for everyone.

"Amalia," says Stefan, as she hands him an elephant-shaped pancake. "Ah, very nice." He looks down at it and tweaks her cheek. "What exactly is wrong with Emily?"

"I don't know, Papa. She said she's not feeling well. She didn't want to be disturbed."

"Hmm," he takes a seat, "I'll check on her before I leave. No one's going to tell me not to disturb my daughter. Even her."

"She said it wasn't serious."

"Still, still." His tone sinks when he says this, and immediately the mood in the room shifts. "Like you said, nothing serious." He grins and continues eating.

After breakfast, I creep up to Emily's room. "Flowers too?" She smiles as I step through the door, tray in hand. "Thank you." She pushes herself up against the headboard and pulls several pillows behind her back. "You didn't have to do this. I could have been home soon."

I look at her, my head cocked.

"Oh, down soon, I mean. I could have been down soon." She waves her hand in front of her face and the motion isn't a smooth one.

I place the tray down over her legs. "I figured you'd be hungry, and Amalia said you weren't feeling well, so…"

"I appreciate it."

"Is there anything more I can do?"

"No." She looks at the ceiling and inhales softly. Her curls settle around her face in thick ringlets, and with all those big pillows around her, she looks younger and more fragile than I've ever seen her. "It's just a hard day. A hard couple of days. I'll do better soon. I need to see my doctor. I'm sure he'll help me figure things out."

"What is it?" I perch on the edge of the bed. "If you're okay to talk about it."

"The medication," she says. "At least I hope it's the medication. It might be that I need a higher dose or even a different one altogether." I don't have to ask to see that the shaking is worse. "I saw my dog yesterday afternoon. Freckles. He came right up on the couch. Cuddled with me. I tried to pat him."

"What? I didn't know you—"

"He died when I was thirteen."

"Oh."

"I'm lucid now." She shrugs. "I've read that the drugs can do that sometimes—hallucinations, delusions. I'm lucky, really. At least I know that's what they are. Some people don't."

"That must be…umm…scary."

"It's not fun. It's very," she hesitates, "unsettling. I know that was a hallucination, but what if there are other things? What if you're not even here right now?"

"I'm here."

"So you say." She gives me a suspicious look then laughs. "Like Farfar says, where there's life, there's hope. I'm sure I just need to get off of my butt and get into that appointment."

"Want me to go with you?"

"Nah." Emily takes her first bite of pancake. "These are really good. If you stay with Farfar that'd be best. I'll be more relaxed if I know he's taken care of."

"That I can do."

She smiles with her eyes closed. "It really tires me out

though. I feel like I just ran two marathons."

"I'm sorry, Emily, that you're—"

"Did you find any good-looking flats?"

"Not yet." I sigh. "I didn't look much more after we spoke the other day. I will though."

"Well, as far as I'm concerned, it's no rush." She takes a few more bites. "Amalia said you helped get Farfar to bed yesterday?"

"Yeah. I didn't want to disturb you."

"How'd it go?"

"It was fine," I say. "I think maybe he tried to do more of it himself than he would with you."

"Probably." She takes several more bites. "Any news from home?"

"Not much." I glance at the tree outside the window. The leaves are starting to fall but haven't reached that bright brilliance I'm used to seeing back home. "Apparently my brother and his new girlfriend are getting really serious. My cousin is seeing a guy too. She seems happy."

"Love is in the air."

"I guess so." I smile at Emily, half-lying there, so feeble yet so lovely. "Anyone in your life?"

"Don't you think you'd know?" She laughs. "There was someone a couple of years ago. He's in Australia now, doing his Masters. We said we'd keep in touch." Her voice trails off.

"It's easy to drift apart."

"That it is." She takes the last few bites. "Don't look so worried, okay? You're making me uncomfortable. I don't like it."

"Sorry, I—"

"I'm not dying or anything, okay? Not yet."

"Don't say that."

"We're all dying, Autumn. I might just be lucky enough to know how I'm going. But who knows? I could be lying here, having a pity party because I'm seeing my old puppy and thinking this is a harbinger of the things to come, of my end, when for all I know I could get hit by a bus on my way to that appointment—all the lamenting for nothing."

"That's true."

A laugh bursts out of her. "I didn't expect that."

I shrug. "Well, it is true." She stares at me, and it feels like she's waiting, or maybe I'm just waiting to see if I'll finally tell her. I don't. "I'm going to go see how Farfar's doing." I rise from the bed.

"Sure. Thanks for coming up. It's delicious, and the flowers smell great."

"My pleasure."

"I'll be down soon."

I nod and step away from her, thinking how she really does have a point.

With the thoughts of the last few days lurking in my mind, I decide to distract myself with a little sightseeing before my shift at work. It doesn't work as well as I'd like and so, while walking through Trafalgar Square, I put that little piece of me that's truly worried about my mother, that knows I should go home—or at least call—somewhere deep inside of me, in that same place where I stuff everything that has to do with Matt. I know this isn't reliable. I know it can and will squeeze out again, but it's what I have for the moment and, for the moment, I feel a tad better. My co-workers notice the smile I'm still wearing when I return to the Andrev's later that night. I help Farfar, just to take the load off of Emily, though she's feeling somewhat better. I laugh with Amalia as she diagrams the innards of a ferret. I listen to talk radio with Jakob and Stefan. I go to bed. And then I wake up the next day and the next, and each is similar to the last. The one thing that tells me this contentment is a farce is the conscious decision to stay away from my email—I despise myself a bit more each day because of it.

❧

"ARE YOU OKAY?" JAKOB approaches me as my shift is ending.

"Yeah, I'm good." I laugh. "You startled me."

"I didn't mean to."

"Yeah, of course. It's fine. How are you?"

"I'm good." His voice is hesitant. "But you don't seem to be."

"Oh." I take a step back from him. "Is it my work? Did someone complain? I want to learn to be the—"

"No," he waves a hand in front of him, "you're doing great. That's not it. You just seem…I don't know." He runs his fingers through his hair. "Less, or something. Muted."

"I seem less?"

"No, that's not what I mean." He swallows.

"It's okay," I say. "Just say it. What's going on?"

"There's nothing going on. Just the last week or so, maybe since the night of the walk, you haven't seemed quite the same."

"I still don't follow," I say, though of course I do, and feel like a failure. My concealment techniques aren't as great as I hoped.

"Is something worrying you?"

"No." I lie again and am amazed at how easily I can do this now.

"Okay. Well, I mean I don't think it's just me. I hope it's not me. I didn't do anything to—"

"No," I say. "No."

He looks at me, and it's the first time I think maybe he does care as more than just a brother. "Well, I hope you're telling the truth. If you're not, it's okay. I get it. It's hard to…just, I hope you're okay."

"I'm okay." I smile at him and let my hand rest on his

shoulder. "Thank you for asking."

"Sure." He laughs, and it's one of the rare moments when he looks self-conscious. "I probably shouldn't have brought this up at work. I mean, it's not that kind of issue. Wasn't very professional."

"It's fine. I should get going though. I don't want to miss the tube."

"Yeah, of course." His face remains serious. "I'll see you at home."

"See you there."

"Autumn," he says as I'm heading to the staff room. "Why don't you take tomorrow off? Maybe you're just a little overwhelmed. A little tired. I know you've been working a lot lately. And then helping out with Farfar…Have a day to yourself."

"No, that's fine, I—"

"I insist." And there's that smile.

"Okay, thanks." I enter the staff room and change out of my uniform, unable to deny the effect his smile has on me. And why shouldn't it? I'm single. I whisper this to myself. "I'm single." And I'm still desirable. Dominic thought so. Jakob could too…but I'm not ready for the possibility, despite the fact that every time I see him I want that possibility…which makes me feel like a cheater. Maybe it's just how much I'm around him. That may be one more reason to find an apartment. I'll go hunting on my day off. It's time to get on with my life.

⁂

THE NEXT DAY IS exhausting. I've forgotten how tedious apartment hunting can be. This one is too small. That one is way too big—and too pricey. The other one smells like stale cheese. But as I walk up to my last viewing of the day, I'm actually hopeful. It's only three blocks from the Andrev's, on a cozy street, and is the second floor of a three-storey house—complete with kitchenette and private entry. I walk up the steps and ring 1a, as instructed in my correspondence with the landlord. A woman maybe a few years older than me opens the door. Unlike some of the other landlords and apartment managers today, she doesn't even give a second look at my scar. I've become so used to it at the restaurant that I find her lack of notice almost unnerving. "Hi!" She sticks one arm out straight to me while using the other to keep back two fluffy white dogs. "Don't mind these mongrels."

She slips her feet into Hello Kitty slippers and pushes the door closed on the dogs. One gives a low whimper, but neither of them yap. "Let's just go on up." She laughs. "I'm Katya, and you're Autumn, right? Gosh—I didn't even ask."

"Yeah," I say. "Autumn."

"Great. So, you're not from here I take it?"

"What gave me away?"

"A funny one," she says as I follow her up the stairs at the side of the building. "That will serve you well in this country." She unlocks the door and opens it into a bright and airy apartment. A cross breeze blows through the open concept kitchen/dining area and out the living room. "It's basically move-in ready," she says. "The last tenant left a few weeks ago and I'm a bit picky about who I let live here. I have a fairly thorough application. Just want to make sure we're a good fit."

"Oh, of course." I give her my best smile in the hope that she'll like me. "It's lovely."

"I like it," she says, crossing her arms. "Follow me."

She shows me the kitchen appliances, which are new, and says there's a washer and dryer in the basement that the three units share. Next she takes me into the bedroom and the bathroom—both tiny, but I could definitely fit a queen-size bed in the bedroom. When we step onto the balcony I fall in love. Potted plants line the space and vines creep up the wooden trellis. "It's still looking pretty good," says Katya, "despite the late season. The last tenant really had a green thumb, but she said it was just too much to take them all with her. I've been watering them. If you end up taking the place, though, you could get rid of them if you want."

"No, they're great."

"Yeah, it's nice." Katya leans against the railing. "A little oasis."

"It really is." The view looks out on a yard with a large willow tree, a small pond, and several benches.

"She helped me design the backyard too. I like it."

"It's gorgeous. What do I have to do to get this place?" I turn back to her. "It's just what I'm looking for."

"I don't know," she says. "I have a good feeling about you, Autumn. And I can usually trust my gut. Still got to go with the application though. But tell me a little about yourself. What brought you here?"

"I was backpacking Europe," I say, trying to sound as interesting and light as I can. "And I met this brother and sister who were backpacking too. We ended up travelling together. I stayed with their relatives in Italy and then they invited me to come and stay with their family here, and I have been for the last several weeks. I'm working at their restaurant and loving it so much I decided I want to stop my roaming."

She stares at me a moment. "You just met them travelling, and they invited you to come live with them?"

"Yeah," I say, her shock making me realize for the first time that this is somewhat of an unusual thing.

"And even gave you a job?"

"Yes." I shrug.

"Well, that's quite the recommendation."

"I guess. We grew close."

"And now?"

"Well, they're happy for me to stay with them, but if I'm going to settle, I'd like a place of my own."

"So you are settling then? This isn't just a stopover? I know life changes fast, but I'd want at least a six-month lease, preferably a year."

This scares me. It really does. But I expected it. Not many places are month to month. "That's fine," I say without a blink. "I have a plan. I'm on a two-year visa and I'm working at the restaurant while I try to figure out how to start my own business. I want to open up a small fitness studio, maybe start with just some individual clients at first. That's what I used to do back home."

"Okay, okay," says Katya. "It's sounding pretty good. Well, come downstairs and I'll give you an application. We'll take it from there."

"Great." I follow Katya and we chat for several more minutes before I leave. We're both laughing by the end of it, and she pats her hand on my shoulder as I say goodbye.

Tingles of excitement flow through me as I walk back to the house. Not only may I have just found my apartment, I can see myself finding a friend in Katya. It's the best I've felt in weeks. Getting this apartment would signify real growth, real progress. It's completely separate from my life with Matt—a new start. When I see Jakob's car in the driveway, I can't wait to tell him, to let him see how the day off really lifted my spirits. I open the gate, almost skipping up the path, and enter the house. Voices in the living room draw me in and I head toward them. My jaw drops.

# CHAPTER TWENTY-TWO

Eloise," I breathe.

She flings herself toward me, embracing me so hard it hurts, then takes a step back. "You're okay. You're fine? Your hands work." She grasps them then releases. "So what the hell's going on?"

"I—"

"Did you not see the emails? And that's not even an excuse—there are phones. Oh." She draws her hand to her mouth. "Did you see the emails? You might not even know…" Her eyes tear up and she pushes out a puff of air. She trembles and hugs me again. Over her shoulder, I see Emily, Jakob, and Amalia sitting in the living room, watching us. Farfar is noticeably absent, he must be having his nap. I start to tremble. *They know.*

"My mom?" I ask. Out of the corner of my eye I see Jakob shake his head.

"You do know," says Eloise. She steps back from me again, like she's not sure what she's seeing. "And you didn't reply? You didn't—"

"Mom's always so healthy. I thought it was just them trying to get me home, trying to manipulate me to—"

"It's not."

I try to breathe and it literally feels like a hand is pushing into my throat, squeezing off my attempts for air. "She's…"

"It's really bad," says Eloise. She sits. "They're pretty sure she's going to make it, but it's bad. She might never be the same."

I stand in the centre of the room as everyone stares at me and squeeze my eyes shut, trying not to sway. When I open them, Emily's hands are on my arms. She pulls me onto the couch beside her, her hand grasping mine.

"Your father said he made it pretty clear. They were going frantic. He sent you like ten emails. He didn't know how else to get a hold of you. He didn't even know the last name of…the Andrev's. How could you—?"

"I'm sorry." I cut her off. "I only saw the first one. He just said she had a stroke, that I needed to come home, that—"

"And that wasn't enough?" I've never seen Eloise look at me like this. I'm not sure I've ever seen anyone look at me like this, but then her eyes soften. "Look, okay. I know you've gone through a lot. I know this must have been hard to hear. Maybe you just wanted to pretend it wasn't real or something, I get that, but it is."

"I thought…"

"You need to come home, Autumn."

I look up at her, at them all, and feel lost in a world that's too big for me. "I don't know if I can. I have a job and—"

"It's just a job," says Jakob. "If you need to go home, you go home."

"It's not just a job," I say. "It's a responsibility." I hate myself even more as the words come out.

Eloise comes over to me. "I'm not sure if you understand." The tears brim over her lids, fall down her cheeks, and I can see she's trying to stop them. "Your mom is not doing well. You need to see her. You need to be with her."

"I can't." I realize my own face is wet. I don't know when I started crying.

"Autumn."

"I just can't, okay." I stand. "I can't go through this again. I can't." I run through the house to the backyard, thinking how stupid that was, thinking how I haven't run from anything and they'll be behind me in a moment. But they're not. No one comes.

When I walk back in sometime later, they're all still sitting in the living room, the fire making it seem like a much warmer occasion. Farfar has joined the group and gives me an encouraging half smile. I turn to Eloise. "How did you find me?"

"The last group email you sent. You said the name of the restaurant. I thought it was weird enough that you never replied to me, but I figured maybe you'd moved on again. Then Daniel called me a couple of days after I got here. He told me everything that had happened and asked me to look for you. I went to the restaurant and met Jakob."

"Oh. Why didn't they call the Lombardi's? Mom has their number."

"Your mom can't speak, Autumn. She can't really do anything. Maybe your dad didn't know she had—"

"Oh." The wind feels knocked out of me. Everyone stares as I sink into the nearest seat. "So, it really is bad."

"Yeah, it's bad."

I look to Amalia and can't read her expression at all. Jakob's looks almost angry. Emily's is a look of pity. Farfar seems thoughtful.

"I'm here for three more days," says Eloise. I have meetings again tomorrow, then I'm free the next two days." These must be the days she added to her trip to visit with me, but she doesn't say this. "Why don't we try to arrange a flight for you on the same one as me. I can look into that tonight if you want."

"I don't know if I can go back." The silence in the room is heavy. It pushes down on me. "I just...I'm not ready." Do they know? They must know. I avoid eye contact with everyone but Eloise. "I'm sorry, I—"

"Don't apologize to me." She stands and walks over to me. Her hand rests on my shoulder and she crouches down so she's eye level, speaking to me as if she's speaking to a child. "I know it's hard, okay. I know you miss him, and I know that's why you're scared to go home. Jenn explained it all, what this trip is really about." I glance to the others, wanting her to just be quiet, and feeling stupid for it. "But this is your mom, Autumn. Your mom." She looks away and I can only imagine what she's thinking. "I have to get back to the hotel, prepare for my meetings, but I'll come by again tomorrow night, okay?"

"Yeah," I say, "yeah, thanks."

"You're welcome to stay for dinner," says Emily, standing as Eloise does.

"Thanks, I really need to get back though. Big prep for tomorrow."

"Sure. Well, come to the restaurant before you leave," says Jakob, standing as well.

"I will." Eloise smiles at them and heads to the door.

Emily follows her and I hear the two talking quietly but can't make out the words. I need to say something but don't know what it should be. Rising from my seat, I finally speak. "I'm going to take a shower. I'll be down later."

The hot water almost scalds my skin, beating down on me as hard as the settings will allow. The pain acts as a welcome distraction and I stay under the onslaught longer than is reasonable. I wash and condition my hair—twice. I shave. I tweeze. When I get out of the shower, I floss. I do anything I can think of to stay protected behind the door. When I emerge, the house is quiet. I debate hiding out in my room but decide that's weak. I can't hide out forever, and my stomach is so empty I almost feel sick. I make my way downstairs and still no one. Muffled voices float through Farfar's closed door. My hunt through the kitchen reveals a dinner someone left for me. It's maybe the first meal I've eaten on my own since I've been here. Once I've finished, I grab a sweater, head to the back porch, then lean against the railing and look out into the yard, remembering how I leaned on my own back porch several months ago.

"Hey," says Amalia.

I turn to see her curled up in the large wicker chair against the house, a book in her lap, a sleeved blanket surrounding her. "I didn't see you there," I say.

"I'm little." We stare at each other for a moment before I walk over and pull up a seat. An extra blanket sits next to her and I wrap it around me. "Why would you want to forget him? Didn't you love him?"

So Eloise did tell all.

I let out a long exhale. "Of course I loved him."

"Then why—"

"It hurts…I just didn't want it to hurt so much."

She's quiet for a moment, her head down. She looks up with intense resolve in her face and, again, she looks older than her years.

"Well, I think it would hurt him that you act like you forget. That you try to live like he wasn't this huge part of your life. I never want to forget my Mom, never. Then it really would be like she never existed. That'd be worse than losing her. That'd be like she died all over again."

The sound of a throat clearing makes me turn. Jakob stands by the door. "I think she's right, you know. It seems like what you two had must have been good, precious. You should be thankful for that, Autumn. Not everyone finds that kind of love."

"Who are you to tell me what I should be?" I snap, instantly regretting my words.

"I'm just saying I think you should be thankful for it. Hold the pain, you know, and the beauty."

I make a sound that's something like a laugh. "That's easier to say than to—"

"I never said it was easy." He shrugs and puts his hand on Amalia's shoulder. "We all have sorrow, and it's always hard." His hand squeezes and I see the love in Amalia's eyes as she looks up at him, the admiration. "It's life. It's meant to be lived. Not acted. Acting, pretending the pain is not there, it's not real. It's basically," he pauses, shrugs again, "wasting life." He squeezes Amalia's shoulder again, looks from me to her. "You mind giving us some privacy?"

She wants to protest, I see it in her eyes, but she gets up, book and blanket in hand, and closes the sliding door quietly behind her.

"I don't have anything to live for if I let myself think of Matt, okay? If I think of him, of all the plans we had, all the things we were going to do, and," I breathe, "it reminds me I'll never have any of it. All my hopes were in him."

"No, they weren't." His tone is casual, sharp.

"How the hell do you know? You didn't even know him. You didn't know us."

"Maybe not. But if all your hopes were actually in him, if they relied on him, then they weren't your hopes, anyway."

"What are you talking about?"

"Tell me, Autumn. Tell me what hopes, what dreams, are impossible for you to carry on if you acknowledge that Matt was a huge part of your life? If you don't keep it some big secret, even to yourself? What dreams were so wrapped up in him that you can't follow through with them now that he's gone?"

"Everything."

"Cut the crap, Autumn." The words hit like a slap, especially coming from him.

"Tell me one. Just one."

"The studio. We were going to open a studio together."

"And he's the only person in the world you could have done this with? There's no way for you to reach success with anyone else or, God forbid, on your own?"

"Well, no, I'm not saying that, but it wouldn't be the same, we had—"

"Yeah, it wouldn't be the same. But you can still do it. Aren't you even thinking of doing it here?"

"Children." I know how stupid this sounds, how stupid

I've been, but I can't say the biggest thing I'll never have now, so I just keep talking. "We picked out how many children we wanted to have. We discussed their names and—"

"And maybe you wouldn't have been able to have children, anyway. Maybe one or both of you would have been infertile. Maybe your child would have died. Would you have just given up on life then?"

"No, I…but we would have dealt with it…together."

"Give me another one. Come on, hand it over."

"Fuck you." The words are out of my mouth before I can stop them.

He stares at me a moment, smiles. "So that's what you're going to do? Really? You're going to resort to profanity? You're going to cuss at me? Well, guess what? 'Fuck' means next to nothing over here. Children say it with abandon. So if you want to piss me off, if you want to offend me or get rid of me, you've got to do better than that."

"What do you care, anyway? Why are you attacking me like this?"

"Because someone needs to. Your family and friends may be tiptoeing around you like you're a little ice princess who is going to crack into a million pieces if they push you too hard, but they're wrong."

"They're not—"

"Oh, are you defending them now? Good. If you care that much, why don't you go be with them before it's too late."

"My mom's not going to die or anything. You heard Eloise. She's going to be fine."

"Yeah, you know that, do you? You know she's going to be fine? Eloise said she wasn't going to die. She didn't say she was fine. And was Matt fine?"

"Don't say his name."

"Things happen, Autumn, crappy, unfair, unexpected things. It happened to Matt, now it's happened to your

Mom. And maybe this won't even be what takes her, maybe it'll have nothing to do with it. But what if it is? Do you want her last thought of you to be that you were too selfish and too absorbed in your own grief to be there for her?"

"Stop it, okay? Just leave me alone."

"I won't leave you alone." His voice softens. "And I won't let you stay here either. I won't help you do this."

"What do you mean?"

"I mean your job at the restaurant is done. After the next two days, you're not welcome here anymore."

"What?"

His jaw is solid, resigned, but his eyes look hurt to say these words. "You're not welcome to stay here anymore."

"I found a new apartment anyway…well, maybe. But if it doesn't work out, I can find another one…" My words trail off and I'm on the verge of breaking. "Why do you care? What does it matter to you if I go home or not?" These last words come out in a little sob.

"I care because I've been you." Jakob sits. His shoulders slouch as he rests his arms on his legs. His head hangs, shaking, then he looks at me and it's like I see right inside of him. "I hated my mom when she was sick. I hated that I couldn't sit on her lap anymore. I hated that she didn't read me stories. I hated that she smelled funny and that she got so skinny and bony and that she was in bed all the time. Most of all, I hated that she wasn't taking care of me.

"I don't know—maybe some part of me thought if I acted out enough she'd be forced to get better, so she could do something about my behaviour. Punish me, anything. I caused so much trouble that eventually they sent me to live with Nonno and Nonna. That's why I was there. I wouldn't even go to my mom before I left. I refused to say goodbye. I turned away from her outstretched arms. I denied her kiss. And then she died. She died and I was away and I never got to tell her what a foolish, stupid boy I was. I never got to say I was sorry. I never got to feel her soft hands caress me."

His voice wavers and he inhales deeply then breathes the words out. "Never got to sit with her when she needed me—get her water or bring her cooling cloths. I was old enough to do those things."

He looks down, his brows pushed together. "I hated myself for years. I didn't like to think of her either. I didn't want to believe that my mother had existed, because if she did then it meant I really had treated her the way I did. I wished I was Amalia instead, too young to even remember her sickness clearly, too young to have guilt.

"Thinking of my mother reminded me that I didn't show her love when it was most important. I spent a lot of years not engaging in life because of this—it's hard to when you're lying to yourself. You just kind of live on the peripheral, live this fake, half-life."

He looks up at me again. "Now I know this isn't the same situation as you and Matt, okay? I know what happened was a horrible, tragic accident, and it's not like you deserted him the way I deserted my Mom. But you're deserting him now."

"What?"

"Just bear with me. You are deserting him, and you know what? Whether you accept his death and how much he means to you or not, you'll probably never stop feeling pain. You're probably never going to be a hundred percent okay. But no one's a hundred percent okay. You're not the first person to suffer loss, to have dreams dashed, and you're not going to be the last. And now you're on the verge of making things a lot worse. Whether your mother fully recovers or not—and believe me, I hope and pray she does—you are never going to get this chance to be there for her, right now, again. Never. You can be there for her twenty years from now, but if you don't go home, you won't get this chance again. And this could be your last. Maybe she'll be fine, but maybe you won't.

"We don't know anything. Nothing. All we can do is try our best. Be our best. And you're not doing that. Not even close."

# CHAPTER TWENTY-THREE

Sitting on the porch, the night growing darker, Jakob expels a breath of air and raises his hands as if in surrender. "Go home, Autumn. You can always come back again. I hope you do, but when you're ready, when you're here for the right reasons, not because you're running away. And if you do come back, you'll have a job here waiting for you and friends to support you. But for now, just go home."

He stands after saying this. I can't speak. He smiles sadly, like he's disappointed in me but has hope I'll do better. He brushes his hand on my shoulder, like a father would, not a man two years my junior, a man whose smile makes my heart skip a beat. He goes back in the house and I'm left sitting with the sun disappearing over the rooftops, the dead vines on the trellis crinkling in the breeze. I stare at the vines, the dried and withered leaves. They're not dead, though. They just look like it. They're dormant. Deep inside, they're brimming with life. I listened to most of Jakob's tirade with my face inflexible and now it cracks. I don't want to admit what his words mean, what they force me to acknowledge—mostly about myself—but I'm going home.

When I step back inside I head to the den, open the computer, and send Eloise a note. *If you're still willing, arrange that flight, okay? I'll pay you back.* Next, I scan through all the other messages. Frantic is right. They've turned from concern about my mother to concern over me. My father sounds desperate as he asks me to get back to him, to let him know the best way to reach me. Anything. My brother sounds pissed. I don't read the emails from anyone else. I can only handle so much. I know it's weak, I know I should call home right now, but I don't. Instead, I write my father and Daniel back, apologizing, and say I'm coming home on a flight with Eloise. Just writing these words terrifies me. Everything Jakob said was right and I know it. It's been over four months and I still haven't dealt with Matt, not at all. Even here, when I'm reminded of him, I feel something akin to panic and, always, sadness. I don't know how I'll survive life back home. But back home isn't about him, I tell myself, it's about Mom. That will be my focus. That's why I'm going. One thing at a time.

After shutting down the computer I lie in bed for hours, imagining what I'll find when I get home. She can't talk. She can't walk. She's getting mobility in her hands again. The doctor is hopeful she'll get mobility back in the left side of her face soon—all things I learned from the emails. My stomach twists. I want to puke, but feel I deserve this discomfort. Jakob's words play again and again in my head, like a reel, and behind it all is the dying hope that he would have been a way out of it all for me, that I could have possibly found something of what I lost in his arms. The way he looked at me though, the disappointment in his eyes, a life for us will not be possible.

I curl over, wrapping the sheets around me. For the first time in a long time I wonder what Matt would think of me right now, at this moment. Would he understand? Would he have looked at me the way Jakob did? Would he still love the person I've become? A person who can ignore her family, can pretend the person she claimed to love most never even mattered. With these thoughts rolling in my mind, at last sleep overtakes me.

When I wake I feel as if I haven't slept at all, though I know I have. My dreams prove it. I could have sworn Matt was here last night, his arms around me like they used to be, but as I see the sun stream through the window, the curtain gently blowing where I left the pane ajar, I know it was only a dream, one I want to slip back into. I don't though. I get up, head downstairs, and face the Andrevs. Conversation halts as I enter the kitchen. "Morning," I say, noticing Jakob is the only one missing.

"Good morning," says Stefan. "How are you feeling today?"

"Tired." My hand shakes a little as I pour a glass of orange juice from the pitcher on the counter. "I'm sorry about yesterday. I'm sure that was…uncomfortable for you all."

"You d…d…don't have to apologize to any of us," says Farfar. "You have no obligation to share your business with anyone."

I look over at him, thankful. "Well, anyways," I say. "I am sorry. I may not have had an obligation, but—"

"It's okay." Emily rests her hand on my arm. "Really. We understand."

I serve myself some eggs and slide into the seat beside Stefan. "I'll be leaving on Sunday, with Eloise. I know that's not a lot of notice to find a new—"

"Nonsense," says Stefan. "We'll be fine."

"Okay, well—"

"So you're going home. You're leaving?" asks Amalia.

"Yes."

"We'll miss you. But I'm glad you're going to go be with your mother."

"Mm-hmm," I say, glad but scared. "Me too." I look to Stefan. "I'll still do my last two shifts if that's okay with you. Maybe get to see some of the regulars, say goodbye."

"You don't have to, but if you want."

"I do."

"All right then. Well, I better head in." He stands. "Jakob's been there for several hours organizing a big shipment. I suppose I should give him a hand." He winks at Amalia. "That big brother of yours is really something."

As Stefan leaves, the rest of us stand as well. I pack the dishes while Emily wheels Farfar away.

"I'm sad you're going," says Amalia, backpack in hand. "But maybe I can come visit you someday."

"That'd be great," I say. "I'd love it."

"I'm sorry I said what I did last night, about your husband." The word makes me suck in my breath. It's maybe the fifth time I've heard anyone call him that. "I don't know what it's like…"

"No, you were right." I cut her off.

"Okay, I—" She shifts her feet back and forth. "I have to go to school, but maybe tonight we could do something. A movie or walk or…I can get my homework done during free period."

"That'd be great."

She turns to leave, then turns back. "I'm proud of you."

I smile at this and watch her walk away. A fourteen-year-old is proud of me. I guess that's something.

My final night in London Eloise joins us at the restaurant, her presence adding a festive feeling to the air. She laughs at Farfar's jokes with pure delight and encourages Stefan's charm. It's as if she's just a friend here to visit me and we're just out having a good time. It unnerves me, how normal everyone seems, how commonplace this is, while I sit here terrified to leave. And as I sit, I wonder if maybe I'm making the wrong choice, if I'm jumping to conclusions about what's best. Mom has Dad and Daniel and Jenn and all of her friends from work and from, well, her whole life. She has so many people to help her, whereas I've been a big help to the Andrevs. Who knows, if Emily starts to go downhill again, she could really need my help with Farfar. These people have taken me in, they've made me a part of their family, and I owe them something for that.

As I'm thinking these words, Jakob laughs at a story of Eloise's misguided notions of what was acceptable behaviour in a Japanese business meeting. He squeezes his father's shoulder, who is laughing too, and I see the connection there, the underlying support in all their thoughts and actions. This family is going to be just fine without me. It's my family who needs me. Any thoughts to the contrary are the rantings of someone who is seriously unhinged…or lying to herself. Home is where I need to be. And besides, according to Jakob, I'm no longer welcome here.

When Eloise finishes her story, leaving everyone chuckling at how she managed to remain barely more than tipsy by 'watering' a nearby plant in a dinner meeting where everyone else stumbled out of the restaurant, Stefan clears his throat. "I promise we won't be stumbling out of here, but I do want to raise my glass—to Autumn." The others pick up their wine glasses and Amalia her Shirley Temple. "You have been a welcome addition to our home, our family, and we are sad to see you leave," he gives me a fond smile, "but we wish you all the best as you go back to your loved ones. And we know you will be just as much a joy to them as you have been to us. To Autumn." He raises his glass.

"To Autumn."

OUR FLIGHT LEAVES EARLY in the morning, and since Eloise's work is paying for her taxi, I'll take a bus the few blocks to her hotel before the sun rises. Emily, Farfar, Amalia, and I arrive home from the dinner past eleven. Amalia, who'd been asleep in the back, rouses when Emily turns off the car. "You'll email me?" she yawns. "And add me on Facebook?"

"Absolutely." I give her shoulder a squeeze. She leans on me as we make our way into the house and then hugs me tightly before trudging up the stairs. I watch her go before following Emily's path to Farfar's room.

"I may not see you again in this life," he says, "but I know I'll see you again." He grins at me. "Come here, give an old fart a hug." I do, and he whispers in my ear. "Remember what I told you, my dear, where there is life, there is hope. Where hope, life." I nod. "I'm sure your mother will be just fine."

"I hope so."

He grins.

I wait in the living room while Emily helps Farfar. The room is lit only with the light from the hall, but I like it like that. Dim and cozy. Emily joins me several minutes later and curls herself into the chair across from me, wrapping an afghan around her. "So, you're really going."

"I'm really going."

"How do you feel?"

"Scared."

"Of what exactly?"

"I don't know." I laugh. "Of everything. Of how bad my mom really is, of whether I'll be able to actually help her, of figuring out my life over there. Of Matt." I pause. "Of how he'll be everywhere. His memory is everywhere."

"Isn't he already everywhere? Isn't he still within you…in the memories you carry?"

"Yeah." I pick up Amalia's blanket and play with the fabric. "It's just different somehow."

"It doesn't have to be. I mean…okay, yeah. There'll be more to remind you, but why does that have to be a bad thing?"

"Can we just not talk about it," I say, careful to not let a snap enter my voice.

"Sure."

"What about you?" I say. "The new medication seems to

be doing well."

"Yeah." She smiles and holds her hand out. "No shakes. And no dead dogs."

"And have you looked into the courses?"

"I don't know. I mean my life is full with Farfar right now, anyway." She drops her head and the curls fall over her face. "I've been thinking of taking some distance courses, maybe getting my Masters, focus on the research side of science. You had a point. I may not be able to be a surgeon but—"

"That's awesome. That's amazing. Emily, that's so—" I grin. "Do it." I slam my hand on the couch between us. "Don't think, do."

She laughs at my exuberance. "You too, all right? Get back into it. I mean you're a great hostess, becoming a skilled waitress, but I know you have better skills to offer the world."

"I'll think about it," I say, my exuberance lessening. "I mean, if Mom gets better quickly, maybe I'll be back here soon."

"I hope that's the case, that she gets better soon. That would be wonderful." She yawns, pushes aside the afghan, and stands. "I need to turn in." She waves her hands for me to get up. "You're not getting away without a good hug."

I stand and we embrace. "I love you," I say.

She pulls her head away and smiles at me. Her eyes glisten. "I love you, too. All right, enough of this." She gives me a wide-mouthed smile then bites her lower lip. "We'll meet again."

"Yeah." I wipe my eyes. "For sure."

I curl back onto the couch and tuck the blankets around me. I said goodbye to Jakob at the restaurant, but it wasn't enough. Reaching up, I flip on the lamp to make sure he doesn't miss me when he comes in and am almost asleep when the sound of the door opening, followed by Jakob and Stefan's soft voices, rouses me. Footsteps make their way up the stairs and I pray they're the right ones. A moment later a figure stands in the entrance to the living room. It's nothing more than a silhouette, but I recognize it. "Hey," I whisper.

"Hey." He steps into the room and his face slowly comes into view. "You're up late."

"Yeah." Some part of me wants him to come sit on the couch beside me. The other part is relived when he settles where Emily sat. "I wanted to make sure I got to say goodbye…again."

"It was a little rushed at the restaurant." He runs both his hands through his hair then shakes his head, letting the strands fall away freely. "I'm still getting used to the professional look," he chuckles. "Maybe one day it'll feel normal." I nod. "So how are you feeling?"

"Your sister just asked me the same thing."

"And what was your answer?"

"I told her I was frightened." I take a breath. "I'm sad too."

"To be leaving, or to be going back…to what you might find there?"

"Both."

"I'm sorry about the other night, if I was too intense. I don't know that I had the right."

"No." I lean forward. "It's what I needed. Thank you. I don't know if I would have—"

"You would have." He leans back in the chair. "Definitely."

"I'm glad you think so."

"I know so." We're both quiet.

"I really loved him," I say.

"I know."

"I haven't stopped."

"That makes sense."

"But I don't let myself feel it. I don't know…it's like I need to pretend it wasn't real…"

"I've gathered that much."

"This sounds so stupid. I don't know what I'm saying. I just feel like I need to explain."

"You don't need to explain anything, Autumn. Not to me, anyway."

I take a deep breath, my voice sounding like a child's. "Life is supposed to be beautiful."

Jakob is quiet a moment, and in the silence I feel so alone. I look over to see him staring at the family portrait across the room. "It is."

We're silent again. "I'm going to miss you." I want to say more but don't know what to say or how to say it, so I let my words hang there, just as they are.

He turns his gaze from the portrait and back to me. "I'm going to miss you too." He takes a deep breath. "And maybe we'll see each other again. Hopefully."

"Yeah."

His tone changes, becomes more distant. "Shouldn't you get to bed? Don't you have an early bus?"

"It's in two-and-a-half hours." I laugh. "I think I might as well just stay awake."

He nods, stands, and his face softens. I know what I want to read in his eyes, but don't know if it's actually there. "I'll stay with you." He sits beside me and pulls Amalia's blanket around the both of us. I nudge myself into his side as he places his arm around me. It's not sexual. It's not exactly a brother-sister thing either. It's just nice.

We don't say much. He talks about plans for the restaurant. I talk about my family, things I haven't told him before, and about the dreams I'd had for the studio, how I wanted it to be a real community, a place of change and energy and hope.

When the time comes, he offers to drive me but I decline. Despite my protests, he walks me to the bus stop and waits with me there. I almost wish he hadn't, because when the bus turns into view our goodbye is rushed. He leans in after a tight hug and I think he might kiss me. He does—his lips brush across the side of my cheek, right along the crinkled and ridged skin. And in that moment, the fear I couldn't speak before almost consumes me. The biggest dream I lost with Matt's death was a life of love, because I still love him and I don't know if I'll ever stop, and so how can I ever love another man? It would be a betrayal to at least one of them. Yet when I step into the bus, I can almost feel Matt beside me, inside of me, and for the first time it's not a feeling I want to push away. It feels like he's smiling.

By the time the bus travels the three blocks to Eloise's hotel, however, the feeling has passed and in its place is that familiar urge to push any thoughts of Matt away, to deny the hurt, because it hurts again. It burns. Jakob is Jakob and maybe in another life we could have worked, but I don't have another life. I only have this one and, although I've tried to deny it, in this one I was meant for Matt, which means now I'm meant for no one. That's not a feeling I want to hold on to.

# CHAPTER TWENTY-FOUR

I try to wipe the thoughts from my face as I step off the bus and see Eloise through the revolving doors. She yawns when I walk up to her. "I stayed up way too late." With her mass of curls pulled into a bun and wearing glasses—a sight I haven't seen since our University days—she looks casual in her Lululemon tights and puffy sweater. Again, not a look I'm used to seeing on her. "How'd you sleep?"

"I didn't."

"Oh, really." She smiles and grins with one eyebrow raised. "Up with a handsome Brit, perhaps?"

"Don't."

"Sorry." Her light tone vanishes. "The driver should be here in a few minutes."

"Great." I stare ahead. "I'm sorry, I—"

"It's okay." She glances at me and her eyes tell me it really is fine. "I think that's him. Let's do this."

When we step into the cab, I know we're on our way to the highway where it happened. As the driver takes the on ramp, I close my eyes. It's only when Eloise slips her hand in mine, squeezes it, that I realize my body has gone rigid. A whimper escapes my throat. Eloise squeezes harder.

We step out of the cab and my head spins with memories. This isn't the spot where Matt and I stood as we left the airport, flagging the cab that destroyed everything, but it looks so similar. It looks— "Come on," says Eloise.

"This way."

I adjust my backpack and follow her. This is stupid. So stupid. It's just an airport. We stand in line. It's just the last place I stood with him. The last place any slight variation could have made things turn out differently. Stupid. Stupid. Stu— "Your passport, please."

"Yes, sure." I respond to the attendant and she looks at me with suspicion in her eyes. "Is everything all right?"

"A fear of flying," says Eloise. "That's all."

"Yeah." I shrug at the attendant. "It'll be over soon though, right?" She nods slowly and waves the next person in line toward her. "Thanks," I whisper to Eloise as we head to the gate. She squeezes my hand again.

As we're approaching security, I try to make light of the matter. "Time for the show."

"The what?"

"I'm going to beep," I say to the security officer.

"Ma'am, please get rid of any metals, any—"

"I'm bionic," I say and hold out my arm. "The best medical technology has to offer. Right here."

"Oh." The young man looks squeamish. Shouldn't he be used to this? "Okay, then." He waves me through and, of course, the alarms sound. It only takes a moment for the next officer in line to have me spread my legs, my arms, and take extra attention to scan the arm in question. I push up my sleeves, hoping they won't have me fully undress like once before, and am waved through, the process complete.

I drift off almost as soon as we're in the air and it's not until Eloise nudges my shoulder when the seatbelt light dings that I fully emerge from slumber. It's an easy landing, but my stomach churns, anyway.

"Your dad said he'd pick us up, right?" Eloise asks as we make our way down the aisle. "I don't need to notify my driver?"

"No," I say. "He'll be here."

"Great."

"You have a driver?"

She laughs, looking a little embarrassed. "Well, it's the company's driver. They make him available for stuff like this. It's kinda weird, I know."

"No," I say. "That's cool. You must be doing well."

"Yeah." She lets out a little smile. "I am."

People fill the baggage area—talking, hugging, wiping away tears. My eyes scan for my father's waiting arms. On every trip I've taken he waited at the gate, eager for my return, but Dad is nowhere to be seen. Eloise makes her way to the baggage carrel and I follow behind her but keep glancing around. At last I see Daniel. He's leaning against a wall. My face brightens into a smile. His doesn't. I wave, making sure he's seen me, and he steps over slowly.

"Hi!" I make my voice bright and lean in for a hug. He reciprocates, but barely. "How are you?"

"Tired. Busy. Taking time off from work that I don't have."

"Oh," I say. "You didn't have to come. I mean we could have taken a taxi or Eloise has a driver."

"Dad said I had to be here."

"Where is he?" I rub a hand along my arm, nervousness flooding me. I've never seen Daniel look at me like this.

"Mom had an issue with her feeding tube. She had to be rushed back to the hospital."

"Feeding tube?"

"Yes. Feeding tube. She can't swallow."

"I…I didn't know."

"You wouldn't."

Eloise reaches for her bag and Daniel steps over in front of her, grabs it, then gives her a quick hug. He looks happier to see her than me.

"I'm sorry, I—"

"Whatever. Do you see yours yet?"

"Yeah, it's there." I point several bags away and he waits, then grabs it.

"Let's go."

As we head to the car, no one speaks. I feel bad for Eloise. Whatever is going on, she doesn't deserve to be part of it. Almost as soon as we hit the highway, thoughts of Daniel are forgotten as my mind floods with memories of Matt and all the times we drove this same road. After a time, the silence in the car makes the force of the memories worse. I break it. "So, Mom said you and Mallory were getting pretty serious. That's great."

"How long ago did she say that?" He casts me an annoyed look. "I know you haven't been speaking with her lately."

"I don't know, a few weeks. Are you two not—"

"We're fine. We're good. Great."

I swallow and try to ignore the dismissive and angry tone in his voice. "What's going on?"

He looks at me with disgust. "You're so selfish."

"What?"

"What's going on? God, Autumn. We had no idea where you were. No idea why you weren't responding." His eyes crinkle and I'm not sure whether he's going to cry or yell or what. He does neither. His voice is quiet. Even. "What's your problem?"

"I don't know."

He shakes his head. "Well, at least you're here now. Thanks to Eloise. Would you even have replied yet if she hadn't shown up at your doorstep?"

"I don't know."

He glances over at me then turns his eyes back to the road. "Yes, she has a feeding tube. She can't swallow. She can't talk. She can't walk. She can move her right hand, but not well enough to write. She points at an alphabet board."

Right. I knew she couldn't talk. I turn from him. "I'm here now."

"Yeah. And just in time. If Dad takes any more days off work, he'll lose his job. He would have already if Jenn hadn't come over so many times to watch Mom."

"What about you?" From the look he shoots me and the sharp inhalation I hear from the back seat, I know it was the wrong thing to ask.

"I go over in the evenings. I've already used up almost all of my vacation days. Today is a sick day."

"Yeah, of course." I turn my gaze to the window then close my eyes. We ride the rest of the way in silence. When Daniel turns off of the highway, I wonder if Eloise has moved—neither of us lives in this direction. "Where are we going?"

"I'm dropping you off first," he says. "You can go home from the hospital with Dad."

"Shouldn't I take my stuff home," I whisper. "I mean..."

"Are you kidding me?" He whips his gaze at me. "You actually want to wait longer to see Mom? God, Autumn. It was probably stress over you that put her in this state."

"Daniel," says Eloise.

"I don't know," he mumbles. "It's not conclusive what caused it."

I nod, trying to breathe as he pulls the car into the drop-off zone. "Thanks for the ride," I say, stepping out. I look back at Eloise. "Just send me the receipt for the ticket and I'll make the transfer." She nods at me. I get my bag out of the trunk and Daniel is gone before I've even made it to the hospital doors. Uncertain where to go, I head toward a sign pointing the way to information.

The receptionist gives me a room number and points me in the right direction. The scent of the hospital—antiseptics and stale, warm air—is all too familiar. I step slowly, wanting to prolong the unknown. She doesn't walk, she doesn't talk, she doesn't eat...is she even my mother?

She is my mother. She always will be. My hand hesitates in front of her closed door. No matter what, she is my mother. And I'm her daughter, and she'll want to see me. Despite how my legs are trembling, I have to make my face look like I want to see her too. Because I do. Just not like this.

I push open the door, step into the room, and there she is. Her eyes look blankly out the window. Her face droops to one side, like it's caught in a perpetual frown. Her shoulder hangs weakly. A faint trail of spit dribbles along her chin. Her head turns at the sound of me. Her right arm raises and a squawking sound escapes from her throat as her eyes light up with recognition and joy. She is my mother. I rush toward her and lay my head on her chest. Her hand pats my head as she murmurs something unintelligible. It's the best sound I've heard in months. Her hand is the feeling of home and, until this moment, I had no idea how much I missed it.

"Autumn." I turn at the sound of my father's voice. I hadn't seen him, sitting there in the corner. I let go of my mother and step into his arms. Unlike my mother's feeble embrace, my father's arms are firm, strong. Everything from the past few months wells up inside of me, fear and pain and shame, and even with all of that I feel safe.

"I'm sorry," I squeak into his chest. He doesn't say anything. He just holds me tighter, his hand against the back of my head, massaging it gently, not even fazed by the raised and rigid scar he must feel beneath my hair. Since the doctors, his is the only hand to have touched that one.

After several moments, he releases me and pushes me away from him in that way he has. "So, you're all right," he says, his voice retaining gruffness that doesn't make its way anywhere near his eyes.

"I'm okay."

He nods. And I can see he's torn. He's angry at me, but he's also glad I'm standing in front of him. He has a right to be angry, I realize. As does Daniel. As does everyone I've abandoned. I have my excuses, my reasons, but some things can't be excused. "Your flight was okay?"

"Yeah, it was great. Fine. Eloise got me a seat right next

to her."

He nods again, his hand drops from my shoulder, and in a flash he's sitting beside my mother. His two big hands envelop her small, nearly useless one. "See, I told you Lucille. You don't have to worry anymore. I told you she was fine. I told you she'd come home." His voice is the softest I've ever heard it. "Our baby's home now. She's okay, and you're going to be okay, okay?"

My mother nods her head awkwardly and makes a garbled noise. She looks at my Dad with such love, like she's the one who is trying to comfort him. They continue to gaze at each other as I stare. I've never seen such intimacy between them.

At last I break the silence. "Daniel said there was something wrong with Mom's feeding tube? Is it okay now?"

Dad pulls away from Mom's gaze and looks up at me. "It seems to be. They want to keep her overnight for observation, but then we should be able to take her home.

"Good. That's good."

"I have to go back to work tomorrow." He stands. "But I'll show you everything you need to do. It's not that hard once you get the hang of it."

"Uh-huh." My stomach tightens. I've never had to take care of my own mother. I think of Farfar, and what I did for him. That wasn't that bad. It actually felt good to help him. But to me, Farfar was always somewhat of an invalid. My mother has always been so…able. She's the one who takes care of us. She takes care of everyone.

"Well," Dad squeezes Mom's hand before letting go, "we should probably let her nap. Do you want to go home and get changed? Unpack a little? Then we'll come back for a few hours before bed."

"Sure." I step toward Mom, lean over, kiss her forehead, then join my father who waits at the door. Not wanting to see the sickness around me, I keep my eyes focused on his back as we walk down the hall.

I'm home. I'm in the hospital where Matt received rehabilitation for his knee, where he still came once every several months to talk to and inspire other patients with similar injuries. I'm home and he's everywhere and nowhere all at once. Last night's draw to Jakob seems a distant dream. Yet again, my feelings for Matt consume me. I can't let go, but I have to. He's now a man from my past. I can't change that. My plan is what's key, what's real. I have to live my life like it's my own.

But, as I've been learning over and over again, forgetting Matt is easier said than done. The scenes that pass by the car window pull the strength right out of me. I slouch down, exhausted. "You mind if I try to rest? Close my eyes?" I ask. My father shakes his head, looking over at me like I make him nervous, like he wants to say something but can't. He pulls onto a street in our subdivision and I notice for the first time that the season is further along here than in London. All the trees are bare, with that stark, spindly look that always makes me slightly uncomfortable. When I was younger, I used to think they were naked. I told Matt about it once and he laughed, kissed me on the nose, called me cute. I don't even need my eyes open, I can feel in the turns of the car the scenes we're passing—the memories of Matt wash over me like a tidal wave. They sweep aside all the other memories I've had along these roads.

I don't need to let this happen though. I'm not the same woman who ran alongside Matt, pushing past him down this street to win one of our impromptu sprints. That woman is gone, just like he is. My resolve sounds weak to me, feels weak, but it's all I have, that and my plan, though now it needs adjustment. Mom's going to need a lot more help, a lot more rehabilitation, than I expected. But it won't be my whole life. I can still prepare for my studio.

It's clear I won't be going back to England any time soon, but I can sharpen my skills for when I do. I'll study all the latest techniques when Mom is resting during the day—research business strategy and marketing plans—and I can take on some clients to insure I have recent references. When I return to London, I'll be more than ready.

As I formulate this plan, my stomach twists again. I'm not positive I will return. I'm not sure of anything. But I already miss Jakob, that much I know—and Farfar, Emily, Amalia too.

We pull into the driveway. I walk up the path, then enter the house, making a beeline for my old room. It doesn't feel like home. My eyes scan the photos, the bookshelf, the flowered bed spread…this is no longer my life. Despite the feeling of home in the hospital, with my head on my mother's chest, I'm no longer certain this is where I'm meant to be.

# CHAPTER TWENTY-FIVE

"Autumn." I turn to the sound of my father's voice. The circles under his eyes look like smudges of ash, they're so dark. "I know you just got home, but I'm going to take a nap if you don't mind. It was a long night with your mother. I didn't sleep at—"

"It's fine. Not a problem, Dad."

He hesitates a moment. "It's good to have you home. We're glad you're safe."

"Thanks," I say, bending over to open my bag. He stares at me a moment longer then shuffles down the hall. I sit on the bed, not wanting to spend my first day back alone. I pull out my phone and take it off airplane mode then remember I discontinued my service. I sigh. That's not something I want to deal with my first day back either. I head to the sewing room for the portable there. When I step in, some part of me still expects the array of gifts, but the space is empty, and this is somehow worse. I reach for the phone then leave the room quickly.

"Hello?"

"Jennifer, hi!"

"Autumn?"

"Yeah, I'm back, hi."

"Wow, uh…yeah, I guess I knew you were coming. I forgot it was today."

"It's today."

"So…you're okay. You're…back."

"Yeah."

"Good."

"Are you okay?" I ask.

"Yeah, yeah. I'm fine. Just," she sighs, "it's good to hear your voice."

I'm quiet on the line and an awkward moment passes. "Are you pissed at me too?"

"I don't know. No. Just…worried maybe and…it was weird, you know? I mean Aunt Lucille's so nice and…"

"I didn't know. I mean, that it was so bad, you know?"

"Well, yeah, though he sent you all those…But I get it, right? I know what it's like to just want to be away, to disconnect from the world, your life. I remember. I'm sure you weren't even checking your email—"

"I wasn't."

"Right. You didn't know."

"Yeah, I didn't know." The words are partially true. "So, I was wondering what you were up to today? This house is so empty." I try to make my voice sound light.

"Where's your mom?"

"Back in the hospital. There was an issue with her feeding tube."

"And you're not there?"

I tense at this, the accusation in her voice. She's hardly one to talk. "I was there. Dad wanted to come home for a few hours. We're going back tonight."

"Oh right," she says, "yeah." And I wonder if she realizes how hypocritical her words just sounded. I'm not petty enough to bring up Billy, but I think it. He was in the hospital for months, and she didn't visit him once.

"So, yeah, did you want to get together? Maybe watch a movie or go for a run. I need to get back in shape."

"You're out of shape?" I can almost see her eyebrows rise.

"My cardio needs work I'm sure. My endurance."

"Oh."

"So?"

"I'm sorry, Autumn. I've been at your folks a lot the last couple of weeks. I'm really behind on my assignments. And then Rajeev and I have plans tonight. I can't." There's silence on the line. "But maybe we could this weekend. It'd be good to see you."

"Sure, I'd love that." I say, trying to sound chipper. "So you and Rajeev are still going strong?"

"Yeah," a softness enters her voice, and it's like all the tension she was holding melts away, "I think I'm in love."

"Really?"

She giggles, a sound I'm not used to hearing from my cousin. "Yeah. Isn't that crazy? Me. In love. With a guy who I think may love me back."

"It's not crazy at all." I smile. "Not at all."

"Thanks." She's probably closing her eyes right now, getting that dreamy look on her face she gets when talking about her favourite movie men. "I mean two years ago I never would have imagined it. He's just such a good guy too, you know? A quality guy. He even wants me to come to India with him next summer. Meet his parents."

"That's amazing, Jenn."

"I know." She laughs, then it cuts off. "Is it okay? Me talking about this…with you, I mean."

I close my eyes, swallow, but don't let too much time pass. "Yeah, Jenn. It's fine. I'm happy for you. I want to know."

"Okay." She's hesitant now. "Good. I mean I want to be able to tell you about this stuff. I've missed being able to tell you. To talk with you."

"I've missed you too." Rajeev really has changed her. Softened her. Though some of these changes started after her mom. Still, I couldn't imagine the Jennifer from two years ago telling me she missed me.

"And I know it still might be hard to think of yet, but

you will find someone again too. Not like those other muscle obsessed jerks, but someone like Matt. Someone wonderful."

Has she forgotten my scar? I almost reference it, but then think of Jakob. I don't know that he thought of me in a romantic way, but he might have. There's also the fact that I used to say this same thing to her when she carried about a hundred extra pounds. I imagine she would have thought the weight was just as repulsive as my scar.

"Maybe I shouldn't say that yet," she says. "But it's true, I—"

"It's okay," I say. "It's fine."

"Okay." She expels a breath of air. "So this weekend then? We can watch a movie, or I'm going over to my Dad's place for dinner Sunday night. Billy will be there too. Maybe you can come? I'm sure they'd both like to see you."

"How is Billy?"

"He's good. Really good. He barely even has a limp anymore. Found another great trainer."

"Good," I say, remembering that Matt started training Billy shortly after he'd finished his major round of rehab. Matt set Billy up with one of his colleagues for the time we were supposed to be away. I imagine that's the person Jenn is referencing.

"Well, so do you think you'll come Sunday?"

"Sure. Sure thing, for the movie, as long as Mom's okay, if Dad or Daniel can—"

"Yeah, of course. Just let me know when you know, all right?"

"I will."

"Okay. I've got to go, but it's good to have you back, really."

I hold the phone in my hand after she disconnects the call, but there's no one else to phone. It's a Monday afternoon and everyone else will be at work. It's possible one of my trainer friends will have a gap in their schedule but that's all it would be—a gap. I head to the kitchen and scan the fridge. Nothing looks appealing. In the living room I plop down on the couch and for the first time I let the reality I've entered hit me. My mother has had a stroke. My mother may never be the person she once was. And if it hadn't been for Eloise tracking me down, I'd still be in England, unaware of it all. Well, unaware of the severity of it all. I *am* selfish. Daniel had every right to look at me like he did, with such distaste. What kind of daughter ignores an email that her mother has had a stroke? I curl up on the couch and close my eyes, wanting to escape but knowing I have nowhere to run.

Sometime later, I'm roused by my father. "It's time to go, Honey." I squint my eyes open to see him standing above me in the dark.

"What?"

"Time to see your mom. We'll go spend a couple more hours with her before she falls asleep. She's expecting us." In addition to the bags under his eyes, his shoulders are slumped. He looks more tired than before.

"Did you sleep at all?"

He shrugs.

"I can go, Dad. Why don't you try to get more sleep?"

"I want to see her." He stretches out a hand to me and I grasp it, letting him pull me up. My limbs ache. I must have been tensing them in my sleep. "We can eat dinner there," he says. "She can't really join us. But it's the idea."

We make the trip without talking. When he pulls into the parking lot and shuts off the car, I turn to him. "Are you angry with me?"

He keeps his hands on the steering wheel and his knuckles whiten. "I don't think...," he shakes his head, "not angry, not mad. Worried. Confused." He looks over at me, seeming somewhat embarrassed. "Yes, maybe a little angry."

"I—"

"I know that you've been going through a lot, but you

shouldn't have cut us off like that. Your mom was really scared, Autumn."

"I'm sorry, I—"

"It felt like you wanted nothing to do with us."

"No! No, of course not. I just—"

"Your mom was so worried. She'd pace the rooms at night. She'd check her email ten to fifteen times a day. She worried herself sick, she…"

"Do you think I'm the reason this happened? Daniel said…"

He sighs. "I don't…No, Autumn. I'm sure it had nothing to do with that." He squeezes my leg, removes the keys from the ignition, then opens the car door and steps out. He's not sure at all. I close my eyes, my hand on the door handle. I can't be the reason. I just can't.

My mother's smile is peaceful. Her eyes hold no anger or accusation, only relief. I sit beside her and chat about my trip as Dad and I eat.

"Have there been any updates?" I ask, after telling them about the canals in Venice.

"Just that she should be able to come home tomorrow," says Dad. "Like I said, if everything stays okay with the tube." He takes hold of her limp hand.

"Can she feel that?"

"Ask her." He sighs. "Your mother can hear you."

"Mom?"

She nods. She smiles. She holds her working hand up to my cheek. I can see in her eyes she doesn't want me to feel bad for what Dad said, for the way he said it. Here she is, as she is, and she's more concerned about me than herself.

"Do you want a few chapters in your book?" asks Dad.

Mom nods.

"I'll do it." I pick up the book from the table before Dad can argue. "Just start where the marker is?"

Mom nods again.

≈

WALKING UP THE STEPS to the front door later that night, my arms feel like weights attached to my body, my legs like stumps. I have no reason to be so weary. My father clamps his hand on my shoulder as I stand in the living room. His words sound stilted, forced. He's so tired it's an effort just to form sentences. "Going to bed. Taking early shift at work and the late one too. Have to start catching up. Call the hospital in the morning. They'll confirm Mom is okay to come home." He yawns. "If she is, call the home-care worker. I've arranged for her to be here the first day to show you the ropes, then it's all on you. Daniel will come around six, me 9:30." I look up at him as if he just handed me a load my arms are too weak to carry. "You'll be fine," he says. "Just fine."

My father walks up the stairs and I stay at the bottom, scared and helpless, then curl up on the couch again, the darkness surrounding me. I wonder where I've gone, because the old me would have handled this, no problem. She wouldn't have even thought of it as something that needed to be 'handled.' She would have just taken to the task with energy and verve. This new me feels lost. I fall asleep on the couch and don't wake until my father starts moving around in the kitchen. It's four in the morning. He wasn't kidding about early. Rolling myself off the couch, I trudge up to my old room—I have to keep calling it that—and slip under the covers.

When the sun rouses me awake four hours later, I'm not even sure I've slept. The doctor says my mom is fine to come home and so I go through the day as directed. Mom is all smiles: the perfect patient. The home-care worker smiles rarely. A stocky woman with thick arms and a ponytail that has to hurt her scalp. I wonder if it's the ponytail that causes her lack of cheer—perhaps her face is pulled too tightly to change expression. But she's good at what she does, efficient, and she takes the time to explain things, making sure I understand fully before moving on.

Mom has dozens of exercises to do every day and she never complains. As she does them her eyes shine at me, so clearly happy I'm back and safe. It makes me feel wretched. Three days in, after I've given her a bath and we've done the first round of exercises, I stare at her happy gaze. "I'm sorry."

She tilts her head in a way that reminds me of Farfar. The active side of her face smiles, and the inactive side joins in ever so slightly as she puts her hand on mine.

"I was selfish. I know I should have called you. I…" My breath catches. "Daniel and Dad think this is my fault."

She points to her alphabet board and I patiently let her spell it out. 'No fault,' she writes, 'just life.'

"I know, but…we can't know that for sure and—" She waves her hand and makes a noise that I'm pretty sure is 'No.' She motions to the board. 'Understand,' and 'happy u home,' she writes. 'U needed time.'

I nod. She wipes the tears from my cheek. It's an awkward movement, but I'm thankful for it. I hug her and she squeezes back as best she can. I pull away and she places one hand above her heart, pats it, then places it above mine.

Each day Mom gets a little better and the doctors think one day she'll be almost back to normal. With this news, Daniel's distaste of me starts to subside. Dad warmed up after that first day, but I still feel like I don't fit. A few of my friends have come over. Some of them are too normal and I resent it, as if they've completely forgotten about Matt. Others seem like their awareness of his absence is in everything they say and do. I resent this more. To justify being away from these people I used to be eager to see, I spend as much of every day as I can with Mom, which seems to work out well for everyone except her, who I can tell is starting to worry again.

"Go with friends," she manages to say once I've been home for almost a month.

"No, I'm fine." I wink. "Weren't we planning to watch a movie tonight? I can't miss out on that."

She's quiet as Dad feeds her another bite of beef stroganoff. She's been off the tube for a week and eating is a messy though happy affair.

"Want alone with Dad." Each word is such an effort. "Get lost."

I laugh, then see she's serious, at least about wanting me to go.

"Here too much." She shakes her body, smiling. "Make me restless."

"I'm fine here," I say. "I'll stay in my room."

"Go. Go. Go."

I stand and lift my plate then take Dad's. Mom is still working on hers.

There's no point arguing. She won't be satisfied unless I get out of this house. I could pretend to go out with friends and head to a movie alone, but she might have a point. If I ever feel like myself again, I don't want my friends to forget who I am.

I call Jenn and although she had plans with Rajeev, she says she'll join me. While getting ready, I'm forced to look at my reflection in the mirror—one I'm still not entirely used to—and think how Jenn and my roles have reversed. It used to be me who would try to get her out of the house. If she had called me up suggesting an outing, I would have had that weird mix of shock and pleasure I just heard in her.

"Do you mind if Rajeev comes?" she asks when she slides into my Dad's car. "When I told him I was blowing him off for you, he practically begged to come along."

I do mind, but what can I say. "Sure, that'd be great."

"I mean, I understand if…" It hurts, the way her voice trails.

"It's fine."

"Great." She puts on her seatbelt and smiles at me. "It's good to see you."

"You too."

"I like the length your hair is getting. It's always grown so fast."

"Thanks."

I focus on driving and try not to think of the last time I was in a car with Rajeev and Jenn, of how Matt was behind the wheel, of how he'd had my engagement ring that whole trip but never found the perfect moment. I pull up to Rajeev's and am blasted with a round of hugs. It's the first time I've seen him since the funeral and time hasn't changed him in the slightest; he has the same chocolate brown eyes, the same general build, the same way of speaking in a way that's a little more intense than the norm.

"So tell me of your trip to Europe," he says over our vegetarian appetizers, "your exploration into the unknown."

"I don't know that there's a whole lot to tell," I say, picking at my spring roll.

"You were on a journey, right? A trip to discover yourself again?"

"I don't know about that."

"You're not fooling me," he says. "Don't tell me you saw all those sites, met all those people, without learning anything. That would be a travesty."

Jenn rolls her eyes at this and squeezes Rajeev's hand. I know Rajeev's way of talking weirded her out at first, though it never bothered me. It does today.

"I don't know." I let out a puff of air. "It was great. I mean I saw so many things, but more than anything I saw, really, it was the people. The brother and sister I met up with—Jakob and Emily—they accepted me like family. I stayed with their relatives in Italy for a couple of weeks, and then later on I lived with them in London…"

"Beautiful," he says, "and?"

I push out a laugh. "You're really set on me gleaning

something from this experience, aren't you?"

Rajeev shrugs and smiles.

"I guess I learned that people are just people wherever you go. That family is important...I mean, not that I didn't know that before but..."

He nods and I can tell he's not satisfied with my answer. Matt used to tell me that's what he loved about Rajeev, how intense he was, how he made Matt think about things on a deeper level than he usually bothered with. I'm quiet for a moment, we all are, and I really try to come up with an answer. What did I learn? I picture Nonna and Nonno and Farfar, their energetic spirits, their zest for life despite aging bodies and failing health. I think of Emily and the tragedy she lives every day, but how she's living life nonetheless, pushing past her fears. I think of Jakob, his convictions, the pain he carries from his youth, his loyalty and love and sense of duty to his family. I think of how all of them made me feel loved and wanted and created an environment where, for the most part, I could let go of my pain, if only for a little while.

"I guess I learned you can find beauty even in the midst of pain, in the midst of all the crap life throws at us, you can find and enjoy love."

Rajeev leans back, and this time his smile looks satisfied. "Now that's a lesson worth learning." He lifts his glass. "To Autumn's journey. To life and love."

I raise my glass and join in the toast, smiling with my mouth, though I don't think my eyes join in. Something pulls on me. It starts at my skin and draws inward to a place I haven't been to in awhile. That may be what I should have learned from the trip, but I don't know that I really have.

As the night goes on, I watch Rajeev and Jenn interact. It's the first time I've seen them together since the wedding, and this realization shocks me. That was months ago. I'm happy for her, thrilled. They look content, comfortable, on the verge of love or maybe there already, but I can't help feeling an ache as I watch the way they interact: How she rests her hand on his leg, how he casually drapes his arm along the back of her chair. I don't know if I'll ever get past the yearning to have that. While we're waiting in line to pay the bill, Jenn leans over and rests her head on Rajeev's shoulder. The memory of my last night with Jakob pops into my mind. I banish the thought.

"We're going to the Amelia Curran concert next weekend," says Jenn as I pull up to her apartment. "Come." It's more of a command than a request.

"Okay." I stop the car at the curb.

"Okay?"

"Yeah, okay."

Jenn looks at me then grins. "Okay! I'll get you the info."

I nod as she steps out of the vehicle. After a few minutes of driving, I pull into a parking lot, wanting to be alone before facing home again. I'm glad to be taking care of my mom but it's exhausting. It seems she knows me better than I know myself. I had no idea how much I needed this night out, hence the quick concert acceptance. I feel more relaxed than I have in weeks.

When I roll down the window, the scent of oncoming winter passes over my skin. I breathe deep and shiver. The cold feels amazing. It's so real. My phone buzzes against my thigh, reminding me of the call I missed several hours ago. I slide out my phone to see the caller and my smile fades. Carol, Matt's mom, has left a message. I slide the phone back in my pocket. I don't want to ruin this peaceful feeling. It can wait until I get home.

# CHAPTER TWENTY-SIX

I sit in my room, phone in hand, not wanting to play the message from Matt's mom. But what if it's something important? Like the message from Dad. A part of me knows I should have visited Matt's parents when I came home, but another part of me argues that part of my life is over, gone, and so I have no obligation to them now. Dad said both Carol and Mike came over to the house the week after Mom's stroke. They brought two casseroles and a bouquet of flowers but haven't been back since, although they called the house twice. Once I didn't pick up. The other time, when Daniel answered, I waved my hands and then fled to the bathroom.

These people welcomed me into their family from the first time Matt brought me home to a family dinner. They were ecstatic about the engagement. I wore Carol's mother's necklace down the aisle, just as she did. I realize I still have that necklace and groan. Perhaps that's what the call was about. She's sure to want it back.

I dial my voicemail and hold the phone to my ear. 'Hello, Darling. I heard through the grapevine that you're back in town and am so glad you're home safe and sound. We miss you. I'm sure you remember Matt's birthday is coming up soon and we've decided to do something special for it. We're going to have a little party...well, perhaps that's not the right term, but a gathering, a celebration of his life. We'll have people over to the house and will take up a collection for the War Amps—he always loved that charity—and we'll plant a tree in the backyard in memory of him. We'd love to see you. The whole family would. Charlie's coming down for it. We'd like you to say a few words. We're sure no one knew Matt better than you.' Her voice chokes up here. She gives a little laugh then continues, shaky. 'Just give me a call, okay? And I'll give you all the details. We can't wait to see you, Autumn. It's been too long.' She chuckles again, and it's a painful sound. 'And so has this message. Oh my. Well, signing off.'

The message ends, and an automated voice gives me the option to delete, save, or send a reply. I press delete. It's too late to call back and his birthday isn't for three weeks, anyway. Not that I'm going. Just the thought makes me queasy—to stand in front of that crowd, to be around all the things I'm trying to forget, to stare into the inevitable eyes that will wish it was me and not him, to have those eyes look at the way I'm now marred, the constant reminder I carry, but how it's nothing compared to losing a life. There's no way I'm going, but I do have to think of the right way to turn the invite down. Not now though, I don't have to think about it right now. Placing the phone on my nightstand, I turn away from it and rest my head on the pillow.

ON THE DAY OF THE concert I try my hair three different ways before finally deciding on a style. What I thought was going to be just Rajeev, Jenn, and me will actually be about ten people. Some I haven't seen since I've been back, others since the funeral, a few I don't even know.

Jenn and I are the first to arrive. We snag a spot in line and wait as the others slowly join. Arms wrap around me and I turn to Eloise's smiling face. "How's it going?" she asks.

"Good. Great."

"It's good to see you out."

"It's good to be out."

She lets her arms drop and turns to a guy beside her. "You remember me mentioning Moses," she says, motioning to a man who towers above us. He has to be at least six foot three.

"I've heard a lot about you." He sticks his hand out and I return the shake. "It's good to finally meet you."

I feel exposed and look at Eloise warily. Moses was away in the months leading up to the wedding, so I never met him, but I'm sure he knows all about it. He'll know about Matt, for sure, but what else? Does he know about Eloise having to get me in London? I swallow, wishing I could disappear.

"Do you know much about the band?" Moses asks.

"No, not really. I've heard a few songs. She's mellow, does original stuff."

"I can handle mellow." He's smiling at me and I smile back but don't know what to say. The act of talking to a stranger unnerves me. I used to be so good at this.

"Autumn!" Allison shuffles up and wraps me in a tight hug. "You're out! Girl, look at these arms. We've got to get you to the gym." She lifts my arm and makes a tsk, tsk, sound. "Come next week. We'll help get some definition back."

"I know how to get definition," I say, "if I want it."

"Yeah, I know." She takes a step back from me. "I'm just saying."

I inhale. *Keep it together. Be normal.*

"Never mind." She waves her hand, dismissing my words. "It's good to see you out."

"You too." The others arrive and within minutes we're ushered into the concert hall. It's a good show—entertaining, contemplative—and, as we're ushered back out, I feel better than I've felt in weeks.

"Who's up for cocktails?" asks Eloise as we gather on the sidewalk.

All but four of the group agree. We head down Argyle Street to a high-end tapas bar I've not been to. The hostess seats us at a large round table with low lighting and we settle in. The conversation focuses on the news of Tammy and her boyfriend's engagement.

"It'll be small," says Tammy. "Close friends, family. We want to keep costs down, spend the money on an awesome honeymoon."

"That sounds killer." Allison grins. "Definitely a good idea."

"I want mine to be massive," laughs Eloise while Moses rolls his eyes. "Something to go down in the history books."

"Well, you better find a groom first," says Moses.

Eloise looks back at him with a wink. "I'm working on it."

"Jenn, what about you?" asks Jenn's friend, Sophia, who is sitting beside me.

"I don't know." Colour rises up Jenn's face. "I'm not really at a place to think about it."

"Hypothetically," says Sophia. Jenn shakes her head. "You're no fun." Sophia laughs. She turns to me. "Well, hypothetically, what about you, Autumn? Will you go big or small?" The chatter stops. Some eyes turn to me, others look away. "What?" Sophia's eyes widen. "Did I—"

"I went big." I attempt what I hope looks like a smile. "Not massive, but big."

"Oh, you're married?" says Sophia. "Where's the hubby tonight?"

"I'm not married." I look at my glass, try to breathe. The silence at our table is amplified by the other noisy diners.

"Autumn's husband passed away," says Eloise, who is on the other side of me. She rests her hand atop mine, but I slide it away. "It was a beautiful wedding. Perfect."

"I didn't know, I..." Sophia stammers. I want to say

something, tell her it's okay, but I can't speak.

"There's a memorial coming up for him soon," says Eloise. "A celebration—for his birthday, right Autumn?" I look at her, confused by the words, then look away. "I just got the invite."

"Yeah, me too," says Allison. "It's such a cool idea that you guys have decided to do that—honour Matt."

"I didn't decide." I shake my head, confused. "I'm not going."

Silence again.

"But..." Jenn's voice trails off. I look up and she's staring at me with the same confused look I imagine I just had. "Aren't you—?"

"Carol called me about it but I don't want to. I'm not..." I stand up, shaking. "Excuse me."

My purse tangles in something and I yank it from the booth then step away from the table. I want to be angry but don't know where to direct my anger. It's not Tammy's fault. Of course she should be happy she just got engaged. Of course she wants to share that with her friends. And Sophia, she didn't know. I just met her tonight. I don't want my friends to have to warn their friends about me—*be careful what you say around the widow*. I'm glad Jenn didn't. Should it be Carol who deserves my anger? She has a right to have as many memorials as she wants for her own son and to invite whoever she chooses.

In the bathroom I stand in front of the counter, my hands pressed against the slick surface, my eyes staring at the bubbled remains in the sink. I want to escape it all. I look up then turn away, sick of my own face and its constant reminder.

The door creaks open. "Autumn?"

"Yeah."

"Are you okay?" Jenn and Eloise step in. I keep my eyes on the tiled wall.

"Yeah, I...I just needed a minute."

"That was really ignorant," says Eloise. "I shouldn't have been talking about wedding plans like that. I just—"

"No, it's fine. Don't apologize."

We stand there a moment.

"Are you really not going?" Jenn takes a step closer to me. "Carol was saying she wanted you to say a few words and—"

"No, I'm not going. I can't. That's fine if she wants to dwell on the past like that, I'm not—"

"She's not dwelling on the past." Eloise cuts me off as she rests a hand on my shoulder. "She's celebrating the life of her son."

"I know but—"

"You should rethink this," says Jenn. "I think you'll regret it if you don't—"

"I don't want to go, okay?" I look over at them. "I'm not going to go. That's my choice, right?"

"Yeah, of course. It is," says Eloise. "You need to do what you need to do but," she pauses, "we're just saying think about it. I mean, at first you thought you didn't want to come back home, right? But now you're so glad you did, aren't you? That you're able to help your mom and—"

"This is entirely different."

"Yes, it is, but—"

"I'll be okay. Okay? Just give me a few minutes."

"Sure." Jenn puts her hand on Eloise's arm and draws her out. She knows what it's like, to need to be alone. Jenn pretty much became a recluse after her mom died, though once she started getting out, doing things, she turned into a different person, a better person.

I'm out. I'm doing things. I'm just not going to do that one thing. There's nothing wrong with that. Carol wants me to talk in front of all those people. Me, the tragic widow. What would I even say? What is there to say? He's gone. Is refusing to go, to talk, really that awful? I fall back against the counter, staring at the stall door in front of me. I guess

I'm not as strong as Jenn. Rather than better, I'm becoming worse.

Amalia's quotations pop in my head—Preparing a face to meet the faces that I meet. I return to the group with a smile and sit down to hear Eloise's story about this old British CEO who tried to convince her that the slave trade and colonization propelled society forward, created the possibility of all the advancements we enjoy today. That there's no way 'her' people would be where they are, enjoying the life they enjoy, if it weren't for slavery. "It was like he actually wanted me to say thank you," she laughs. "I was dumbfounded. I mean he's the big guy, the person I was sent to Britain to schmooze up, and he's spouting this crap. Who says that?"

"What'd you say?" asks Tammy.

"I told him if my great-great grandmother ever comes to me in a dream, I'll ask her opinion on it, and until then I'll keep silent on the matter."

"And did your company get the contract?" asks Allison.

"Oh yeah, not only did we get it," she laughs that big laugh she has, "he recommended us to one of his sister companies and we're in negotiations. I'm heading back in a few weeks to finalize that deal. He said I was original. He liked that I had spunk and wasn't afraid to speak my mind. If he thought that was spunk though, I'm glad I didn't say what I was really thinking." She laughs again, making her curls shake around her face. "Probably would have been too much for the old chauvinist. He also said it was nicer than he thought to get some fresh young colour in the office."

"He didn't…and he meant?" Tammy covers her mouth, a look of horror splashing across her face.

"Well, who knows what he meant, right?" Eloise winks and shrugs. "Ah well."

"That's awful," I say, wondering how much it really bothers her. "But I'm glad you still got the gig. So you're going back?"

"Yeah. I'm going to have dinner at the Andrev's restaurant too. So if there's anything you want me to take them or any messages or anything, just let me know."

"Yeah." I keep the smile on my face but wish I could be there, serving at their restaurant, instead of here, where Matt should be, being served upon. "That'd be great. I'll think on it."

Less than an hour later we pay the bills and engage in a round of hugs. Plans are made for next weekend. I stand by as Jenn, Rajeev, Eloise, and Moses make plans to meet for lunch before the memorial service. None of them ask if I want to come along, thankfully. I decline the offer of a drive home from Rajeev and take a bus instead, wanting some quiet time before entering the house. When I get home, I pick up the invite that arrived in the mail earlier this week and rub my thumb across the embossed text. I still haven't called Carol back. I should at least do that. Tomorrow.

MORNINGS ARE BUSY, what with Mom's feeding, sponge bath, and exercises, so it's noon by the time I even think of calling Carol. But then lunch needs to be eaten and after that Mom's nap, and since she's sleeping, I might as well get a snooze in too. I've only been lying down for about thirty minutes when the doorbell rings. I groan, roll out of bed, and head to the door, expecting to ward off a salesperson or political canvasser.

"Carol."

"Hi Autumn." She steps inside. "May I?"

"Of course, yes, sure."

She wraps her arms around me and I want to push her away but, of course, can't. "It's so good to see you." She steps back, gently brings her hand up to my cheek. "It's healed well."

"It could be a lot better."

"It could also be a lot worse." She tilts her head the same way Matt used to. "Be thankful."

"Sure, yes. You're right." Shame washes over me. Who am I to complain? I'm still here. I lead her into the living room and she takes a seat. "Can I get you anything?" I ask. "Orange juice? Soda? Tea?"

"Water would be lovely." I return from the kitchen with two glasses. "How is your mother doing?" she asks.

"Oh, a lot better." I sit down across from her. "She's really improving. She's been off the feeding tube for a while now and she's getting some feeling back in her left side. She started talking again too. She struggles, but still."

"That's wonderful," says Carol. "We've been praying for her. My prayer group as well. She's such a good woman. And strong. I'm sure she'll be almost as good as new before you know it."

"We hope so."

She nods and I think of the way she looked at me when I showed her the ring on my finger, how her face lit up with joy. "And how are you doing?"

"I'm all right." I look at my hands—free of a tan line, free of any visible reminder. *Keep it together.* "It's nice to be home. It's good to be here to help Mom."

"And your trip? Was it all you'd hoped?" Her voice has the slightest crack.

"It was good." I'm hesitant. Should I have been exploring the world while Matt's body grew cold? "I met some great people. I saw some great sites."

She smiles, and it looks genuine. "Mike and I were so glad you decided to do that. We'd love to see pictures, if you have them."

"I didn't really take many," I say, shifting in my seat. "I was just trying to soak it all in, you know?"

"Oh, of course. Sometimes that's a better way to do it." She takes a sip. I take a sip. She sets her glass down and now she's the one who seems hesitant. "What about the wedding pictures—did you end up getting them back? I know you'd had that package deal. They were supposed to provide so many prints and do up an album, a DVD with video clips?"

"I haven't opened it."

She nods. "Did you get my voice mail? Last week? I wasn't sure whether to call again, so I just thought I'd stop in."

"I got it. And the invite. Thank you for thinking of me."

Pain and disappointment flash across her face. "Autumn, how could you——?"

"I was going to call today."

"Mm-hmm." Her expression is serene again. I guess she's been preparing a face as well. She looks at the holly along the mantel. "Getting ready for Christmas early, I see."

"Mom likes it."

"We'd really like it if you said a few words. It would mean so much. You knew Matt better than anyone and we all thought he'd found such a treasure in you. You two seemed made for each other."

I purse my lips and look out the window.

"Of course you don't have to talk. There's no pressure. Just being there is enough."

"I'm not coming," I say, my hands folded. "Thank you for the invite. I think it's a really nice thing that you're doing. I just…I'm trying to move on with my life. I…I don't know. All those people, all…thank you for the invite."

She lets out a long breath of air. Her eyes crinkle, just like Matt's used to. She smiles. "I think it would be good for you too, Autumn. It was so sudden, what happened. You were still recovering yourself at the funeral. It must have all been a bit of a blur. This would be a proper chance to remember him the way he deserves. To say goodbye again, to——"

"I've said goodbye." *I hate this.* "With all due respect, Carol, I've decided not to go. I'm sorry but——"

"It's your choice." She clutches the glass like it's a precious treasure. "I hope you change your mind, but it's your choice." I nod. "Is your mother around? Could I say hello?"

"She's napping right now."

"Oh, all right. Well, maybe I'll pop in again some other time."

"Sure, that'd be great." I stand. Carol stands too and relinquishes the glass to a side table. She hugs me, pats her hand along my good cheek, as if she pities me. "Thanks for stopping by."

"Of course. You feel free to come by our place too. Anytime you like, okay?"

"Okay." We walk to the door and she hugs me again. She steps out and I lean against the door, close my eyes, and imagine being there—everyone thinking of Matt, everyone talking of Matt, the family pictures that cover their home. I try to imagine his face. I can see it in pictures. In my mind I see the picture above their mantel. I see the photo booth strip I used to keep in my wallet, all the funny faces. We took it on our fourth date. But I can't really see him. Not in a concrete way. He's blurring. I try to hear his voice but I'm not positive I have the right intonation. He's slipping away and I suppose I should be happy about this. Perhaps it means my plan is working. Perhaps it means one day I'll really be able to live like he was just one of the many people who've come into and gone out of my life, like I don't still love him. I touch my hand to my face. It's wet. Yet again, I don't even know when I started crying.

A noise from my mother's room snaps me back to the present. I wipe the tears away then hurry upstairs. My mother is smiling like a little girl. She knocked her water over and it spread over her sheets. My first reaction is frustration that the mess means more work—helping her out of bed earlier than expected, changing the linens—but staring at her expression, I push the feeling aside. She always used to tell us: 'Don't cry over spilled milk.' A common phrase, but one she took to heart. Whenever we had a genuine accident, made an honest mistake, we knew we wouldn't hear a harsh word from her. She did expect us to learn from our mistakes, to make better choices next time, to not live as if the world weren't constantly teaching us how to be and do better. I pull the sheets away. "No worries." I smile back and wonder if there's something bigger I should be gleaning from her lesson.

# CHAPTER TWENTY-SEVEN

On the day of the memorial I sit in the backyard on a lawn chair, trying not to think of all the people who, in less than an hour, will judge me for my absence. The scent of the crinkled leaves comforts me with the memory of simpler times and backyard play. On this unusually bright and mild fall day, the strength of the sun and a light afghan are enough to warm me.

"Shouldn't you be preparing for the service, or memorial, or whatever it is?" Billy's voice breaks me out of my reverie. I turn my head to see him standing in the yard.

"Shouldn't you?"

"I came to sit." Something in his voice makes me tense.

"You what?"

"I came to sit with you. That's what you did when I was in a coma."

I turn my face from his. "What's that supposed to mean?"

"What do you think it means?"

"I don't know."

"You're just letting things happen to you, like you're in a coma." I look back at him, waiting for him to elaborate, but he doesn't.

"I'm not in a coma." I pull my legs up on the chair and tuck the blanket around them. "I went to Europe. I came back. You don't call that making choices?"

"You ran away to Europe. And while you were there, you

hooked up with people who let you tag along on their journey."

"It's not—"

"And then you came back 'cause people pushed you into it. They guilted you into it. You didn't want to, right? That's why you ignored Uncle Leo's emails." He looks so calm and detached, it makes me want to scream.

"It wasn't like that. Going to Europe was a choice, a hard one."

He grabs a lawn chair, brings it over, then sits so we're both looking at the trees that line the property—not at each other. "Okay, maybe you made a choice," he says, "but you made it for the wrong reasons. You *were* running away, and you know it. And coming back here wasn't a choice. You weren't ready to come back. You had to. You were obligated. If you had your way, I'm guessing you would have stayed in England."

"Well, I'm sorry, okay." I'm not sure whether I want to cry or yell, so I say the words without emotion.

"What are you sorry for?" I pull the afghan up so it covers my arms as well, cocooning me. "What are you sorry for?" he repeats.

"I don't know. For getting it all wrong. For disappointing people. For not," I pause, "handling this better."

"That's crap. You don't owe anyone else any apologies."

"Well then, what the hell—"

"You only have to answer to yourself."

"Then what are you even doing here?" My words feel as tired as I do.

"Trying to help you answer to yourself." He grins, still facing the tree line. He sits low in the chair, his legs outstretched. "I've been to the other side and back, Autumn. I know a thing or two. Anyway, it's obvious. Until a few months ago you had a pretty sweet life. A Mom and Dad who love you, popular, smart, successful."

"You don't know my life."

He brushes away my words with a sweep of his hand. "Maybe you had hard times. You dated a few losers, I'll admit that, and I know it was rough when your dad was sick, but he got better and then you found Matt, this amazing guy who was going to keep giving you the fabulous life you were used to." Billy casts a hand in the air then lets it fall. "And now he's been stolen from you, and it's shitty. Really shitty. Your life is never going to be quite as good as it once was because nothing can erase Matt's death, how it's hurt you."

He pauses, as if contemplating. "What happened was horrible, but good can come out of bad. You have to try to look at this as an opportunity. Already you're a stronger person than you were, and you're going to keep growing stronger as you deal with all of this, and that's kinda cool. It's like the reverse of my deal. I always thought everything was shitty and then I almost died and I realized life is only as hard as you let it be."

"I don't exactly know what—"

"We all have pain, okay? We all have things we're scared of, things we don't want to be real, but they are real and we have to deal with that. Don't be sorry, Autumn. Just accept that sometimes life sucks, sometimes life hurts, but you're still alive. I was in a coma when my mother died. A mother I treated like garbage." He shrugs. "But that's just what happened. We have to keep living. We can't let the weight of all the crap life throws at us pull us under, otherwise, what's the point?" He stands and gives my shoulder a squeeze. "Anyways, I gotta roll, Cuz. Don't want to be too late." He releases my shoulder. "You'll figure it out."

He walks to the back gate, stops, then turns back. "Matt's dead, Autumn, and from what I hear you're trying to forget that in a really weird way—by pretending he wasn't this huge part of your life? That's stupid. It won't work, okay? You can't just forget him. Don't bother trying."

He turns again and the sound of the gate slamming

disturbs the quiet around me. Long after he leaves, I'm still staring where he stood. All this time I've been so concerned about my face being hideous, trying to convince myself it isn't, but what's really hideous is how I've been handling the accident and all that came with it.

Farfar's words come to mind once again—as long as there is life, there is hope. As long as there is hope, life. When Matt died I let go of having the life I'd hoped for, but Billy's right, I still have my life. Matt being gone doesn't change that, and pretending my love for him isn't as strong today as it was the day we took our vows hasn't made it any easier. Some days the love feels stronger. Some days my yearning for him is all consuming. My love for Matt's not going anywhere and there's no point trying to hide from the pain of remembering, not that I've been very successful at it, anyway.

I pick up the afghan and walk the steps back inside. It's probably been too long since I checked on Mom. As I pass the sewing room, I can almost feel the weight of the parcel inside, the one Carol wanted to see, the one I've kept hidden away in a room I rarely enter. I tiptoe down the hall and peek into my parents' room; Mom's face looks serene against the pillow. She smiles as she sleeps. I walk back to the sewing room and open the door. The deep-set drawer in this old desk never wants to open and I have to yank at the handle to make it move. At last it does and I lift the bundle out. It's tied with a satin purple bow and feels heavy in my shaking hands. Moving over to the love seat, I place the package on my lap. The bow loosens at my gentle tug, freeing a DVD case, several framed photographs—wrapped in foolscap—and the photo album. Putting the other items aside, I rub my hands over the text of the album cover. The letters of our names are raised, only it says Matthew for his, something I only called him once.

I take a deep breath, close my eyes, and open the album. The moments on the first page bring a smile—Mom fixing a pin in my hair, Eloise touching up my nail polish where it had chipped the night before, Dad wiping away a tear as I pin a corsage on his lapel. Next I turn to moments I never saw—Mike and Matt pinning corsages on each other at the same time, both mid-laugh. Matt sitting, a look of concentration on his face, as he wrote on the card Charlie delivered to me hours before the wedding. Him and Charlie posing with their parents. I keep flipping and get to the shot of Matt as I came down the aisle. I place my finger to the page, moisture flowing down my cheek while I touch the spot where it flowed down his. I'd never felt more beautiful, more loved, than when I turned the corner and there he was, looking at me like that. I could see our entire life in his gaze—all the days before and all the ones yet to come.

I flip the album closed. Those days didn't come. They never will. My hands grip the album, anger coursing through me. They didn't come and they never will. I hold on to this thought, this feeling, until it starts to dissipate, and in its place is the way his face looked when I stepped into the aisle—not from the picture, but from my memory—the most perfect moment of my life. I close my eyes and feel again the gentle touch as he held my hand and slid the ring on my finger. The pressure on my back as he pressed my body into his, tipping me over for our first wedded kiss. The music, the lighting, the shared whispers and laughter during our first wedded dance. I open the album again and find that moment, beautiful, but nothing compared to the richness of my memory. It's not something I want to lose— not any of it. A drop falls on the page and I use the corner of my shirt to wipe it off. I don't want to lose him or the love we shared, and at last it hits me—I don't have to.

I look again at that smiling face then close my eyes and see his face in my mind's eye, feel his touch, hear his laughter. He wouldn't want me to forget him, but he also wouldn't want remembering him to hold me back from life. Without realizing the absurdity of it, I've been trying to do both. No more.

My eyes open and turn to the clock. I have time. Grabbing the album, DVDs, and framed pictures, I place them in a bag and head down the hall to see my mother gazing out the window. "Mom." She turns her head to me and smiles. "I need to go to the memorial. Do you want to come with me?" She nods vigorously. It takes longer than I'd like to get her and her wheelchair situated in the car, but I manage. We're quiet on the drive over, me because I don't know what to say and am trying to retain the strength to not turn back, her, presumably because the few words she can form don't allow for much conversation. But maybe she doesn't know what to say either. Cars flood the street Matt grew up on, but the Evens' driveway only has the family's vehicles and there's space for one more.

I'm struggling to get the wheelchair out of the trunk when Billy and Daniel walk toward me. Daniel wraps his arms around me and I choke back new tears. He looks at me in a way I haven't seen since before I left for Europe. He opens his mouth to say something but then closes it and gives my hand a squeeze before helping Billy set up the wheelchair for my mother.

I reach into the back seat for the bag of pictures and walk up the drive. Daniel and Billy lift Mom up the steps to the front door where one of Matt's cousins stands, holding it open. She nods as I pass by. Just as I feared, when I walk through the crowd all eyes turn to me. I try not to imagine their thoughts. They're not why I'm here, and maybe some are looking at my mother, anyway. But if they're not, if they're looking at me, contemplating the scar I wear and thinking of it as my marker, that doesn't have to be a bad thing. It's my constant reminder, and I no longer want to forget. Carol turns when I tap her shoulder. Her face crinkles up in a smile as she looks at me with eyes that are so much like his. "I'm glad you came," she says.

"Sorry I'm late."

She shakes her head. "You're just on time."

"I brought you something to look at. You can make copies, but I'd like it all back."

She looks inside the bag and makes a noise that's a mix between a whimper and a laugh. "Thank you." She inhales deeply. "Will you say something?"

I nod. She puts her hand on my back and ushers me to the living room where she gathers the crowd's attention. It all feels a little surreal. "Thank you for coming today," she says. "We know Matt would have loved to be here, spending time with each of you. We know he'd feel blessed to know there are so many people who love him and want to remember him. We don't want this day to be about sorrow." She takes a hold of my hand. "We want it to be about celebrating Matt's life, celebrating what he meant to us and the good times we had." She stops and it looks like she's having trouble keeping the smile on her face. I step forward.

"Today would have been Matt's thirtieth birthday," I say. "We were going to go skydiving to celebrate, or bungee jumping—something memorable." I take a breath. "Matt was like that. He wanted to get the most out of life. He wanted to experience and enjoy every moment, to help others enjoy it too. He died too young."

Murmurs of agreement spread throughout the room. "But he still lived, and he lived well. I know he would want all of us to remember him with love, as Carol said, and to go on living our lives just as fully as we were before, more so. I know that's what he would have wanted for me." I glance at my mother, and she nods at me. I look to Billy, wearing a proud, satisfied look on his face. Jenn is trying to keep it together. Dad is beaming...I didn't even know Dad was here.

I clear my throat and continue. "It's been really hard for me these past months. I've been a little lost." I pause and take another breath. "But I want to thank Carol and Mike for holding this today, for urging me, all of us, to hold on to the good times." My voice cracks and Mike takes over. He tells everyone about the tree and, after a few minutes, we file out. Carol, Mike, Charlie, and I all pick up the oak together and place it in the pre-dug hole. We pile the dirt around it with our hands then stand and brush the remnants off our knees. When we go back inside I feel as if I'm floating through the room, listening to stories of Matt, telling some of my own, and saying goodbye to the shell of myself I've been living with all these months. It's hard, but I'm starting to feel like the old Autumn already. Or maybe, as Billy said, a new Autumn, a better one.

OVER THE NEXT FEW months the pain transforms. It's not less, really, just different. I accept it, which seems to take away some of its power. I find myself getting better, stronger. I watch in amazement as my mother goes through a similar transformation. We're both learning how to live again. We were both crippled and are finding the strength to gain back all we lost.

When Mom is well enough that she can get herself to and from the bathroom and in and out of the motorized seat Dad installed on the stairs, I look for my own apartment. I'm not going back to England. Not yet, at least. I still keep in touch with the Andrevs though. Emily and I exchange emails, Amalia sends me literary memes on Facebook, and Jakob and I have had more than a few phone calls. I'd be lying if I didn't say he gives me hope that I'll love again. I miss him. I miss all of them. But for now, at least, my life is here.

On the one-year anniversary of Matt and my wedding, I sit with Jenn and my mom and Carol, looking through the album.

"I laughed so hard when the minister stepped in that

piece of cake," says Carol. "The look on his face!"

"I've never seen a man look more in love," says Jenn as she smiles at the picture of Matt that had me crying months before. "It's beautiful."

We watch the wedding video and sob unabashedly.

On the one-year anniversary of his death I stay in my apartment alone, with the lights dim, and let myself wallow. The next day I draw the curtains open to let in the light and go to my first official business meeting. Allison and I have decided to open a studio together. We'll start small, taking on clients in the park and at our apartments, but today's meeting is about looking at loan options to lease a studio space by next year. It may not be a success…but then again it may. And I know it's what Matt would have wanted me to do, and to do without fear.

I'm walking home from that meeting, feeling pretty good, feeling somewhat recovered from yesterday's descent into misery, when my phone rings.

I slide it out of my pocket and smile at the name on the display. "Jakob. Hi. It's been weeks!"

"I know," he says, his voice low and sad.

"What is it?"

"Farfar." The word hangs in space as I take a deep breath.

"He?"

"Last night."

"I'm so sorry."

"I guess it was his time." In his voice I hear the emotion behind the strength he puts forward, and my heart breaks for him.

"I just thought you'd want to know."

"Yes, of course I…how are you?"

"I mean it wasn't a complete surprise. He'd been getting worse. I just thought he'd hold on longer, you know?"

"Yeah." That silence again.

"Emily's a wreck."

I nod and then remember he can't see me. "She's bad? How is she doing?"

"She's just so tired—that's a big part of it I think. She's sad, and the last few weeks…he was a handful. Being worn out seems to make her meds not work as well. It's the loss of him, the fear for herself. It wasn't a pretty way to watch someone go. But she'll be okay."

I take another deep breath, imagining how scared she must be. "When's the funeral?"

"This Friday."

"I'll be there."

"What? No. That's not why I—"

"I'm coming."

He sighs. "What about your mom? Don't you need to—"

"She's doing great. She's doing so well she says I'm not of service anymore. I got my own apartment a few weeks ago." He doesn't reply. He must be outside, every now and then it seems like a breath of wind makes its way through the receiver. "Jakob?"

"It'd be good to see you." I can almost hear his sad smile, the way his lips turn up ever so slightly. "I don't want you to feel at all like you have to come, but it'd be good to see you."

I hold the phone to my ear and listen to the sound of his breath mixing with the faint breeze. My mind travels back to that last night—the way we sat so close, the way his presence allowed me to imagine a future. I have commitments here, new clients, and can't afford to take off for more than a week. It will make getting the business in order more stressful, but it's time I start making choices that put others before myself. "I'll be there," I repeat.

He exhales, "Autumn?"

"Yeah?"

"Life is beautiful, right?"

"Yeah," I smile, picturing his face. "It is."

# A NOTE FROM THE AUTHOR

Dear Reader,

Thank you so much for taking the time to read *Where There Is Life*. I hope you enjoyed it. Did it make you think, laugh, cry, or take you out of your life for a few hours?

If yes, it would mean so much if you took a moment to write a short, honest review on either your favourite retailer or Goodreads (or both!). Reviews are incredibly important. They encourage readers to give a book a chance, which means your review may just help a fellow booklover find a story to touch their heart!

The next books in the series are available now. In *By What We Love*, follow the story of Eloise as she learns that sometimes getting exactly what you want doesn't mean you have what you really need…

Turn the page for a short description of the book.

If you want to know more about the other books in the series, you'll find information on them following the excerpt. Each book digs deep to look at the heart of a woman struggling with all life's thrown at her.

They're also all stand-alones. So if book 3 doesn't interest you, skip ahead to book 4, but they are chronological, so if you plan to read them all, you'll enjoy them most if you read them in order.

If you'd like to know the next time I release a new book or have a great promotion, please follow me on BookBub. And if you've read *Where There Is Life* as part of a book club, you can visit charlenecarr.com for a Book Club Discussion Guide.

Turn the page to learn about the rest of the books in the *A New Start Series*.

Read on, my friend,

*Charlene Carr*

***When Comes The Joy***
Book 1

**Jennifer's not perfect. Not even close. But she may just capture your heart.**

At 27, Jennifer's out of work, her mom just died, and despite stellar qualifications, every job interview ends in rejection.
Haunted by the teasing, taunts, and fat jokes that defined her childhood, Jennifer blames her unhappiness on her ever-growing waistband.
And she's ready for change.
Messy and real.
Beautiful and harsh.
When Comes The Joy (previously titled Skinny Me) explores one woman's journey along the road of forgiveness, healing, and strength.

# ACKNOWLEDGMENTS

I would like to thank my wonderful beta readers who gave generously of their time and provided invaluable feedback. It amazes me, the little nuances you are able to see that help me make these stories so much more than what they were.  I would also like to thank my editor and her keen eye.

# BOOK CLUB DISCUSSION QUESTIONS

1. Was it a shock to learn Autumn's husband died right at the beginning of the story? Would you have liked to have the wedding described in more detail or would this have made the accident more traumatic?

2. When Autumn came home from London after the accident, what do you think of her behaviour? Did you feel it was normal or typical for her to reject all her friends calls, refuse to eat, or meet with people? Or do you think she handled the situation worse than most due to her relatively trauma free life up to that point?

3. Was there anything Autumn's Mom, Dad, brother or friends could have done to make her grieving period easier for her? Autumn clearly was frustrated with what she felt as her mother's intrusion on her grieving process. Did this frustration seem justified?

4. Autumn decided to act 'as if Matt had never existed'. Do you know anyone who responded to death in that way? Do you think seeing a psychiatrist or psychologist could have helped her at this stage?

5. Autumn meets Jakob and Emily very early in her 'runaway trip'. Do you think this hindered or helped her (albeit odd) grieving process?

6. Dominic hits on Autumn very early on in her visit to the family vineyard. Do you think he noticed that Jakob seemed to already have an interest in her and so thought he needed to act fast to turn her interest to him? What do you think of Dominic and his expectations that Autumn would sleep with him at the hotel?

7. The title of the book comes from some life lessons passed on (in a paraphrased quote) from Farfar. What role do you feel Farfar played in the book and in the story of Autumn's journey? How would the story have been different without him?

8. Autumn eventually learns to deal with her grief and embrace the life she now has. What role do you feel caring for her mother played in this? Were you able to forgive her for not immediately making the decision to head home to help her mother?

*If you have any questions about the discussion guide or would like a chance at having Charlene visit your bookclub through a webcall, email contact@charlenecarr.com or https://invitd.ca/authors/charlene-carr.*

# ABOUT THE AUTHOR

I'm a lover of words. Pursuing this life-long obsession, I studied literature in university, attaining both a BA and MA in English. Still craving more, I attained a degree in Journalism. After travelling the globe for several years and working as a freelance writer, editor, facilitator, and starting my own Communications business, I decided the time had come to focus exclusively on my true love - novel writing.

My goal is to write books that are almost impossible to put down, not because of some great mystery, or high-speed chase, or sexy scene, but because they're full of characters who enrage and delight you; Imperfect people in circumstances that could hit any one of us.

Characters full of human frailties who make awful, sometimes stupid choices …

But who don't give up when they're knocked down. Who struggle and fight and come out on the other side stronger, braver, ready to live a life of their own making.

Read more at www.charlenecarr.com/books

www.ingramcontent.com/pod-product-compliance
Lightning Source LLC
Chambersburg PA
CBHW061620190726
48288CB00007B/2399